A MOSCOW
AWAKENING

A MOSCOW AWAKENING

RICHARD FASSAM-WRIGHT

The Book Guild Ltd

First published in Great Britain in 2022 by
The Book Guild Ltd
Unit E2 Airfield Business Park,
Harrison Road, Market Harborough,
Leicestershire. LE16 7UL
Tel: 0116 2792299
www.bookguild.co.uk
Email: info@bookguild.co.uk
Twitter: @bookguild

This work is entirely fictitious and bears no resemblance to any persons living or dead.

Typeset in 11pt Minion Pro

Printed and bound in the UK by TJ Books LTD, Padstow, Cornwall

ISBN 978 1915122 568

British Library Cataloguing in Publication Data.
A catalogue record for this book is available from the British Library.

For Meg, James and Kate

PREFACE TO A
MOSCOW AWAKENING

A Moscow Awakening is a work of fiction set against the backdrop of the USSR in the 1970s. In writing this book I have drawn on my experience and knowledge of Moscow and Russia whilst living there for five years in both Soviet and post-Soviet periods. All characters are inventions: it is just the setting which seeks to be as authentic as possible.

In researching and writing *A Moscow Awakening* I have benefitted from advice and suggestions from a number of people. I would like to thank literary consultant and editor Lynn Curtis, who provided me with wide-ranging comments and suggestions. I also sought advice from friends in Moscow, one of whom devoted an inordinate amount of time to my project; without this input I would not have been able to complete the manuscript. I can only say a huge thanks. I have also benefitted from detailed suggestions from my wife Meg, who laboriously read through a number of drafts; from my brother Andrew; from my nephew Alex (1) and from my cousin Alex (2). Piers Dudgeon has been very helpful in proffering advice on publishing challenges. To all my heartfelt thanks.

Finally, I wish to acknowledge that, at the start of the book, and purely to set the scene, I have adapted and used some short passages from a section of a very informative brochure, 'Spaso House: A Short History' written by Tatiana Dudina, which was produced by the US Embassy in Moscow on the occasion of a ball hosted to celebrate seventy years of cultural exchanges in this iconic Moscow building in April 2004.

Any factual errors that remain in the book are my sole responsibility.

Richard Fassam-Wright
London
March 2022

ONE

Spaso House, Moscow, Residence of the Ambassador of the United States of America to the Union of Soviet Socialist Republics (USSR), early June 1975

Songbirds and animals on loan from the Moscow Zoo.

Halls bedecked in roses and tulips, delicious food in abundance, and streams of cascading champagne.

Spectacular lighting and dancers from the Caucasus.

All these delights awaited guests forty years ago at the 1935 Spring Ball at Spaso House, Moscow. In attendance was Russian writer Mikhail Bulgakov, whose novel *The Master and Margarita* describes Satan's 'Spring Ball of the Full Moon' associated with this lavish and outlandish party. In the same momentous year Sergei Prokofiev's opera *Love for Three Oranges* was staged in Spaso House, conducted by the composer himself.

Will Lawrence, a graduate student living in Moscow, wondered if similar delights awaited him as he stood flicking through the official brochure of Spaso House. He was standing in the receiving line of invitees to a reception in honour of a visiting delegation of US grain dealers and brokers in early June 1975 hosted at the residence of the US Ambassador to the USSR. Will counted himself lucky: an

1

invitation to this venue was widely sought after in Moscow, not just because of its association with Russian folklore but also because food and drink were known to be of the highest quality.

As the queue inched forward Will, in his smartest shirt, tie and jacket, exchanged pleasantries with a middle-aged, overweight Russian of average height working for the Ministry of Agriculture. The Russian did his best to convey an attitude of indifference to the splendid surroundings but his insouciance did not convince.

After passing the security checks, Will was escorted into the main hall and the chandelier room, where he was immediately offered a selection of drinks by an impeccably dressed waiter in a black suit, white shirt and black bow tie. He opted for a glass of chilled white Californian wine. As he did so he inadvertently bumped again into the Soviet official he had met a few minutes before.

"Ah, we meet again," he said, handing over his business card to Will. "My name is Kuznetsov, Alexei Vladimirovich. I am part of the official delegation of the Soviet Union to this reception."

"And I am Will Lawrence, a British exchange student studying at the Timiryazev Agricultural Academy in Moscow," responded Will, shaking hands with Kuznetsov. "Pleased to meet you." Will didn't hand over a business card as he did not have one.

"And what are you studying at Timiryavskaya Academiya?" asked Kuznetsov.

"I am focusing on sociological changes in the agriculture sector… as you know the rural landscape of the USSR has changed in the last twenty years as collective and state farm workers have migrated to towns in search of a better life, despite improvements in working conditions in the countryside. I am interested in how the USSR is managing these transformations in this key sector of the Soviet economy," replied Will matter-of-factly.

"Interesting but, if I might say, a rather theoretical and unscientific project. Your research will show that the USSR is handling this transition well," commented Kuznetsov.

The propagandist line, thought Will to himself. He decided to switch tack. "On another issue, Gospodin Kuznetsov," Will continued, "may I ask what the prospects are for the Soviet Union's grain harvest in 1975?"

"Uniformly good, young man: the Soviet grain harvest will achieve record levels in 1975 in accordance with the Communist Party's ninth five-year plan which finishes this year. More than two hundred million tons of grain are expected. This reflects the correctness of the Party's course and the wisdom of our political leaders, comrades Brezhnev, Kosygin, Andropov and Suslov," replied Kuznetsov.

Will was about to ask a further question when Kuznetsov drifted off to get another drink. Wendell Randall III, political counsellor at the US Embassy, who had invited Will to the reception, then took to the podium briefly, tapping the microphone to inform guests that the visiting delegation of US grain traders had not yet arrived but were on their way. Their Hungarian-made Ikarus bus had developed mechanical trouble on the Moscow Ring road.

Will observed Spaso House's elegant reception rooms. The ceiling, chandeliers, warm furnishings, ornate tables, paintings and magnificent wooden parquet floor were a revelation to him. The 1935 description was accurate: there was even a ballroom for concerts and dancing. So this was the environment in which top-drawer diplomatic receptions took place in Moscow. *Not bad*, he thought to himself.

As he continued to gaze in awe at the surroundings the US grain traders began drifting into the reception, apologetic for their delay and thirsty. Many opted for a martini on the rocks, a Jack Daniel's or other US whiskies and bourbon. They were dressed smartly in expensive dark plain or pinstriped suits, immaculately starched white shirts and colourful ties, some with tie pins, with polished shiny black or burgundy brogues. This business clan was successful. *And wealthy*, Will concluded.

It wasn't long before the sound of a knife tapping on a wine glass several times brought the murmured conversations of the guests to a stop. It was the cue for the welcoming speeches. In Will's limited experience of diplomatic receptions, these tended not only to be very tedious but also last longer than necessary. With a half-full glass of wine in his hand he steadied himself to listen to what was to come.

TWO

November 1974

Eight months earlier general practitioner Dr Jim Lawrence, MD, MRCPI, eased his newly acquired 3.5-litre maroon Rover P5B coupé car out of the garage adjoining the family house in the suburbs of Birmingham and parked it on the driveway close to the front door. It was just before 4.30am on a dark and damp Midlands morning. Inside the house his son Will was gathering his things together – two large matching Cambridge blue suitcases and a briefcase which contained his personal documents, including his dark blue British passport, a Nagel's travel guide and other reading material neatly arranged for his journey.

"Mother, hurry up, for goodness' sake!" shouted Will from the hall of the four-bedroom detached house.

"I'm ready," said his mother, slightly flustered as she descended the stairs. "Don't get into a tizz," she added. "We have plenty of time."

"No, we don't," replied Will. "I have to be at the station by 7.15am and you are holding things up. Why can't you ever be on time?"

"Calm down and stop getting agitato," said Will's mother. "We're ready to go now. Let me help to bring your things to the car."

"Just take the briefcase. I can manage the rest," said Will grumpily. He proceeded to awkwardly manoeuvre the two heavy suitcases through the front door, in the process scratching the floral wallpaper above the skirting board as he headed outside into the cold air and towards the car. His father helped him put the luggage into the Rover's ample boot.

"Do you want to drive?" his father said.

"I'm a bit edgy, to be honest, Dad. I'd rather you did," answered Will.

"Very well, son," said his father before emitting a rasping cough, not for the first time that morning.

By this time Will's mother had arrived at the car, having locked the front door of the house.

"Who is sitting where?" she asked.

"I'll go in the front passenger seat," said Will. "Dad's driving."

"Very well then. Do we know the way?" asked Will's mother, a veteran of volcanic family rows occasioned by unprepared route-planning and poor map-reading.

"Of course," replied Will's father, taking out a Player's No 6 filter cigarette from its packet and lighting it by striking a match on the side of a yellow, red and green Swan Vestas box. "Simple. Straight down the M1 and then on to central London."

"Central London is a big place, Dad," Will said nervously. "Are you sure you know the route?"

"Absolutely, son," replied Will's father. "I had a chat with a fellow in the Rose and Crown last night. He used to be a cabbie in London. Knows the place like the back of his hand. I bought him a pint of Watney's bitter. He wrote the route down on the back of this pad."

Will looked carefully at the directions scribbled on the back of a crumpled grey pad of medical prescriptions. They seemed clear enough: M1 motorway south, Euston Road, King's Cross, City of London, then follow directions to Liverpool Street Station.

"Do you have a fag, Dad?" asked Will as he settled into the

front seat. His father handed over his virtually empty packet of twenty and Will took out a Player's No 6 filter and lit up.

"What do I do with the green coupon?" asked Will, since he had just taken the last cigarette from the pack.

"Put it on the dashboard, son," his father replied. "Right, all aboard? Then let's go." He turned on the ignition and the Rover's V8 3.5-litre engine purred into life. Taking a last drag of his cigarette he stubbed out the end of it in the car's half-full ashtray. Engaging reverse gear, the car slid slowly down the garage ramp onto the adjoining road. They were on their way.

"I'll kick her into a higher gear on the motorway, son. A special feature of the automatic engine. You'll see the difference when she accelerates." Will's dad had only bought the car a few weeks ago, second-hand from a local patient at 'a special price for you, Doc, all included', and he was proud of it. He called it a poor man's Rolls-Royce.

At this time of the morning the roads were clear, and they made swift, unhindered progress towards London. An hour or so into the journey, Will's mother pulled out a Harrods gift box from her bag and gave it to Will.

"Will, this is for you. You will need to keep warm," she said.

"Mother, you shouldn't have done that. I can look after myself, you know. I'm not a child," said Will, embarrassed that his mother had gone to the trouble of buying him an expensive gift with money earned from her poorly paid nursing work.

Will opened the gift box and found inside a pair of brown sheepskin leather gloves, size XL. He put them on. They fitted perfectly.

"Do you like them?" Will's mother asked.

"That was very kind of you, Mother. Indeed, I do. They will keep my hands warm in the cold for sure. I am now fully equipped for all eventualities." Will blew a kiss to his mother sitting behind him in the back seat.

His father drove on towards London.

THREE

Liverpool Street Station, London

Arriving at Liverpool Street Station with twenty-five minutes to spare, Will grabbed a trolley onto which he loaded his heavy luggage. His father pushed it for him, having lit up again, his eighth cig of the day. His mother followed.

Will joined a small group of postgraduate students, five men and one woman in all, gathered in a rough semi-circle at the entrance to Platform 5 in Liverpool Street Station. Standing amongst them was Mr Gordon Longmore, Commander of the Most Excellent Order of the British Empire (CBE), a mid-fifties, dapper, balding employee of the British Council, the cultural arm of the British Government responsible for disseminating British culture worldwide and promoting educational exchanges. A Scotsman, he was wearing a green tartan cap and carrying a plastic clipboard containing documents which he proceeded to distribute methodically to the six students present in return for a signed receipt. There was an air of both excitement and nervousness among the group reflecting their unusual destination – the Union of Soviet Socialist Republics, the USSR.

The students had come from different corners of the UK and from different universities. They all shared a common interest in

Russia and the USSR, and wanted to experience life there (in some cases for a second or third time) and carry out some academic research. Twenty-three years old, six foot three inches tall, brown-haired with an athletic build, Will was studying for a master's degree at Birmingham University, one of two main centres for studying Soviet Studies in the UK. His chosen field of study was the economic and sociological changes in Soviet agriculture in the 1970s.

Longmore, all bustle and business, called the group to order to listen to his pre-departure briefing and instructions.

"Now then, you five lads and one lassie," he began in his strong Scottish accent. "You're a group of six. Stick together like the contents of a bagged-up haggis until you reach your final destination – Moscow. Clear?" That joke fell flat.

He continued, "Once you reach the port of the Hook of Holland from Harwich make sure you get in the right carriage – the one bound for Moscow not Amsterdam. Your sleeping cars – bunk beds – have been arranged and I've given the tickets and reservations to Evan here – say hello, please." Evan, an unassuming post-doctoral student from Oxford, duly confirmed his role by waving his hand weakly. "You should all now have Soviet customs and currency forms which you need to fill in before the Polish-Soviet border at Brest-Litovsk. There you will have to leave the train. Remember, please, that you are all representatives of, and the outward face of, the United Kingdom in the USSR. Questions?"

There were none.

"Right then, lads and lassie. Let me be clear: *you...*" Longmore hesitated a second to drive home his message. "*You* all will be objects of suspicion at official level in the Soviet Union and people of great curiosity to ordinary Russians, who are generally warm-spirited, generous and welcoming. Don't get into skirmishes, don't engage in lascivious or lewd behaviour towards the opposite sex – or even the same sex – avoid drugs, black-market trading in goods and currencies, debauchery, excessive boozing – a few drams of liquor notwithstanding. In short, steer clear of sin and mischief. We, in the BC, do *not* want to have to repatriate you for bad behaviour or rabble-rousing, which would mean *you*," Longmore again strongly emphasised the '*you*', "reimbursing us for the whole cost of your studentship. You'll have a great experience if you follow these basic rules; enjoy it. Bon voyage. Or as the Russians would say..." here Longmore broke off to quickly consult his clipboard, "*chaste lyie vevo putty*."

Putty? The students, all of whom understood Russian to a decent level, looked at each other with bemusement: Longmore's phrase had flummoxed them.

"I think he meant have a good trip in Russo-Gaelic," Evan whispered quietly to Will.

The students gathered up their belongings and began to make their way towards the Harwich train. Will turned to his parents and hugged them both. His mother suppressed her tears while his father quietly slipped two five-pound notes into his hand.

"Take care of yourself, son. Have a drink on the boat. See you soon," he said.

"Now you will write, Will, won't you, and let us know you have arrived safely," his mother said fussily. "And let us know if there is anything you need. Here, I bought you some Murray Mints you can share with the other students," she added, thrusting the bag of transparently wrapped fawn-coloured sweets, with chewy centres, into his hand.

"Thank you, Mother. I'll be fine. Don't worry. Keep well." Will swivelled on his heels and pushed his trolley past the ticket barrier towards the train. Having deposited his luggage in the compartment reserved for the students, he alighted the train briefly to wave a final goodbye to his parents. They reciprocated.

This is it, thought Will to himself, as he turned to reboard the train. He was on his own now.

Apart from spells away at university Will had never been separated for any significant length of time from his family. A planned absence of nine months in the USSR, therefore, was going to be a stretch. He would have to face the challenges ahead alone without their support. It was the biggest test of his adult life to date. By consciously placing himself into an unknown environment Will would be forced to be more independent and self-reliant. How would he cope?

The train eased away from Liverpool Street.

He was on his way to the USSR.

FOUR

London to Moscow

On a calm sea, the trip across the North Sea to the Hook of Holland from the port of Harwich in the East of England was uneventful. The students quickly identified, on landing in the Hook, the Eastern Express carriage destined for Belorussky Station in Moscow. Will intended to use the journey to establish contacts with his fellow British student travellers, most of whom were destined for Moscow State University, MGU, whereas he was heading alone to an agricultural academy named Timiryazev in the northern suburbs of Moscow, an institution much less frequented by visitors from the West.

Will was allocated a carriage with Tristan de Fallières, Oxford graduate and old Etonian, his father a high-end West End art dealer descended from past French royalty and his mother, a former Russian ballet dancer and gallery owner, now living in Geneva. His parents, Will discovered, had divorced when he was in his early teens. Tristan was, he said, trilingual in English, French and Russian, having been brought up in England while speaking his parents' mother tongues at home. *What an advantage*, thought Will.

"Why Russia, Will? Why not China? Liverpool? Or Barnsley?" asked Tristan.

"I got the bug," replied Will.

"Bug? What bug, you old bugger?" retorted Tristan jokingly.

"Sounds weird."

"Got bitten by the Russia bug, Tristan – desire to immerse myself in the mysteries of a vast, mysterious, enigmatic country occupying one seventh of the world's land mass..."

Actually, Will could not date precisely when he got bitten, metaphorically, by the 'bug', but it was around 1972. That was the year in which he took a lecture course at Cambridge University which covered Russian history from the emancipation of the serfs in 1861 to the present day. Everything in his academic life had flowed eastwards from that point. Will developed a taste for the great music and art of the Ballets Russes and for twentieth-century suprematist artists such as Malevich. He read Russian classics like Tolstoy's *Anna Karenina* and Dostoyevsky's *The Brothers Karamazov*. He was moved by Yevgenia Ginzburg's harrowing story of the 1930s purges in *Journey into the Whirlwind*. He delved into Russian classical music – Rachmaninoff, Tchaikovsky, Mussorgsky and Prokofiev.

"I don't quite know why," Will said, "but Russia has become an inexorable attraction for me. A part of me. I feel drawn into its fascinating historical, cultural, social and political orbit."

Russia had become, in reality, the means through which Will was seeking to better understand the world and his place in it. Placed in an alien environment, unencumbered by family and traditional ties, he was on a journey to find what he wanted to achieve in life without knowing what he was going to discover. It was a deliberate choice but one with an uncertain outlook.

"So, Tristan, tell me about yourself," Will said, as they approached the Dutch-German border. "You are studying the revolution? Who on earth is this Bolshevik agitator you're going to focus on?"

Tristan, already deep into a blue pack of filtered Gitanes he had purchased in the ferry's duty-free shop and sipping a can of beer, replied, "Andrei Vladimorovich Kentilovsky. I call him AVK. Not known in the West. Bolshevik agitator in some provincial towns near Moscow – Tula, Yaroslavl, Vladimir – so I'll need to go to these places. Had an impact. Executed in the Stalinist purges in the 1930s. Knew key Bolshevik leaders, Trotsky and Bukharin, whom Stalin turned against – that decided his fate. Known as a good trade union and workers' organiser. Spent four years in Czarist jails. Mid-level player in the revolution. Want to meet his relatives. Sometime." Tristan spoke jauntily and jerkily in a staccato fashion, the assumption being that his interlocutors would fill in the gaps of his incomplete sentences.

He lit up another Gitane. "And you? What are you researching?" Tristan asked Will.

"Soviet agriculture," replied Will.

"You – agriculture? Didn't see you as a farmer boy, a man of the soil and a country yokel. Don't buy it," said Tristan, laughing to himself.

"Not at all. I'm as urban as they come. But agriculture lies at the heart of the Soviet economy. I want to look at the sociological changes in the farm sector which has been pivotal in Russia's history," answered Will.

Tristan looked away, manifestly uninterested in Will's research topic.

"What do you plan to do after the USSR, Tristan? An academic career? Government? Private sector?" Will asked.

"Shit, no," replied Tristan. "Journalist, politics maybe. Hope to make contacts when away. You?"

"Not certain. I don't see myself being an academic, to be honest – too specialised. And I don't want to teach. I'm thinking of government, but maybe an international variant such as the EEC or NATO or the UN," replied Will.

"Don't want to think about it," Tristan replied dismissively. "My current future is defined by months. Looking forward to a

14

fun-filled nine months in the fragrant cradle of world socialism, generously subsidised by the British taxpayer. Going to sample the local delights in full – gorgeous Russian girls, curvaceous, voluptuous, blue-eyed, sexy *blondinkas*. Plenty of booze, travel and just a tad – I emphasise a tad – of study. Bit of contraband trading on the side to keep me solvent. Got tights, lipstick, lingerie and perfume to sell, and fifty condoms for the first three months."

"Are you serious?" responded Will naïvely. "I never thought of that. You're well prepared. I brought two packets of Durex, just in case. That's it for nine months."

"Won't last you a week, dear comrade, once you get the scent of those Russian fillies in your nostrils," said Tristan, glancing out the window at the flat, wet terrain outside.

Tristan had a short attention span which matched his scattergun thought processes and speech. He laughed a lot, particularly at his own jokes, but otherwise exuded the calm, insouciant air of someone of privilege, confidence and entitlement unencumbered by the vicissitudes of everyday life. Everything was easy and focused on the here and now. Things would fall into place for him no matter what. The world would provide a place for him – indeed, it owed him one. He wouldn't need to go looking for it.

By contrast Will, less confident, edgy in disposition and less experienced with women, intuitively felt he would have to graft and grind for whatever he achieved, both personally or professionally. Yet Will warmed to Tristan – he was amusing, quick, light-hearted, a chancer, but also, seemingly, self-effacing and honest. He didn't take himself too seriously. But he was cut from a very different cloth from Will.

As the train passed into Western Germany Tristan brought out a hip flask of Scotch, offering it to Will and other fellow students who had joined in the conversation. More Gitanes, more beer, wine and Scotch, and the mood lightened and became progressively more boisterous if not rowdy. Tristan was at the centre of things, drinking heavily, laughing and animating the discussion. Will retired to his bunk, exhausted by the early start to the day. He was not at heart a party boy or a heavy boozer. Tristan, by contrast, was in no mood to quit: he was having a good time.

Once into Communist East Germany (GDR) Tristan let out a whoop of feigned joy. "Goodbye to England, capitalist robber barons and the bourgeois Western world! See you again in nine months' time! A toast, my friends, to fraternal friendship with socialist peoples," he cried out, sinking another shot of Scotch.

At the long stop in Warsaw a few passengers joined the students' wagon-lit railcar including two Soviet officials returning to Moscow from a *kommandirovka* – an official government-sanctioned business trip to Poland. Tristan pulled out a full bottle of Johnnie Walker Scotch whisky to lubricate friendly discussions with Fyodor and Viktor. Tristan plunged headlong into an animated, alcohol-fuelled conversation with the two Russians, who reciprocated by producing bottles of German beer followed by two bottles of Green Label forty per cent proof Stolichnaya vodka.

Loud toasts were made to the victors of the Great Patriotic War, England, wartime collaboration in Murmansk, the Red Army, Bobby Charlton, Lev Yashin the famous Russian goalkeeper, Yuri Gagarin, Sputnik, the Queen, the General Secretary of the Soviet Communist Party Leonid Brezhnev, friendship, Russian women and a succession of other miscellaneous subjects, the jollity and hilarity becoming more exuberant and boisterous as the evening wore on. Tristan was unwisely endeavouring to keep pace with the Russians' unending capacity to absorb alcohol. Having already consumed copious amounts of drink prior to the Russians' embarkation in Warsaw, he was getting paralytically drunk, his words slurring and his feet unsteady as he raised himself to offer one more toast before seeking temporary relief in the WC at the end of the carriage. The dreadful sound of retching and vomiting was heard along the corridor: Tristan was paying for his excesses. The train rumbled on towards Brest-Litovsk in Belorussia, the border of the USSR, where it duly arrived at around 9pm on day two.

Considerably the worse for wear, Tristan and his Russian drinking companions joined Will and other passengers in disembarking the train to complete immigration and customs formalities at the Soviet border. Simultaneously a posse of border guards, customs officials and sanitary inspectors boarded the railcars to undertake checks. The panelling in the roof of the corridor was unscrewed to check if anyone was trying to enter the USSR's socialist paradise illegally. Oranges and apples were confiscated for inspection and only some returned. On the platform passports were checked, visas confirmed and stamped. Meantime the wagon-lit railcar in which they had travelled from the Hook of Holland, emptied of passengers, was raised horizontally by a series of winches, the standard-gauge bogies removed from the underside of the carriage and replaced with new ones fitting the eight-centimetre wider gauge of the Russian railway system.

Will looked on, intrigued, as the complicated mechanical operation ran its course. The train was ready to depart for Moscow at 1.30am. It slowly trundled its way out of Brest-Litovsk on the 650-mile journey to the Soviet capital via Minsk and the Vitebsk region in Belarus before reaching Smolensk in Russia. The Smolensk to Moscow line had been opened in 1870. Will knew this because one of the Russian bonds used to finance it was in a frame on his wall at home, an original Tsarist debt obligation rendered worthless by Bolshevik repudiation of all Imperial Russia's state debts.

The rhythmical sound of wheels on rail and chuntering carriages provided a good backdrop for an alcohol-fuelled sleep.

Waking up later that morning Will looked out from his window at a flat landscape turned wintry and snowy. Tristan had already staggered out of his bunk, a yellow-green sickly pallor to his face. He immediately reached for a Gitane before rushing towards the WC.

Returning, he muttered, "Hell of a drinking session, Will. Enjoy? Typical Russian. Drink till you drop. Then start up again." He laughed quietly to himself, reaching for a breakfast beer and another cigarette.

Will could see that Tristan would be part of many such boozing sessions in the USSR. Moderation, circumspection and a measured approach to life were not part of his make-up. He acted impulsively, plunged in headfirst and dealt with the consequences as and when they arose.

Arrival in Moscow was now just several hours away, and Will was beginning to wonder what lay in front of him. In fact, he was asking himself what on earth had encouraged him to make this leap into the unknown and undertake this seemingly madcap venture. He was worried about being isolated in a college far from the centre of Moscow and away from the other British students. Total immersion in the USSR sounded great on paper, but the nearer it came to reality the more Will was feeling uneasy. He would soon find out what he had let himself in for. There were now just fifty kilometres to go to Moscow. There was a general shuffling and stirring in the carriage as passengers began to gather up their belongings, repack suitcases and get organised for disembarkation.

As Moscow's extensive suburbs, mainly comprising endless white apartment blocks set alongside the railway line, came into view, the train began to reduce speed before slowing down to a crawl. Eventually it entered Moscow's Belorussky station, shuddering to a stop with a loud and lengthy screeching of the brakes. On the platform there was much commotion, bustling and shouting, people greeting passengers, porters with luggage trolleys, uniformed railway authorities, with police and other onlookers surveying the scene.

Upon disembarking onto the narrow platform, the students were greeted by the British Council representative, Mr James Pressman, Cultural Attaché at the UK Embassy in Moscow. Of military bearing, chin jutting out, he was dressed formally in a blue cashmere coat and business suit. He welcomed them to Moscow.

"Good to see you all," said Pressman. "For once the train was more or less on time. Now let's get ourselves organised. Those going to Moscow University please stand to my right. Others to my left."

As he shuffled to the left Will looked around this famous station built in 1909–12, his eyes gazing at the green and white stucco decorations in the main concourse area.

"Are you Lawrence, the chap going to the Timiryazev Agricultural Academy?" Pressman asked.

Will, having responded affirmatively, was introduced to Zina and Natalia, two student representatives from the academy, and to Igor, a sullen-looking driver, who helped him by carrying the two heavy suitcases.

"Welcome to Moscow," the two young ladies chimed in unison in Russian, smiling. Zina Ivanova Sverdlova, evidently the senior of the two ladies in the receiving party, was plumpish with a round face and thick-rimmed rectangular glasses. She wore her hair in a bun and was wearing a red wool dress under a loose coat. By contrast Natalia Petrovna Furtseva was slimmer with thick dark brown hair cut to shoulder length, high cheekbones and an angular jaw, above which protruded a toothy smile and gums. Her brown mid-length dress was patterned with small yellow and red flowers, and she was sporting some shiny calf-length black boots.

Will said goodbye to Tristan, Evan and his fellow student travellers. Despite their differences in temperament, he had struck up a good relationship with Tristan. He was now well and truly on his own.

Zina and Natalia walked with Will to a fawn-coloured Volga car parked outside the sprawling station.

Gazing out of the windows from the back seat sitting next to Zina, Will's first impression of the station's surroundings was of a huge square area with buildings displaying a wide range of Soviet propaganda posters, notably ones of Vladimir Lenin exhorting the Soviet people to move forward in constructing communism. There were far fewer passenger cars than he was used to in England, with only three main types visible – Fiat-designed Zhigulis, East German Trabants and Soviet Volgas. Many dilapidated and banged-up vans and small open-backed lorries laden with every imaginable type of material and machinery were scurrying around the square in a flurry of activity. Trolleybuses and buses were heading in all directions from the station. He noticed a few queues comprised mostly of middle-aged and old ladies with fur hats and long boots, or *valenki*, as protection against the cold.

Neither Zina nor Natalia spoke a word of English, so Will was immersed immediately into employing his fragmentary knowledge of the Russian language. Both ladies were young Soviet Komsomol representatives and clearly briefed about how to handle this incoming Westerner.

After a thirty-minute drive to the north-west of the city, they arrived at Listvennichnaya Alleia (Larch Avenue), a straight, two-lane road bordered by larch trees on its eastern side with the buildings of the academy opposite. Will was shown to his accommodation in a five-storey building known as the *gostinitsa*, or 'hotel', part of the academy reserved for visiting guests. His room was on the ground floor and had two single beds. The double-glazed window looked out into a courtyard covered with a light dusting of snow and a few beer bottles protruding from the surface. The light was fading and it was dull.

Will was invited to have supper with the two ladies in a *stolovaya*, or 'canteen', in the academy, where they continued their introductory conversations. Food was basic: Will settled for some meatballs and brown, tasteless gravy nestling in a mini canyon formed by the white, liquidy potato mush.

After a not very peaceful night he was picked up in the morning by a representative of the academy's foreign department and escorted to a nearby office to sort out administrative formalities, including getting a *udostovoreniye lichnosti* – the identity card for the academy – and receiving his first stipend. Will was to receive 150 roubles per month – a decent sum by Soviet standards, well above the average working wage – minus two roubles and thirty-one kopecks for the monthly rent of his room. Will immediately set out to stock up on some basic foods at the local food store with the plain name '*Producti*', where he purchased bread, cheese, milk, yoghurt, smetana and eggs to carry him over the first few days. His accommodation had cooking facilities, a shared bathroom and shower. Hot water supply proved to be erratic from day one – a reflection of the fact that the building was constructed in 1928, when boiler technology was primitive.

Will's task on the second day after arrival was to draw up a study and travel plan with his allocated supervisor Professor Kuzmenov, a well-known expert in the area of the economic performance of state and collective farms in the USSR. There was quite a bit of negotiation needed here. Kuzmenov advised focusing on technological improvements in Soviet agriculture. Will, on the other hand, wanted to focus on sociological changes in the countryside resulting from the new Soviet agricultural policies adopted after the removal of Khrushchev as Party Secretary in 1964. A compromise with the professor was reached a few days later, including a plan for Will to visit the Kuban/Krasnodar region (south-east Russia) and Ukraine in the spring, the precise locations to be determined later.

FIVE

Svetlana Antolevna

On his third day in Moscow Will returned to his room from a morning visit to the local bread shop to find his door at the end of the corridor ajar. Slightly alarmed since he was sure he had shut it before leaving the building, he walked cautiously towards the open door to find a diminutive, rotund lady busily sweeping the floor with an old-fashioned long-handled broom.

"*Zdravstvuyte*," she said as Will entered. "Hello, I am Svetlana Antolevna Dontsova. The cleaning lady. Good gracious – *Bozhe moi* – how tall you are! You are English? Vill? Lavrens?"

"Yes, yes. Pleased to meet you, Svetlana Antolevna. You work here?" replied Will, holding out his hand, which Svetlana took limply in her own.

"Of course," she replied. "I will make some Russian tea for us," and she promptly headed off to the kitchen, returning some minutes later with two glass *stakanchiks* of strong tea, a boiling kettle, some jam and some biscuits on a large tray. "Welcome," she said. "Put jam in your tea. Tasty. Take a biscuit."

Svetlana was in her mid-fifties and not much more than five feet two inches in height. Her ginger, greying hair was tucked behind a traditional orange, silver and white peasant scarf tied under her chin with a few strands protruding onto her forehead. She wore a dark blue smock, a practical choice for the cleaning-up work she was employed to undertake in the academy. The lines on her face and her puffy cheeks suggested she had lived a hard life. Her smile revealed a set of teeth containing a multiplicity of gold-coloured fillings, no doubt the consequence of her penchant for all things sugary, notably in tea. Will initially viewed her as a stern, severe woman – a Soviet female stereotype with orders to keep an eye on him – but he quickly corrected this impression and warmed to her as she sought to make him welcome in his new surroundings while introducing him to some local customs.

She explained some of the amenities of the building, how to seal the windows to keep warm, how to work the dilapidated cooker which was infested with cockroaches – and what to do when the hot water supply malfunctioned.

"If you turn on the gas on the cooker and wait five minutes, all the cockroaches will run away before you begin cooking," Svetlana advised, smilingly. "It's quite simple really!"

Svetlana was a tough, no-nonsense lady but with a warm heart. Her small, black eyes darted hither and thither, redolent of someone keeping her wits about her as part of a carefully developed survival strategy. There would certainly have been times when she would have had to behave obsequiously and deferentially towards authority and power, ducking and weaving for the sake of self-preservation.

"Excellent, tasty tea. Thank you. In England we always take milk with our tea. From what part of the Soviet Union do you come from, Svetlana Antolovna?" Will asked, endeavouring to keep the conversation going as he sipped the sweet brew.

"Milk? Impossible! Well, I never!" Svetlana replied. "What strange foreign habits. Georgian tea is the best. I'm from Krasnodar Oblast, in the Kuban," she said proudly. "Far away in the south in the Black Earth region. Moscow is better, though. I like it here. We have everything here in our capital, and the best food and clothes in the Soviet Union."

"Your family is here too?" asked Will.

"I live with my daughter Valya. She is twenty-three. She studied here in this academy. She is very clever and hard-working. She helps me. My sister Masha still lives in Krasnodar, in the south of Russia, where we were brought up."

"What is Valya's work?" asked Will.

"She works for the Ministry of Agriculture. On information. Statistics. I understand nothing of it – numbers, numbers, so complicated! And you? Tell me about yourself," answered Svetlana.

Will gave a brief history of his life in his broken Russian. Svetlana nodded, interjecting, "*Khorosho* – good," at various points. They continued conversing for twenty minutes or so before Svetlana announced she had to get on with her cleaning work. She gathered up the teacups and plates and headed towards the kitchen.

SIX

Winter Days in Moscow

Will gradually settled into his new environment, travelling regularly to the centre of Moscow to study at the Lenin Library. He adapted to the onset of the cold Russian winter and heavy snowfalls in December and January but had to buy a number of items locally to boost his inadequate inventory of winter-resistant apparel, notably some fur-lined boots and a rabbit fur Russian hat – *shapka* – with ear flaps for the cold winter days.

As Will's life developed into a routine, he decided that once a week he would pick up his post at the British Embassy situated on Maurice Thorez Embankment with a direct and splendid view of the southern ramparts of the Kremlin. Built in the late nineteenth century, the embassy buildings were formerly owned by a sugar merchant, Pavel Kharitonenko, who passed it on to his son, also Pavel, a renowned philanthropist and famous collector of Russian art. In short, a superlative embassy and residence whose occupation by the UK had long irked the Soviet authorities.

Walking back from the embassy across a near-empty Red Square towards the 87 bus stop one bitterly cold winter's day in early January, Will observed to his left a pair of goose-stepping soldiers and a sergeant from the elite Kremlin Regiment moving slowly to relieve their comrades guarding the Lenin Mausoleum, the shrine where Lenin's body was preserved. They were clad in long grey coats, fur hats with hammer and sickle emblems prominent in the middle of the forehead, and elongated felt boots (*valenki*). They marched along the elevated tribune parallel to the Kremlin's eastern wall abutting the mausoleum on Red Square. It was a slow, deliberate march, immaculately synchronised, the arms of the militia swinging across their bodies in time with the vertical extension of their stiff, goose-stepping legs, rifles on their shoulders pointing upwards. It was minus twenty-two degrees centigrade, and the temperature was falling as the winter sun slowly set.

As he walked in the direction of the National Historical Museum, at the far end of Red Square, Will glanced to his right, the east side of Red Square. Giant portraits of Vladimir Ilyich Lenin, the founder of the Soviet state, and Leonid Ilyich Brezhnev, the current General Secretary of the Communist Party, looked down on him from 'GUM', the State Universal Shop, the largest department store in Moscow claiming to sell every imaginable item a Soviet citizen might need in their daily lives. Between these comrades hung an equally prominent large poster with a rallying message: 'Glory to the Soviet People'.

Will was wearing multiple layers of Western-style outer clothing, a scarf covering most of his face, his rabbit fur shapka with ear flaps down and tied at the rear of the hat, a pair of East German-made long johns from GUM, warm corduroy trousers, two layers of socks, fur-lined boots and his mother's Harrods sheepskin gloves. Only his eyes were visible, and they were watering in the cold. His breath steamed on his scarf as he made his way steadily across Red Square, a light dusting of snow scattering randomly and skittishly on the cobble stones in front of him propelled by occasional gusts of wind. Glancing over his shoulder, his eyes focused on the cloudy grey emissions from the power station on the south side of the Moscow River making their way skywards. The calm, eerie yellowy

26

hue of incoming dusk, was accentuated by small ice particles, which danced in the chill air and attached themselves to his outer clothing.

Will stepped up his pace to try to keep warm. He noticed that there were few people braving the cold on the Square; almost all of them were wearing a uniform of some description, a common sight in central Moscow. Chilled to the bone, Will wondered why he was subjecting himself to this biting cold and loneliness. To make the point that he could stand on his own two feet, be independent and act alone? *Must be crazy*, he thought.

Eventually he reached the 87 bus stop in Ploshchad' Sverdlova, not far from the north-east corner of Red Square, more famously known as the square hosting the front façade of the Bolshoi theatre building, home to the world-famous ballet and opera company. This bus took him back to his accommodation and room on Listvennichnaya Alleia. Will had forgotten to buy his five-rouble monthly travel pass for Moscow for January and had no intention to make his way now to a metro station to purchase one, so he was going to have to pay for the bus ride to his academy hostel in cash. Five kopecks, the standard bus fare, was the cost of the forty-five-minute ride. Will had this coin at the ready in his right hand inside his glove. A bus ticket was purchased by putting the fare into a box and tearing off a bus ticket from a roll. When the bus was crowded this operation meant passing some money down the bus via other passengers and hoping a ticket came back in the reverse direction (which it usually did). After a few minutes of waiting the bus arrived. The driver had kept its engine running. Noxious lead-smelling petrol fumes were emitting from its rusty tailpipe and clumps of dirty snow and ice clung to its mudguards. Will entered, got a ticket and seated himself in the middle of the bus, trying to thaw out.

SEVEN

Spirt

The following evening Will had been invited to the academy's foreign club. A special guest speaker was announced.

Arriving at the venue of the meeting five minutes late, Will found that the speaker was a certain Chi´ Văn Minh. A diminutive, fiery North Vietnamese guerrilla fighter from Hanoi, Minh was busy chastising the US and its capitalist backers, including NATO, Europe, Australia and others, for destroying his country with bombs and chemicals, killing thousands of women and children, torturing and murdering prisoners of war and raping women. Fired up by his own fierce rhetoric, Minh's speech built up to a crescendo of indignation and fury, calling on fraternal socialist countries including the USSR and COMECON countries to come to North Vietnam's assistance and resist the capitalist invaders. Prolonged 'stormy' applause greeted the end of Minh's tirade.

His ears reverberating from Minh's wholesale disparagement of the Western world, Will was heading for the exit when Natalia spotted him and invited him to join Zina and some friends for post-harangue drinks and food. Will thought he could hardly refuse, though he felt awkward at not having anything to take to the party. Natalia brushed away his concerns: with Zina she had prepared Russian zakuski, or hors d'oeuvres – stuffed eggs in mayonnaise, herring, cheese, pickled cucumbers, beetroot salad, pickled mushrooms, red sturgeon caviar and rye bread – together with two bottles of Extra vodka, Moldovan wine and beer. It was quite a spread and Will was embarrassed to have been added to the guest list only as an afterthought.

The party was lively, with much joking, frequent telling of Russian anecdotes, not many of which Will understood, toasts including to all and sundry, including the leaders of North Vietnam, Leonid Brezhnev, the Communist Party of the Soviet Union, the Viet Cong, international cooperation, peace between comradely nations and so forth. Will began drinking cautiously but joined in the good-natured revelry as the evening evolved. A tall Russian postgraduate student, Tolya, who spoke good English, disappeared at one point and returned with a flask of clear liquid – *"spirt"* – brewed from industrial alcohol in one of the academy's chemical laboratories, to widespread applause amongst the guests. About ninety per cent proof in terms of alcoholic content, Will was chosen, much to his embarrassment – he did not like being the centre of attention in social gatherings – as the evening's guinea pig with the task of tasting and certifying the transparent brew as fit for human consumption.

"*Davai*, Vill," went the chorus. "Drink up! Everything in one gulp – but sniff this black bread while you swallow it."

As the party interloper Will was not in a position to act as a killjoy, so he slipped a small vodka glass of the spirt liquid down the hatch while clutching and sniffing the bread for comfort.

"Jesus Christ, Mother of Mary," gasped Will to widespread amusement amongst the guests, slowly coming to his senses after the toxic brew had coursed through his body unleashing shuddering alcoholic waves.

"Bloody lethal. Where did you get it?" he asked, barely able to string two words together.

"Made with care, craft and refinement in chemical laboratory number three, Timiryazev Academy!" replied Tolya with pride, smiling mischievously.

"No," someone cried out, "it was made in laboratory number two! That is why it's so weak in alcohol. Bring us a stronger brew worthy of the name *'spirt'!*" This engendered much laughter and ribaldry among the partygoers, as well as lewd calls for the women to take part and drink the fiery mixture.

"Comrades, I hear your message loud and clear. By general proclamation you demand the ninety-six per cent proof variant. As toastmaster, your appointed *Tamada*, I must solemnly fulfil your request," said Tolya before disappearing to find an even stronger brew.

Returning a few moments later with a flask of ninety-six per cent proof firewater, Tolya asked, "*Yesho*, Vill – would you like to be official taster once again?", an invitation which Will this time batted away with firmness.

"Tolya, it was simply delicious, but… British decorum and modesty obliges me to desist," joked Will.

No wonder, he thought to himself, *that Russian men's life expectancy is less than sixty years. This spirt stuff is virtually pure alcohol.* The Russians present – men and women – continued to drink and passed the *spirt* around the table with reckless abandon. Tolya returned with another, larger flask, at which point Will decided to opt out from further participation in the evening's drinking. He bid goodnight to the group and thanked Zina and Natalia for their hospitality. A good Russian experience, though there were limits to the extent he could absorb some local practices. Death by alcoholic poisoning was not the way he intended to pass into oblivion.

EIGHT

British Embassy Club, Kutuzovsky Prospect 7/4, Moscow

Will wandered down to the British Embassy Club most Fridays to meet and catch up with other British Council students, including Tristan, who had travelled with him to Moscow. It was located off Kutuzovsky Prospect to the west of the Moscow River within one of the high-rise compounds housing Western diplomats, businessmen, journalists, teachers and others over whom the Soviet authorities kept a close watch, and opposite the Hotel Ukraina. Entering the compound required presenting identification such as a diplomatic pass, or *propusk*, to the Soviet security guards on duty. Anyone suspicious or 'non-conforming' was turned away or checked again by means of a phone call from the guards to the Ministry of Internal Affairs. There were cameras everywhere and extensive listening devices in most apartments.

The club consisted of not much more than an elongated bar area with some stools, tables and chairs, a dance area for those so inclined when things livened up, normally on Fridays or Saturdays after 10pm. Drinks were cheap and subsidised by Her Majesty's Government – half a rouble or fifty kopecks could buy you a Worthington Pale Ale, a pint of Watney's bitter or a shot of Extra vodka. One rouble would get you a generous gin and tonic. Seven to eight roubles, therefore, were enough for a good night out – about five per cent of Will's monthly income.

Will arrived at the bar around 7pm on a cold night in late January, having spent the day at the Lenin Library reading some books on the economic and sociological changes in collectivised and state-run agriculture in the late 1960s.

The Lenin Library was cavernous but warm in winter. It was perpetually busy. Its canteens were heavily frequented, as, on a good day, without warning, food items for general sale might appear, such as oranges or pears. The study halls tended to empty when word got around that a new consignment had arrived, and queues rapidly formed. Never enquire what was being queued for, the Soviet dictum went, just get in line and ask questions later.

Back in the British Embassy bar, things were quiet. Will ordered a Worthington Pale Ale and waited to see who would arrive. He had made a loose sort of arrangement to meet up with Stephanie, a petite Scottish secretary from Glasgow whom he had met on a previous visit to the club. She worked in the Chancery, the heart of the British Embassy, but often had to stay late to ensure that cables were dispatched to London before the end of the day. There was no sign of her.

The evening appeared to be going nowhere. It was now 8.45pm. Stephanie had not arrived, there was no-one he knew hanging out in the bar and he didn't really want another drink on his own. He was on the point of leaving when there was a slight commotion and flurry of activity at the door.

In walked Stephanie, accompanied by some colleagues. She did not see Will initially as she headed towards the bar but, glancing sideways, she caught his eye. "Hey, Will is here; come and join us. Let me introduce you: Tom Dawson from the economic section, Charles Fortescue, who works with me in the Chancery, and Wendell Randall III, political attaché at the US Mission."

Wendell immediately jumped in: "Political adviser to the US Ambassador actually, Stephi. Gotta get my title right, honey! So who's having what? Stephi – G&T, guys, beers?" Tom and Charles opted for pints.

"And for you, Billy boy? Small beer? I assume you are old enough to drink it, buddy!" said Wendell loudly, which provoked sniggers all round.

Will took an instant dislike to Wendell: arrogant, condescending, egocentric and self-satisfied were some of the adjectives that immediately came to mind. Will objected to being called Bill or Billy (the more so as they were the names of his family dog). And he resented the fact that Wendell appeared to have Stephanie locked firmly in his grip.

Will helped Wendell carry the orders back from the bar to the small gathering, resisting the temptation – not without some difficulty – of feigning a slip on the polished bar floor and pouring the mixed drinks over Wendell's immaculately pressed business suit.

Stephanie asked Will when he was going away on his trip to the south of Russia and Ukraine. He was about to answer when Wendell butted in to ask if this was a typical student vacation or something more serious.

"Actually, Wendell, it is a study trip related to my research on Soviet agriculture. I will be visiting collective and state farms and looking into sociological changes in rural life in the USSR since the implementation of the Brezhnev agricultural reforms."

"So you are writing some kinda book or something?" asked Wendell.

"No, Wendell," replied Will, "that would be way beyond my capability. The research is for my master's thesis at Birmingham University. In the UK, that is."

"Oh, I see. I would like to hear about your travels, Billy boy. Soviet agriculture is important in this country. The US Embassy keeps track of harvest developments. Call me when you are back from your travels. You can get me, if I'm not busy, at the ambassador's office," replied Wendell authoritatively.

At this point Tristan barged clumsily into the group, manifestly the worse for wear. "Hey you bourgeois capitalist lackeys," slurred Tristan. "Fraternal socialist greetings from MGU, Moscow University, home of Soviet brains, Russian beauties and foreign spies. How are we all?"

Wendell looked disdainfully upon Tristan, manifestly irritated at the heavy-handed and boorish way he had muscled his way into the conversation. Stephanie, who knew Tristan from past encounters in the club, was also annoyed.

"Now, diplos," Tristan continued, "the socialist paradise is no place for closet capitalist intrigues. Work with our Soviet brethren, not against them for a change... you'll be surprised what can be achieved. Need more Reds *in* beds not *under* beds, I say, hah, hah, hah. Who's buying the drinks?"

Silence ensued. Tristan was making a pig's ass of himself, and no-one wanted to engage with him. Wendell, looking scornfully upon this unwelcome interloper, grasped the bull by the horns: "Stephi, Tommy, Charlie – drink up, buddies, we're outta here. I reserved at the Metropol. Cheers, Billy boy – call me with the harvest news," and with that Wendell ushered his companions out of the bar to his waiting car, totally ignoring Tristan. Stephanie cast a short, backward glance at the hapless Will, as if apologising for having shunted him aside and intimating that 'you can't say no to this hotshot slicker, Wendell, can you?'

Will, irritated and humiliated, decided to settle scores with the disruptive Tristan. "Tristan, your barnstorming entrance was deliberately designed to disrupt and provoke. You succeeded in dispersing the group with masterly efficiency. I'm glad you saw off that US Embassy prick, but you screwed up my chances with Stephi. You should stop playing the club bore and cut down your boozing before you seriously damage your health."

"Piss off, Will. I don't need a fucking lecture. You're just a prim and proper, sanctimonious, pampered typical petit bourgeois Brit.

So boring and safe – just play everything by the English middle-class book. Loosen up. Live life to the full. Drink and be merry. Take some risks, for God's sake. Enjoy life – it's short enough, after all," responded Tristan so loudly that the attention of others hovering near the bar was drawn to his outburst.

"Well, thanks, Tristan," said Will sarcastically. "That's just what I need to hear. A fine example you set. If I'm so sodding boring why waste your time with me?"

Will made to pick up his things and head for the exit. What made it worse was that Tristan was hitting home to some degree – it was true that he was all coiled up, cautious, serious and reserved, and he knew he needed to open up and live more adventurously.

"Don't go, Will. I'm sorry, man. I went overboard… these arrogant diplomats piss me off – treat us students like shit. They know sod all about Russia, its people, its history, its culture and its struggles. Who saved us from fascism – America, Britain? Get me a drink, Will."

"I'll get two beers, that's it," replied Will, still smarting from Tristan's verbal attack on him. Tristan, smoking heavily, slapped Will on the back and apologised again. He knew his outburst had hurt his friend.

Will drank his beer quickly, not wanting to hang about the club with Tristan any longer. He made his way to the stop on the other side of Kutuzovsky Prospect for a connecting bus to Sverdlov Square and his 87 bus ride home. As he did so a motorcade of sleek luxury Soviet Zil limousines, accompanied by police cars and outriders on motorcycles, swept past him at speed along the middle lane of the Prospect heading west. A big-shot Soviet leader – perhaps Party Leader Leonid Brezhnev himself – was heading home.

A chastened, small-shot British student was doing the same.

NINE

Siberia

Ten days later, at very short notice, Will was asked by the foreign department of his academy, Inotdel, if he would like to join a group of postgraduates on a six-day trip to Siberia leaving that evening.

"Siberia?" Will asked somewhat incredulously. "In February? In the middle of winter? Is that a good idea?"

"Yes," Julia Timofeevicha, head of Inotdel, replied. "A chance for an exceptional experience. Yes, or no? Reply needed immediately!"

Why not? Will thought to himself, as he wouldn't have another chance to visit such a faraway place. *Be adventurous. Take a chance.*

"Well, I accept, thank you," said Will. "I would be happy to join the group."

That evening he boarded a Tupolev aircraft at Vnukovo Airport at midnight for the six-hour flight east to Irkutsk, which was to be the base for the group 'excursion'.

There were about fifteen foreign students on the trip, mostly men and mainly from socialist countries Poland, Hungary and Czechoslovakia, plus Will himself and a couple of Russian lecturers from the academy to manage the group and the logistics. Arriving in Irkutsk about midday local time, Will immediately felt the colder temperature – minus twenty-five degrees centigrade. They were shepherded to an institute with whom his academy had links and shown to bunk-bed accommodation. Will's was on the top, by a double window, through which the cold air outside penetrated.

During a few days' sightseeing in snowbound Irkutsk, the group visited the wooden homes of the Decembrist rebels who had attempted to overthrow the Czar in 1825 before being exiled to Irkutsk where they were joined later by their devoted wives. The students then tried some cross-country skiing (Will nearly got some minor frostbite from inadequately lined boots) and witnessed some of the spectacular scenery and taiga of Siberia with frozen rivers, forests of fir trees and lakes with a thick carpet of snow everywhere. Against a blue sky and bright but weak and watery sun, the landscape was truly breathtaking.

The next day they set out to visit Lake Baikal, the largest freshwater lake in the world, its surface frozen with metre-thick ice. Will found walking on the lake was an extraordinary experience.

One of the Poles on the trip got out a bottle of vodka to celebrate. "*K Baikalu, davai!*" they said in unison, paying homage to this wonder of nature.

In the distance Will observed a small van making its way across the frozen ice to Olkhon Island, whose lifeline to the mainland in winter was the frozen road carefully marked out by wooden posts drilled into the ice. At a restaurant by the shores of the lake the group tasted baked omul, the species of flat white fish unique to Lake Baikal.

Will was overawed by the environment, which he found invigorating but intimidating. The vastness of the taiga and the harshness of the climate might have suggested that only the hardiest of souls could survive here. Not so, Will noticed. People were accustomed to the winter and dressed appropriately. Irkutsk and its environs, though more than five thousand kilometres from Moscow, did not feel Asiatic at all but rather European, like Western Russia. As if to make the point one of the local guides was the son of a German prisoner of war sent to Irkutsk in penal servitude after the Great Patriotic War. His dream was to live in the German Democratic Republic, an opportunity currently denied to him. The vastness of the territory of Russia was bought home to Will even more when they visited Bratsk, a huge hydroelectric power station six hundred kilometres from Irkutsk on the Angara River, after a short plane ride.

Will joined in the drinking bouts piloted by a few Polish and Hungarian students with some reserve. He did not feel integrated in the group. Rather, he felt an outsider, lonely and isolated, in a physical and cultural environment very far from home. He wondered what his family would be doing at home at that moment. Cut off from his roots, he wished, there and then, that he could be whisked back to familiar and comfortable surroundings.

The experience of living in the USSR would be bearable with more companionship, preferably female. Tristan, though he was wild and unpredictable, was his best mate in Moscow but lived on the other side of town. Will needed someone he could rely upon nearer to hand.

Siberia had brought home to him the scale of Russia. It was inspiring that people had found a way to eke out an existence there, many of them forcibly travelling thousands of kilometres by wagon and on foot from western Russia in the nineteenth century to endure penal servitude and exile, a testament to the hardiness and adaptability of the human race. Exposing himself to this environment reminded Will that at heart he was a West European urban dweller. Seeing and experiencing the vast expanses of Siberia made him realise that this would not change.

TEN

Valya

Shortly after returning from Siberia Will began to feel unwell and progressively developed influenza-like symptoms. He resorted straightaway to taking antibiotics provided by his father coupled with Benylin syrup for loosening coughs. But this bout of influenza was unlike any other he had experienced before. He found himself sweating profusely on the floor of his room, lying on the mattress from his bed which he had placed there to avoid the rigid springs of his bedframe that drove into his back.

Svetlana Antolevna, the cleaning lady, found him the next morning on the floor. "Well, I never," she exclaimed. "What is going on, Vill?"

"I'm unwell. Fever. Temperature," replied Will, lying prone on the mattress in a night shirt and scarf.

"You need a traditional Russian remedy," Svetlana insisted. "Lemon, milk, garlic and honey, to rid yourself of the fever. I will get them and return straightaway."

Will thought no more about it, drifting in and out of sleep, but was awoken when Svetlana arrived with a strong garlic, hot milk, lemon and honey mixture, insisting that Will swallow it wholesale and take it three times a day. Will thanked her for her efforts but was sceptical if this remedy would do the trick.

Overnight he sweated even more profusely, his sheets becoming very damp as his body sought to dispense with the fever. But after twenty-four hours he began to feel better. Svetlana returned with more of the potent garlic, hot milk, lemon and honey brew the next day. The fever slowly left his body, he ceased aching and he started to feel up to resuming his normal activities. He recovered his appetite. He didn't know which treatment had worked but strongly suspected that the traditional Russian one had played the major role.

Two days later Svetlana appeared again with some homemade biscuits and jam. "Take them, Vill, good for your health. And I have brought my daughter with me to introduce you to her," said Svetlana, who opened the door and shouted to Valya to come to Will's room.

At the door a few moments later appeared Valya, a fresh-faced, good-looking Russian girl of medium height, pink cheeks and a warm smile, about Will's age. Beneath her silver fox-fur hat with grey-silver and black spiky, vertical strands and wraparound scarf Will noticed her dark long hair. Her thick knee-length dark blue coat was a familiar style in Moscow, as were her calf-length boots, which were like those that Natalia had worn on the day he was met at the Belorussky station.

"*Ochen' priyatno* – pleased to meet you," began Will, somewhat disorientated by this attractive young woman appearing on the threshold of his unkempt and messy room with medicine bottles and the debris of Svetlana's magic potion scattered over the table.

"*Ochen' priyatno*," reciprocated Valya, holding out her small hand hesitantly once inside the room (Russians, Will learnt, avoid handshakes across the threshold of a room as it is believed to be portentous). "Welcome to Moscow. My mother said you were unwell. Are you better now?"

"Your mother has looked after me very well, and, yes, I feel better now, thank you. I have heard a lot about you; it is nice to meet you in person," said Will.

"My mother told me about how tall you are. And your strange English habits – milk with tea! We Russians eat more simply – bread, eggs, meat, smetana, cheese, fish, kasha… and we drink a lot. Too much. The winter is harsh. People resort to vodka and alcohol to beat off the cold."

Valya was looking around the room and her eyes fell upon Will's box of cornflakes. She looked at the picture of a young mother and children at the breakfast table on the outside of the box and the curly letters of the accompanying text and asked, "*Shto takoi* – what is that?"

"Ah, Valya. Those are cornflakes. I have them in the morning with milk and sugar for breakfast. On the box there is advertising – *reklama*. To sell it to the customer. To encourage a purchase. To make you think you will be tasting them again for the first time."

"I am not sure I understand," said Valya. "Here we just say: bread, cheese, smetana. People still buy them."

The conversation meandered on between the two of them. Will's Russian was improving but there were swathes of Valya's softly intonated phrases that passed him by. Svetlana re-entered his room with a special chocolate cake she had baked at home, together with tea, hot water and lemon, and the three of them continued to chatter away. Valya had dispensed with her hat and coat, revealing a slim, well-proportioned figure in a one-piece blue-grey woollen dress on which was attached a small butterfly brooch as well as a Komsomol badge of Vladimir Lenin.

Will found Valya attractive though cautious and withdrawn. He sensed there were layers of personality beneath her calm, reserved exterior which were not currently accessible to him. She was in that sense traditionally Russian, watching her back, not revealing much about herself and speaking in a passive voice as she carefully and metaphorically circled around Will and assessed who he was. There was nonetheless a straightforward, honest and pleasant engagement between the two of them, devoid of expectation.

Taking a bold step, Will said, "Valya, I have bought two tickets for a classical music concert at the Moscow Conservatory next week. Would you like to come with me to the concert?"

Valya hesitated while passing a sideways glance at her mother for a sign of approbation or disapproval. Having received a positive eye signal (how exactly it was transmitted was beyond Will's comprehension), she replied, "That is very kind of you, Will. I haven't been to a concert for a while – so much work. I shall look forward to it."

They agreed to meet at 5.30pm next week at Will's residence in time for the concert at 7pm.

Svetlana busied herself round the room doing some clearing-up while Valya and Will chatted away. Dusting the solitary cupboard Svetlana came upon Will's razor and a blue can of Gillette shaving mousse. "And what is that?" asked Svetlana, pointing at the cylindrical tube.

"Ah, I'll show you," interjected Will, and proceeded to take off the lid and press the top of the tube, from which emerged some thick white shaving foam.

Svetlana looked on, bemused. "Well, well, well," she exclaimed. "*tekhnologiya na predelakh fantastiki...* today I have witnessed technology bordering on the fantastic," she exclaimed. "Amazing. We must be able to develop this product in Russia after the success of our Sputnik satellites."

The two ladies prepared to depart at this point.

"Until next week," Valya said, putting her coat back on.

ELEVEN

Concert

Will met Valya, as planned, at his hostel to go to the concert and they set off to travel into town by 87 bus on a cold, late February evening. Valya was wrapped up and looked very Russian in her silver fox-fur hat, white scarf, thick blue coat and padded gloves. She was quiet, reserved and polite, answering Will's questions but not initiating any conversation herself. Upon arrival at Ploshchad' Sverdlova they headed eastwards towards Bolshaya Nikitskaya and the Moscow Conservatory, home of Moscow's famous musical school and a concert hall.

"What music are we going to hear?"

"Tchaikovsky violin concerto and Shostakovich Symphony Number 5, I believe," replied Will.

They headed for the *garderob* run by busy *babushki* ladies dressed in grey smocks who issued a coat tab to each concert-goer.

After depositing her coat and hat Valya went to one of the nearby long mirrors adjoining the *garderob*, carefully combing her hair, adjusting her dress so it sat correctly in place over the curves of her slim body and touching up her makeup, an interminable process with Will looking on awkwardly not quite knowing what to do or where to look.

"Can I offer you a drink before the concert, perhaps?" suggested Will, half hoping that Valya would decline as his student stipend was running low.

"That is kind. I will take a glass of champagne," replied Valya. "Half sweet. And maybe we can get some *butterbrod* with cheese and ham too?" Will duly bought two glasses and the *butterbrods*, which cost eleven roubles, leaving him with just eighty-three roubles for the rest of the month.

They examined the programme of the concert together on the circular upright table, sipping their drinks and munching their *butterbrods* while keeping a respectful distance between themselves at opposite sides of the table.

"I haven't been to a concert in a long while," said Valya. "Too busy at work. My mother does not like classical music, only Soviet songs, mainly wartime ones. She goes to a club with friends on Fridays and they have a good sing-song and reminisce together."

Will said, "I go to concerts quite often here: the musical and theatrical life here – ballet, opera in particular – is very good. My dream is to see the ballet *Spartak* at the Bolshoi Theatre, but it is very hard to find a ticket."

At this point the bell rung to summon the audience to their seats. Valya and Will found theirs towards the back of the stalls. It was quickly evident that the concert hall would be half full at best, which subdued the atmosphere ahead of the arrival of the orchestra and conductor.

As the musicians shuffled onto the stage some sharp-eyed members of the audience, seeing that more expensive seats in the auditorium were unoccupied, moved forward to occupy them. This unedifying scramble continued well after the Tchaikovsky piece had began and led to disputes when some of the bona fide ticket holders, arriving late, attempted to secure their rightful places. It was a good ten minutes before the audience began to settle down. Russians appeared accustomed to this free-for-all, which, Will thought to himself, would not be tolerated in more regimented Western concert halls: meanwhile, the orchestra played on regardless of the commotion in the audience. Making things worse, two coiffed *babushki* in front of Will and Valya chattered incessantly through the violin concerto, making it difficult to concentrate on the music.

Modest, polite applause greeted the end of the performance of the famous Tchaikovsky work, which had failed to inspire, before the audience returned to the bars for interval refreshments.

Will and Valya had another two glasses of champagne, further depleting Will's tottering stipendiary reserve.

"Well, to be honest, I didn't think that performance was very uplifting, did you, Valya?" asked Will.

"It was, how should I say, *normalno*," replied Valya, smiling and trying to be polite. She appeared to be preoccupied, not looking at Will, her mind elsewhere.

"Perhaps the Shostakovich will be more inspiring," offered Will hopefully.

"Yes, maybe," said Valya, looking over her shoulder. "Excuse me for one minute. I will see you back at the seats," she said, heading hastily, Will presumed, for the cloakrooms.

Will returned to his seat after five minutes. The orchestra reassembled. No sign of Valya. The conductor strode out to take the podium and just as he took a short bow Valya arrived, flustered and out of breath.

"Are you alright?" said Will quizzically.

"Yes, yes," replied Valya hurriedly. "Alright. Headache."

That doesn't sound very convincing, thought Will.

Before speculating any further the dramatic opening bars of Shostakovich's Fifth Symphony summoned the audience to attention. This time there was an immediate stop to the pre-concert hubbub and merry-go-round of exchanging seats. Everyone's attention was focused on the music almost instantaneously.

The contrast with the first part of the concert was extraordinary. There was a sense that everyone was being swept away by the drama of Shostakovich's famous symphony, his 'creative response to justified criticism'. Will felt drawn in and emotionally connected to the composer's brave resistance against oppression and his desperate assertion of his right to artistic freedom. The entire concert audience was in harmony with the conductor and orchestra and found themselves in a timeless world, under a magical spell. Will was deeply moved. At the end of the symphony the audience stood, clapped and cheered. They had experienced something special.

As they gathered their belongings after a lengthy wait at the *garderob* Will asked Valya if she had enjoyed the concert.

"I am sorry I was late, Will. Something came up. A work matter. Yes. I feel invigorated. Shostakovich was a brave, courageous man. During the music I felt that I must do everything to uphold the things in life dear to me," replied Valya quietly as they walked towards the exit.

"Time stood still. The music took over my soul, Valya. I won't forget it. Why were you away so long?" asked Will casually.

Valya's mind was elsewhere. She was not listening to Will. "Did you ask me something, Will? Excuse me, I was not concentrating," she said.

"It doesn't matter," said Will.

As they prepared to leave the Conservatory and emerge into the cold, damp darkness, Will suddenly heard a greeting from a familiar female voice behind him.

"Will, Will, hello there, hello, were you at the concert too?"

TWELVE

At the Metropol Hotel

Will hadn't expected to be hailed by name as he left the Moscow Conservatory with Valya after the Shostakovich concert, nor did he welcome it. He turned quickly and caught a glimpse of Stephanie, submerged between a forest of dark coats, fur collars and hats of Moscow concert-goers, pushing and shoving their way through the sturdy swing doors and the accumulated black slush on the floor as they exited the building.

Having passed the threshold between the inside and the outside of the Conservatory building, Will waited for Stephanie to emerge, which she duly did after a few seconds.

"I thought you were going to disappear there in that Soviet-style rugby scrum. How are you, Steph? Oh, this is Valya, a friend of mine from the academy," said Will.

Valya duly smiled sheepishly.

"Did you see Wendell?" said Stephanie, looking about. "He went off to find his car and driver ten minutes ago and I haven't seen him since."

Will's heart sank – he had no desire to see Wendell.

To his consternation and right on cue, Wendell arrived in his chauffeured black Buick bearing US diplomatic number plates. Bystanders looked on with a certain deference as Wendell emerged from the car. He said a cursory hello to Will, who then introduced him to Valya. The sight of a young, attractive Russian lady had an instant impact on Wendell's demeanour and body language and produced a broad smile and greeting from him. "Well, great to meet you, Valya," said Wendell, unctuously displaying his shiny white teeth while looking her over and ignoring Stephanie. "I'm Wendell Randall III from the US Embassy."

Valya, whose English was weak, replied, "Good evening, sir, Randall."

Wendell, never one to let an opportunity to ingratiate himself with a pretty girl, proposed that they all go and have a drink at the Metropol Hotel. "We can all squeeze into the car. Let's go. Boris, move the front seat back, please, so big boy Billy can get in the front."

Valya and Will barely had the time to draw breath before being whisked into the vehicle with Wendell positioning himself strategically in the middle of the back seat between the two attractive women. Will was marooned in the front. *This guy Wendell*, Will thought to himself, *is used to getting his own way.*

Valya appeared impressed by the American diplomat's display of smooth, decisive action and easy-going conviviality. Exuding authority, Wendell barked an order to his Soviet driver: "Boris, Metropol Hotel. Quickly. We are thirsty."

They arrived after less than ten minutes at the landmark Metropol Hotel and headed for the main bar after disposing of their overcoats at the *garderob*.

"Bottle of dry champagne," Wendell barked to the barman in English. "Four glasses. Nuts. If you have them, that is."

They found a comfortable spot in the lounge. Will noted that the Metropol was not far from the 87 bus stop, so he and Valya would not have to go far to bail out if Wendell became excessively overbearing and irritating.

The champagne and glasses arrived after an inordinate delay and Wendell proceeded to pour out the bubbly and offered a toast to friendship. Glasses were clinked and refilled.

"Well, I didn't think much of the concert," opined Wendell loudly.

"I thought the Shostakovich was wonderful," retorted Will. "Moving. What did you think, Stephanie?"

"Not bad," she said, taking an equivocal position between the two men. "And Valya. Did you like it?" enquired Stephanie.

Valya, embarrassed by her poor English and smiling nervously, replied, "Yes, thank you," and remained reserved and quiet for the rest of the evening, cautiously sipping her champagne while carefully observing the surroundings and all those present, mostly Soviet apparatchiks, Western businessmen, diplomats and attractive Soviet women in their twenties. She tried to project an image of self-confidence and ease with the surroundings, but Will thought this was a façade: she was nervous about being the only Russian in a group of foreigners. Her presence with the Westerners would be noted.

"What do you do, Valya?" asked Wendell.

Valya, with the help of some rudimentary translation by Will, explained that she worked as a junior statistician compiling technical information on Soviet harvests for the Ministry of Agriculture.

"What is the harvest outlook for this year?" blurted out Wendell, who was, as usual, dominating the conversation and not letting anyone else get a word in edgeways. "Our information is that it will be pretty good – even a record. Can you confirm that?" he added.

"Oh, I cannot say," replied Valya.

"Cannot say? Or will not say?" Wendell shot back; Will translated.

"Both," said Valya, feeling herself pressured. "I am not allowed to discuss state matters."

"Understood," replied Wendell, surreptitiously smirking at her and suggesting that, if he had free rein to deploy his multiple charms, he would find a way to loosen her resistance and extract some useful information from her. And more besides.

"Billy boy," continued Wendell, "your round. Another bottle of Soviet bubbly – double quick – dry, not the cheaper half-sweet variant," Wendell barked.

Will had been dreading this moment because a bottle of Soviet champagne in this upmarket central Moscow hotel would deplete his monthly monetary reserves below a critical level. Sheepishly he approached the bar to be informed that a bottle of dry champagne would cost twenty-three roubles, leaving him just fifty roubles for the rest of the month.

Returning with the bottle Will noted that Wendell had drawn both young ladies even closer to him. Will was left to sit on a single armchair, isolated. It was a three-plus-one situation and he was the one. This evening was not panning out as he had intended.

Valya, increasingly aware of the risk of being seen to be overindulging and fraternising in bourgeois Western company in an upmarket Moscow hotel frequented by KGB watchers and informers, eyed Will with a flash of her dark eyes, deftly communicating that she would not tempt fate any more and wanted to leave.

"Well, Gospodin Wendell, Gospozha Stephanie, I will go home now. Thank you for your hospitality," she said in Russian.

Will, who had barely taken a sip of champagne from the second bottle, had already got the message. He would have to accompany Valya home. It irked him that virtually the whole bottle of pop he had bought was now left for Wendell and Stephanie to imbibe at his expense and that he had wasted his money. He said his goodbyes and helped Valya on with her winter coat retrieved from the *garderob*. They exited the Metropol Hotel and headed for the 87 bus stop on Ploshchad' Sverdlova, on the other side of the vast square, where a bus was fortunately waiting.

"What did you think of Wendell Randall, the American?" asked Will a few minutes later as the bus trundled towards their destination.

Valya's reply was cagey. "He is the first American I have ever met," was all that Valya would offer in reply.

That's hardly a ringing endorsement of him, thought Will. He wondered if Valya had concluded that all Americans were like him.

The 87 bus arrived at Listvennichnaya Alleia and they alighted at Will's stop.

"Can I see you home, Valya? It's dark. Do you live nearby?" asked Will.

"I am fine," said Valya. "I will take the bus back six stops and get another one to our home. You don't need to come. I am used to this short journey: remember, I used to study at the academy."

"Well, at least let me wait with you. I would like to see you safely onto your return bus," insisted Will.

"*Ladno-clear* – thank you," replied Valya, and they crossed the street to wait at the bus stop close by. "What a gallant, classical Englishman!" she joked, lightening the tone.

The bus emerged in the murky distance, its headlights shining jerkily as it bumped along the uneven road surface. It was partially obscured by the damp, heavy atmosphere as it trundled its way slowly towards them before shuddering to a halt after sliding the last few metres on compacted black ice.

"Thank you so much, Will. I enjoyed our evening together," said Valya, offering her hand. Will took her hand and leaned tentatively forward, seeking a brief touching of their cold cheeks, which Valya duly reciprocated albeit, though without any obvious affectation of closeness or warmth.

"Well, thank you for coming, Valya. I enjoyed it too. Please give my regards to Svetlana Antolevna."

"I will," replied Valya as she boarded the bus. It set off. Valya waved as it headed off into the distance.

Will had enjoyed Valya's company, although the evening had been hijacked by Wendell and Stephanie. He was not convinced that a more serious relationship with Valya was on the cards. There were too many barriers between them. Valya was reserved and careful during and after the concert and had been rather formal, tense and stiff; there was little laughter or merriment between them. It was as if she was testing him out to see if he was trustworthy. Furthermore, she had been distracted by something or someone work-related, or both.

THIRTEEN

Linguistic Somersaults

After his foray to the conservatoire and a large outlay on 8 March for flowers on International Women's Day for Svetlana, Valya, Natalia and Zina, Will was struggling to manage his expenses. So he was pleased to find some paying work, through Tristan, at the Maurice Thorez Moscow Pedagogical Institute of Foreign Languages, which was recruiting mother-tongue English speakers to read some phrases out loud and pronounce them in their natural voices. The pay was twenty-two roubles for two hours' work.

Will went along with Tristan. They were in turn placed before an old spool tape recorder and asked to recite into a microphone sentences like:

"Edward likes the cornet."

"Where's the troubadour's trumpet?"

"Who stole my horse dung?"

"Dolly danced the tango."

"Firm bubbles make a louder pop."

"These sentences would never be spoken by an Englishman – or even by a Scotsman," Tristan said to Maria Fedorovna, the middle-aged stern, silver-haired and humourless linguistics lecturer from the institute who was supervising the session.

"That is not the point, Gospodin de Fallières," replied Maria. "We are a scientific linguistics institute. We want to hear how you pronounce vowels, such as 'o', 'a', 'u', 'e', in English. This is important for our research. Now let's get to work. I want you to say these phrases in different moods. The first mood is sad. Then normal. Then excited. Then happy. Then angry. Then frightened. Then inquisitively. Ready to begin?"

Tristan said it was tautological to ask where the troubadour's trumpet was in a happy voice when the underlying problem was that it was missing.

"How can I possible express joy about missing my horse dung or be angry if Edward likes his cornet?" asked Will mischievously. "And how can bubbles be firm?"

Maria Fedorovna dismissed these concerns out of hand as irrelevant. "Concentrate, please. This is important state-sponsored research," she said.

Will and Tristan dutifully recited the phrases into a microphone for registration onto the spooled tape, in different moods, before being set other linguistic assignments. *What is this research going to be used for?* thought Will. *To train interpreters? Or maybe to enable KGB spies to adapt to the nuances and intonation of the English language in the country to which they were to be assigned?*

They took the payment, inflated to thirty roubles, as the session had lasted half an hour longer than planned, and went off in search of a restaurant or café for supper.

They found a modest-looking *Stolovaya* canteen relatively quickly.

"*Vam shto* – what do you want?" barked an ample-bosomed, rotund, gruff lady serving behind the counter clad in a stained white kitchen uniform with matching cap, beneath which her black hair was stacked up and supported by hair clips.

"Well," said Will, glancing at the lengthy menu spread over ten pages, "I'll have the meatballs, please."

"*Nyeto*," responded the lady.

"OK," said Will, "how about the *tefteli*?" which were basically meatballs masquerading under a different name.

"*Nyeto. Rybni dyen'* – fish day," replied the serving lady with a sigh, amazed that her customers were not aware that *rybni dyen'* rules were in force. *What was the world coming to?* her expression suggested.

Tristan, not really listening, opted for minced meat and potatoes.

"*Nyeto*," in a shriller voice, was the response from the serving lady.

Tristan, in a mood to confront, replied, "Why not? It's on the menu. I want minced meat or meatballs or *tefteli* or whatever else you call them."

"Citizen, for the last time, it's *rybni dyen'*. No meat. Only fish is available today," replied the increasingly irritated lady serving at the counter.

"Only fish? Why?" asked Will.

"State regulations. Only fish on Tuesday and Thursday. These are fish days. What fish do you want?"

"Did the cows go on strike or what?" asked Will, getting exasperated.

"Since only fish are available I'll go for pike perch as a main course with Caspian Extra caviar and blini as a starter washed down with a glass of Dom Perignon French champagne, vintage 1969 – no, no, perhaps, on balance, I'll opt for the crisper 1968, which is fuller on the palette." replied Tristan, knowing full well there was nothing of the sort on the menu.

"*Nyeto*," shouted the counter lady.

Tristan, exasperated, replied, "Comrade citizen, why don't we apply a new approach regarding menu choice? How about you tell us – that is, your imbecilic, trembling customers standing here before you, the ones who have, unwisely, chosen to eat here – what cordon bleu fish dishes are on the menu and then we can choose what we want from your wide-ranging selection."

The lady, becoming even redder in the face, spat out, "*Shproti v maclo* – sprats in oil. *Bolshe nichego* – there's nothing more. One rouble. *Da* – yes – or *nyet* – no?"

"*Shproti.* Wow. *Shproti.* My favourite," Tristan replied sarcastically, dancing on the spot, whooping and hollering up in a feigned moment of pure jubilation. "I'd go a million miles for one of your smiles and a plateful of *shproti.* And with greasy oil too! Yes, please," added Tristan, now fired up for a confrontation.

The serving lady duly put two greasy portions of scraggly sprats hiding under a heated serving container onto much-used blue plastic plates with a dollop of oil, and added some sort of thick carrot and potato mix with a splat.

"Two roubles altogether," she stated.

"Thank you," said Will, handing over the money and trying forlornly to take the heat out of the atmosphere.

"Could I possibly have a knife, please?" he added, noticing that he had been supplied with a fork only.

"*Nyet,*" replied the irate counter lady. "*Nye nado* – knives are not necessary on fish days."

Tristan intervened, "Esteemed canteen worker, what is the rule that prohibits my comrade here from using a knife to cut up his fish?"

"Soviet regulations," she replied.

Will chimed in, "Could you give me the precise number of the regulation? Then I can look it up and make sure it definitely applies to sprats."

"*Nyet,*" she replied.

Bemused and pummelled into submission by the 'no knife on fish day regulation', the two friends found a table and with trepidation tentatively poked at the shrivelled, oily sprats and veg mix with their forks.

"Inedible," Tristan pronounced after one mouthful. "Utterly disgusting. I'm going to ask for my money back."

Will said, "Wait, wait, Tristan. I don't think that's a terribly wise move given the general mood and hospitality shown by the serving staff here, which I would not characterise as one being excessively friendly or welcoming to members of the human race."

"Sod it," Tristan responded. "I wouldn't feed these slops to a starving dog." He walked quickly over to the counter of the *stolovaya*.

"Young lady," said Tristan, referring flatteringly to the middle-aged server, "these *shproti*, in which I had such high expectations, are not fit for human consumption. My friend and I would like to be refunded, please. Two roubles back. Thanks."

The lady looked at Tristan incredulously. She left the counter and brought back a tallish, beefy, middle-aged man with slicked-back black hair and moustache, clad in a poorly fitting, tight, well-worn black suit, his belly protruding over his belt – presumably the manager.

"What is the problem, citizen?" he asked formally.

"The food is revolting. I want my money back," Tristan said, confronting him head-on.

The manager was unimpressed. He'd heard it all before. Cheats trying to defraud his *stolovaya*.

"We serve only the highest-quality Soviet products here. Are you trying to eat for free? We've had this ruse many times before here. Foreigners trying to swindle the USSR. You've touched your plate. No refund. And I will give you five minutes to finish your meal and get out or I will summon the militsiya. There will be no trespassing by foreigners in this *stolovaya*. Understand?"

By this time Will, also revolted by the oily sprats, had decided to call it a day. "Come on, Tristan. Let's leave. We don't want to create more trouble. Let's write it off to experience."

Tristan would have none of it. Seething, he approached the manager aggressively and, speaking in a mixture of English and Russian, he said, "Listen, you prat, or should I say sprat? This is the biggest shit I have seen on a plate in my twenty-three years on this planet. In my country you would be put in jail for serving such pigswill to humans or even to animals. So, esteemed comrade, shove your fucking sprats right up your rear orifice," and with that, and the manager looking on quizzically, having understood only a few words, Tristan threw the entire plate of sprats at the restaurant wall, where they, the potato mix and the oily gravy splattered and began sliding downwards towards the floor. Tristan stormed out of the canteen with Will following behind.

"Brainless git," Tristan continued outside, still fuming. "No wonder this country is falling apart. The people deserve what they get. Treating us like that. Fuck it, let's get a drink."

Will agreed that the food was inedible and the service appalling even by the abysmally low standards of the USSR, but he was becoming unnerved by Tristan's hot-headed recklessness. There was a tightly coiled confrontational streak to him which, when trip-wired and released, unleashed a volcanic temper, causing nothing but trouble for him and for whoever was with him at the time. He would get himself into serious difficulty one day.

FOURTEEN

Party Time

Stephanie was throwing a birthday party at her apartment in the diplomatic compound in Kutuzovsky Prospect for Gloria, a friend of hers at the Canadian Embassy. She had invited Tristan and Will along, probably to make up the numbers with the added benefit of having a few different faces present than just the usual embassy crowd. They clubbed together and bought a bottle of Soviet cognac and some flowers, which they presented to Stephanie upon their arrival at 9pm. The party was well underway, and Stephanie invited them to help themselves to the buffet supper and grab a drink.

For Will, entering any lively gathering was always awkward. Shy and withdrawn, he did not propel himself forward in moments such as these, whereas Tristan, harbouring no such scruples, plunged into the party and began sizing up the women, arming himself with several stiff drinks on the way.

Will spent a few minutes with Gloria before noticing that Wendell was spouting forth at the other side of the room in the company of a predominantly female audience. Will shuffled over in his direction.

"...It runs in my veins and in my upbringing. I am a bona fide true-blue capitalist trader. You cannot survive in the shark-infested waters of global gold trading – as I did in Zurich for three years – or in volatile commodity markets in Chicago without entrepreneurial drive. Dog eats dog. Zero-sum game. Your money or mine. Governments should serve the people and get out of the way of business. That's very different from the people serving the state, which is what happens here in the USSR and why the system doesn't work."

"Well, Wendell," replied Charles Fortescue, a stiff, mid-ranking, rather formal British diplomat dressed in an unfashionable tweed sports coat, checked shirt, brown tie and grey flannel trousers whom Will had met briefly before, "I'm with you most of the way, old chap, but not all of the way. Government has to provide basic services – health, housing, education, utilities, security, defence – and these cannot all be subcontracted to the private sector. It's a question of degree. And judgement. In the US, more of these services are parcelled out, leaving people to fend for themselves. We in the UK have struck a different balance."

"Government is the problem, not the solution. Personal effort is what counts," continued Wendell, pontificating in a loud voice. "Governments do not create wealth; the private sector does. Take my case: I made big trading profits for my Zurich-based bank by taking open-ended trading positions on forward markets on Soviet gold sales. That is value creation. The Soviets sold their gold. Everyone was happy."

Will decided to needle the puffed-up Wendell whose boasting about his prowess as a hotshot trader was getting on his nerves. "I'm confused, Wendell. How can everybody be happy if, as you said earlier, markets are snakepits where 'dog eats dog'? How does that benefit the man in the street? Isn't this commodity trading just a financial merry-go-round, a convoluted betting game dressed up by barrow boy traders who pretend they are doing sophisticated things which are, in reality, not much different from flogging ripe bananas from Columbia in a suburban fruit market in Brooklyn?"

"That's because you're a socialist and you're opposed to wealth creation," snapped Wendell in reply. "Traders bring creativity, bespoke trading concepts and strategies, agility, investments in spot and forward markets to the table, all underpinned by client development and customer care. That's the skill of the entrepreneur, which reaps its reward through trading profits and bonuses. Few guys possess it."

"Financial traders' excessive profits are dependent on privileged access to information. I fail to see the broader benefit to society. None of this stuff takes place here in the USSR, Wendell, at least not legitimately. So why are you a diplomat here in Moscow? I don't get it," interjected Will provocatively.

Irked by someone he regarded as an inferior, who had the gall to challenge his presence in Moscow, Wendell replied testily, "As a young student just out of college with no knowledge of US politics, I wouldn't expect you to understand that when the top leadership of the Republican party, the Grand Old Party in the US, comes calling for your services you don't say no. No, sirree, you do not. As a political insider and selected appointee you respond, 'When and where do I start to serve the GOP?' Our US government needs to draw on outside talent and expertise, which is why I am here advising the US Ambassador on key political and economic matters. I bring dynamism, imagination, initiative, innovation, risk-taking and nimbleness to the often immobile and statuesque State Department machine. In the UK outside talent should also be recognised like in the US."

"Well, I don't think we regular, boring UK civil servants are quite as talentless as you imply, old boy," retorted Fosdyke drily and defensively, getting in on the act. "It's just that in the UK we rely more on a permanent civil service which has served us well for centuries. Happily, outside advisers – big-shot 'Johnny-come-lately' types with inflated egos and ill-thought-out ideas to upend the existing order – have a very limited role in our system. Quite rightly as, in my experience, they do a great deal more harm than good."

A neat putdown, thought Will to himself, *and one in the goolies for Wendell.*

"I couldn't disagree with you more, Charlie boy," replied Wendell.

Will had noted that whenever Wendell wanted to belittle someone he always resorted, patronisingly and condescendingly, to employing familiar and diminutive versions of their name without seeking their consent, thereby seeking to assert his assumed superiority in knowledge and experience.

"The market should decide. Government needs to draw on the brightest and best talent and support business. On that happy note, let's drink to financial success," proposed Wendell, raising and clinking his glass with those in his vicinity, but notably omitting Will's empty glass, which he had held out, in any event, with scant enthusiasm.

Will couldn't stomach listening to any more of Wendell's self-glorification and worship of money, and drifted off from the group in search of Tristan. He wondered what on earth Wendell was doing here in the USSR if he was so obsessed with lining his pockets from trading profits in gold and grain markets. He'd be better off in Zurich, New York or Chicago peddling his wares.

At the other side of the room Will found Tristan, true to form, in the preliminary stages of attempting to seduce an attractive, well-proportioned, dark haired young diplomat of Mediterranean pedigree, probably an Italian, who, Will suspected, was not fully cognisant of his double entendres and British jokes.

"Maria, Maria," blurted out Tristan, "the most beautiful sound I ever heard. Will, my friend," Tristan continued boorishly, "I've just met a girl called Maria plucked directly from the set of Bernstein's *West Side Story…*" Tristan never failed on flattery and one-liners, and Maria herself laughed nervously at Tristan's joke.

"Pleased to meet you," said Will.

"Maria, Maria, maketh Will here smile… introduce him to your twin sister Mirella from Firenze…" carried on Tristan in garbled, slurred gobbledygook on the edge of respectability for such a gathering. "Oh, sweet, fragrant Maria, fail me not in my modest quest…"

Maria, increasingly bemused and uncertain where this bizarre conversation was heading, began to emit unmistakeable distress signals as Tristan rambled on incoherently, oblivious to the impression he was conveying to her or her reaction to his gibbering nonsense. The Maria and Tristan show was heading for a car crash and Will didn't want to be around at the denouement. Taking his leave, Will headed for the exit, having thanked Stephanie for the invite.

As he did so Wendell unexpectedly appeared from behind. "Hey, Billy boy, not leaving yet, are you? First up, I need some insight on that cute Russian gal Val – the one who joined us for drinks after the concert. Remember?" he said, his chest protruding outwards in a gesture of preening manliness. Wendell was oblivious as to whether Valya might have any close ties to Will.

"You mean Valentina. Or rather *Valya*, the Russian diminutive of her name, which is used by those who know her well," replied Will.

"I'm talkin' 'bout Val. I want to meet her. I need to ask her something about her work. Do me a favour and arrange it, please. It's kinda urgent," demanded Wendell.

This guy has got a nerve, Will thought to himself. He wondered how he should reply to this audacious request. He decided to play a straight bat. "I don't have her contact details, Wendell. She tends to call me or pass on messages via her mother, who works at my student residence. But, if you like, give me your private telephone number and I will pass it on to her." Will was pleased with himself at this reply, which kept the matter of Wendell's relations with Valya strictly under his control.

"You don't have her telephone number? Wow you're really on a fast track to the 'win' column there, Billy boy – hah, hah, hah…" said Wendell, laughing at his own tasteless joke. "OK, here's mine," and he gave Will a US Embassy business card, writing his private number on the back. "It's confidential and not to be shared with anybody, Billy boy, but give it to her when you next see her – when will that be, by the way?"

Inquisitive pillock, thought Will. "Oh, sometime in the next week probably. Or the week after that," Will answered, endeavouring to put Wendell firmly off the scent. Not wishing to lose an opportunity to get one over on Wendell, he added, "Valya doesn't speak much English. I do enjoy conversing with her in her mother tongue, which she speaks so beautifully."

"Just do it for me, OK?" said Wendell.

Moments later Stephanie, approaching her American boyfriend from the rear, slid her arm around his waist and whispered in his ear, "Let's dance." In the background David Bowie's 'Rebel, Rebel' blasted out from the Pioneer stereo record player in the living room at maximum volume.

Will, self-conscious and never keen on shaking his hips on the dance floor at the best of times, thanked Stephanie for the party and made a timely exit.

As he headed home Will realised he needed a break from Tristan – which he would get now, as his trip to the south had just been approved by the Timiryazev Academy authorities – and from Wendell, whose effrontery at trying to muscle in on Valya with big talk and bluster infuriated him.

FIFTEEN

Southern Preparations, May 1975

Will found out a few days before heading to Krasnodar in southern Russia, and Cherkasy in Ukraine, that the academy had arranged for him to be accompanied by Tolya, purveyor of the pure alcoholic spirt, whom he had met at the impromptu evening at Zina and Natalia's some months before. Anatoly 'Tolya' Grigorovitch Mashkov was to assist – in reality to 'mind' – Will and ensure he avoided the temptation to deviate from the planned meetings that had been arranged for him or get up to any mischief.

It was at this moment that Svetlana Antolevna, surprisingly well informed in advance about Will's travel plans (there were few comings and goings in the residence she was not fully aware of), appeared at Will's door with a bulky brown paper package tied up with string. It must have weighed close to ten kilograms.

"Vill, would you be kind, please, and take this package to my sister Masha Antolevna who lives in Krasnodar? I have told her you are coming. She will meet you when your train arrives so you won't have to carry it across the town," said Svetlana, having calculated that Will could not possibly object.

"It's quite large and heavy, Svetlana," responded Will, eyeing the package with suspicion. "May I ask what it contains?"

"Only household things that are difficult to find in Krasnodar, such as good-quality *kolbasa*, cheese, coffee, chocolate, biscuits, shoes, perfume and things like that. Masha will be very grateful. She can tell you something about the region as she has lived there for nearly fifty years."

Will did not feel in a position to refuse, but lugging a bulky parcel around in addition to his own luggage was going to be burdensome and, to put it mildly, a pain.

"Very well, Svetlana, I will take it," sighed Will. "How will I recognise Masha?"

"Good question," replied Svetlana. "Masha is two years younger than me, a bit taller but with similar ginger-coloured hair. She is slimmer than me. I will tell her to wear a red headscarf and a Lenin pin so you will recognise each other."

"And how is Valya?" asked Will, changing the subject. "I haven't seen her since our very pleasant evening at the Moscow Conservatory."

"Work, work, work," replied Svetlana, "...on the Soviet harvest so this is a busy time for her. She leaves early, comes home late, she has meetings with comrades out of office hours and I barely see her. The worst thing of all is that she is still unmarried. Twenty-four years old now and unmarried. Can you believe it? As a single mother I worry about her all the time. She needs to settle down and have children. I want to be grandmother before I die."

"And your sister, Masha, is she married?" asked Will.

"She was once married but no longer is. She lives alone and has no children," Svetlana said in response, somewhat sadly.

"Well, I look forward to meeting her in Krasnodar. I leave tomorrow. I will see you upon my return in ten days."

"Safe journey," said Svetlana, putting on her smock and readying herself to begin her cleaning duties.

66

Just at that moment there was a quiet knock at the door. Will opened it and, to his surprise, Valya stood there in a floral dress.

"Valya, what a surprise, *privyet*, nice to see you," said Will.

"You too," she replied, smiling.

"My apologies for not being in touch. I have been working late. When do you leave for Krasnodar?" she asked.

"Tomorrow," replied Will.

"I thought so. Could you possibly add this card and book to your luggage for Masha, my aunt? I am very fond of Masha and I wanted her to have a small present from me," said Valya.

"Ah, OK, I suppose," said Will unenthusiastically. "Your mother has also given me a large package for your aunt."

"That would be so kind," said Valya, hovering outside his room.

"Do you have time to take a stroll?" asked Will.

"Yes, for half an hour," replied Valya.

Leaving the *obshezhitye* Will and Valya walked along Listvennichnaya Alleia towards Timirayevskii Park behind the main semi-circular nineteenth-century buildings of the academy. There they sat on a bench enjoying the warm spring day.

"So, Will, are you enjoying life in our country?" asked Valya.

"It is very different from England. I am learning a lot about Russia and its people. But also about myself."

"What are you learning?" said Valya.

"Well, that would be a long story. Be honest to oneself. Be who you are. Respect others," answered Will.

"That sounds very noble and very nineteenth century," said Valya teasingly in reply. "Can you maintain your principles whatever environment you live in? When it is a question of life and death would you behave so honourably?"

"I can't vouch for how I would behave in extreme circumstances. Who can?" replied Will.

"No-one," replied Valya, leaning casually on Will's shoulder.

They stayed awhile relaxing in the spring sunshine. Valya shifted position to stretch out her shapely legs on the bench, her head resting on Will's shoulder and chest. She was very slim, a bit on the bony side. For Will the experience was highly pleasurable, something to build on with Valya after his return from the south.

"I have to go now," said Valya, raising her head to kiss Will lightly on the cheek. "Come with me. To the bus stop."

They got up and began ambling towards the stop two hundred yards away, Valya's hand lightly holding on to Will's arm.

As they walked along Listvennichnaya Alleia Will said, "Let's get together again when I return from the south in ten days' time."

"I would like that very much," said Valya as they approached the bus stop.

Valya seemed pleased to be with him. It was a reciprocally shared feeling. Outwardly, there was a lightness and gaiety to Valya that Will found attractive, not to speak about all the mysterious layers of her personality that remained to be unravelled.

The bus eventually came. Valya put her hand on his shoulder and said, "Until we again meet again, Gospodin Galant. All the best," and she kissed him lightly on the lips. She waved to him as the bus departed.

Will returned to his room with a spring in his step.

Will saw Svetlana again before she left for the day. He thought about scribbling down Wendell's telephone number on a strip of paper and asking her to pass it on to Valya. But then he thought again about it. *Sod it.* He wouldn't do it. He wasn't going to be a messenger boy for the odious Wendell.

SIXTEEN

Masha Antolevna

Will and Tolya left the next day on the 750 miles journey to Krasnodar. leaving at 11pm from Moscow's Kazan Station and travelling overnight in third class. This category provided three-tier bunk-bed accommodation in an open carriage. Passengers brought their own food with them – including *kolbasa*, dried fish, boiled eggs, pickled cucumber, tomatoes, potatoes and plenty of vodka and beer. The collective smell of these food items permeated the whole carriage, resulting in a rather pungent and lasting odour which remained throughout the journey. The atmosphere livened up after midnight as the train headed south with anecdotes and much laughter, animated discussions, and the singing of patriotic and popular songs. *Forget about sleeping*, thought Will to himself as the train trundled southwards, at a steady pace.

Upon arrival in Krasnodar in the early evening of the next day Will and Tolya were met by Svetlana's sister Masha, as well as by a driver from the Krasnodar Agriculture Institute, who was to take them there for their overnight stay. They were to share a graduate student room. Masha invited Will and Tolya to an early supper. Tolya, not keen at all and in a rather irritable mood, said he was feeling unwell and set aside his 'minding' duties. He would proceed directly to the institute by car. He requested Masha to accompany Will there after they had had supper.

Masha lived in small, single-bedroomed, compact and functional apartment near the centre of Krasnodar, a tram ride away from the Agricultural Institute. It was the first Russian home that Will had ever visited. In a typical display of Russian hospitality, she had prepared a table full of *zakuski,* fish dishes and salads for Will. She asked him to open a bottle of half-sweet chilled Russian champagne. Will's first impression was that Masha did not receive many visitors. Like her sister Svetlana she was warm-hearted but her taut and yellow-tinged sallow complexion suggested she had suffered personal tragedy in her life. Her brow was particularly heavily lined, and she was evidently a compulsive worrier.

"Thank you again, Will, for bringing the parcel and the gift from Valya," Masha began. "za *vashe zdoroviye* – to your health," as they clinked glasses. "And how are Svetlana and my niece Valya?"

"Thank you for providing this delicious supper, Masha. You should not have gone to so much trouble," said Will, tucking into some red caviar, pike perch and salads. "Your sister and niece are well. Svetlana Antolevna has been very kind to me and helped me settle into Moscow. She was particularly helpful when I was ill in winter: her Russian remedy – garlic, lemon, milk and honey – helped me get rid of my influenza. I have met Valya a few times and once we went to a concert together. She is very occupied with her ministry work." It was a formulaic answer, giving nothing away.

A couple of glasses of champagne later Masha's tongue loosened a bit and she blurted out, "Valya is a ridiculously spoilt girl. Her mother is obsessed by her, clings to her and won't let her go. She's twenty-four now! Can you imagine it? Twenty-four! By now she should be married with at least one child. She had a fiancé once, Yuri, a nice lad, but he wasn't not good enough for Svetlana. No, not at all! Only a railway administrator. I told her to encourage Valya to marry him. She wouldn't. She said Valya could do better.

Now look at the situation – twenty-four and unmarried. Almost an old maid! Unheard of for a beautiful Russian girl."

"Valya is an interesting and intelligent person," said Will, choosing his adjectives carefully, "and she does deserve, for sure, to find a good husband. But, Masha Antolevna, twenty-four is not old! In England many people don't marry until their late twenties or thirties even."

"What a strange country you must come from, Will," opined Masha. "Perhaps it is because we don't live long in our country. Time in Russia has a different meaning. Russians are always worried about portentous events; they have a foreboding of disaster around the corner, a fear that things will not turn out well. People are superstitious. They seek partners early in life. You should remember that the Great Patriotic War is still fresh in everyone's memory. All families in this region lost someone, sometimes all family members. Our parents died in the war. Svetlana and I were orphaned. It was a miracle we were able to stay together."

Will, emboldened, asked, "And who, Masha, is Valya's father?"

Masha hesitated, took another sip from her glass and wondered if she should reveal more of her family history to this stranger from a foreign land.

"Her father's name, I believe, was Anatoly Ivanovitch," whispered Masha. "He never married Svetlana nor took any interest in his daughter. Good-looking, sharp-witted, ambitious but totally untrustworthy. A fixer. He is now a Party apparatchik in Gorkii. He used Svetlana for his own purposes and caused her a great deal of unhappiness. She has struggled on her own ever since with no financial support from Valya's father at all. I don't think Valya has even met him. Svetlana's life is Valya, Valya, Valya. This is all she lives for. God forbid that anything should happen to her daughter – it would be the end of Svetlana. She could not live without her."

"Valya is equally devoted to her mother. She recognises all the sacrifices Svetlana has made for her. The feeling of love and respect is mutual, I believe," replied Will.

"Yes, but Valya must peel away from her mother sometime. She must become independent, live her own life and not be continually cosseted by her mother."

The evening had turned to dusk as Will and Masha chatted away. The mood had become sombre and serious but was lifted when Masha began teasing Will about his own marriage plans.

"Too young," Will said jokingly. "I'm only twenty-three."

"Not at all." Masha laughed. "I could find you a good Russian girl. A good-looking man like you should marry before it is too late. Russian girls are the best."

On this jovial note they left for the tram and a thirty-minute ride to the Krasnodar Agricultural Institute. Masha identified the corpus block where Will would be staying.

"Will, it has been a pleasure to meet you," said Masha. "Take care. Enjoy our country. Convey my love and best wishes to my dear sister Svetlana and my niece Valya."

"Masha, thank you for your kind hospitality and introduction to Krasnodar. It was a pleasure to meet you," replied Will.

Masha stood on tiptoe and gave Will a peck on the cheek. "*Vsevo dobrovo* – all the best to you," she said, and then she turned and headed off into the night.

Will had enjoyed the evening. Masha had been generous and welcoming. As he climbed the stairs to his third-floor room, Will figured that, although he would probably never see this woman again, her sincerity and the hospitality she had shown him would not be erased lightly from his memory.

SEVENTEEN

Southern Soviet Farms

After a good night's rest Will and Tolya headed out of Krasnodar into the Kuban plain, with its rich, fertile, black earth soil, known locally as the *Chernozemlye* region, to visit a state farm and a collective farm producing wheat and other grains, sunflowers and sugar beet.

In warm weather they travelled about 60 miles north towards Rostov for the first port of call, the 'Kubanets' State Farm – a *sovkhoz* – where they met the chairman and staff. It was a farm primarily producing wheat. They took a journey with the chairman around the vast farm and met some workers, all of whom pronounced themselves satisfied with their working conditions. Last year's harvest had been reasonable, not as productive as 1973 but decent nonetheless. When Will asked about the prospects for this year he noticed an uneasy shifting of glances amongst staff before being told by the chairman, a Party appointee, that it would be *normalno*. Will then received a lengthy briefing on how the Party was promoting greater intensification of agriculture, the application of more fertilisers, better drainage, land improvements, greater mechanisation. It was an upbeat but propaganda-driven narrative.

Will and Tolya left the state farm and headed for a collective farm – a *Kolkhoz* – an hour's drive further north-west named 'Oktyabr' commemorating the October Socialist Revolution of 1917. This farm spanned an area of 16,000 acres, seventy per cent of which was sown, and employed nearly six hundred collective farm workers.

The *kolkhoz* had gone to some trouble to provide refreshments and another Russian-style buffet ready to welcome them. Will soon ascertained that he was the first ever Westerner to this collective farm, which the staff considered to be a great honour, and they were curious to meet such an unusual visitor. They tucked into the buffet – *zakuski*, sturgeon, carp and bream from the Don River, salads, pickled cucumber, beer and soft drinks. The chairman of the *kolkhoz* had been called out to deal with an unspecified matter on the farm. Consequently, Nina Petrovna Vashenko, his assistant, acted as host in his place pending his arrival. Will stuck to non-alcoholic drink options as he wanted to be on his mettle when the official visit began.

Grigoriy Timofeyevich Donchenko, the *kolkhoz* chairman, eventually arrived. A big barrel of a man in his mid-fifties, medium height, brown swept-back hair, expansive chest, and booming voice, he wore a battered old black leather jacket and open-necked white shirt. He exuded authority. He introduced himself to Will and Tolya and apologised for his late arrival.

"A minor fire has taken place at one of the silos, necessitating a rapid intervention with fire hoses. The problem has been resolved but some minor damage had occurred to the roof of the silo. We do not need these problems at this point in the agricultural year but there you are. We had to act speedily," said Grigoriy Timofeyevich.

Nina Petrovna handed him a plate of *zakuski* from the buffet, for which Grigoriy thanked her. He scoffed them down quickly with a bottle of Georgian Borjomi water. This was a man in a hurry.

"Tell me about yourself, young man," said Grigoriy as he ate. "Your nationality, age, educational background, from where you come, what you plan to do in the future. Perhaps work on a collective farm?" he asked jokingly, to widespread mirth amongst those present. "What is your research topic, your impression of the USSR? When will you return to England?" This questioning was not carried out in an aggressive fashion but simply reflected Grigoriy's interest to know and understand his visitor better. A shorter, snappier list of questions was addressed to Tolya.

Will replied to Grigoriy's questions and asked him about his background in return.

"We will speak about it later," replied Grigoriy, finishing up his rapidly consumed meal. "Let us visit our farm first."

They proceeded to take an extensive tour of the Oktyabr *kolkhoz* in Grigoriy's Volga car, stopping at various points for him to greet and acknowledge workers and explain to Will the crops they were growing (principally wheat and barley), the increased inputs they were applying to improve productivity and agricultural yields, the need for more investment in machinery, fertilisers, storage equipment and the need for more financial incentives for *kolkhozniki* workers.

"We need better housing, local amenities and schools to persuade people, especially young people, to stay and earn their livelihoods and bring up families on the land," he said.

Grigoriy noted realistically that it was natural that the agricultural workforce would eventually reduce as productivity improved. The country could not develop into a modern state, he argued, if nearly thirty per cent of the working population were employed on the land. The tour round the *kolkhoz* took three hours. Victor and Will thanked him and said that they would now head back to Krasnodar.

"Absolutely not," insisted Grigoriy. "You must stay for dinner as honoured guests. We have arranged dinner at our local *osobnyak* – guest house. My wife will also attend."

Settling round the dinner table, Grigoriy ordered a range of dishes for his guests, with a heavy meat component this time, plus beer, cognac and vodka. Two rounds of vodka shots were swiftly dispatched before the food arrived. Will asked Grigoriy about the region, its history, its place in Soviet agriculture. They were in for a long night. And many toasts.

Grigoriy was nothing if not loquacious. He sallied forth on the history of the region, its rich black earth, the central place it had occupied in the brutal fighting in the Great Patriotic War from 1941–44 which had convulsed this region and beyond.

"The human and material losses in this region were unimaginable," said Grigoriy soberly. "Everyone suffered and lost family members. I was amongst those fighting in the Red Army to resist the German Wehrmacht. I was only eighteen when I joined up in 1941. We began defeating the Nazis from 1942, starting with the heroic resistance and defence of Stalingrad. I was a young infantry corporal in the Red Army and in 1943 I fought for the liberation of Kursk and Kharkov. In battles I lost my two best friends Ivan and Dmitrii, both blown up by fascist artillery. I was then transferred to a new infantry battalion on the Romanian border. I fought at Borisov, Minsk, Vilnius in Lithuania and in East Prussia in 1944, and arrived in Marienburg, Germany in 1945. I miraculously survived. I was wounded once near Minsk in the leg but I recovered. It was brutal, bare-bones, violent combat, a fight to the death. Many Soviet prisoners were starved or shot in violation of the rules of war."

Grigoriy's wife Sofia, a diminutive middle-aged lady dressed soberly in a two-piece grey suit with her auburn hair in a neat bun, must have heard Grigoriy recount his wartime escapades many times and was evidently proud of his achievements.

"He won't say, but I will tell you that my husband received, by the command of the Commander-in-Chief Generalissimo of the USSR, Comrade Stalin, a letter of official thanks, signed by his commanding officer, for participating in fourteen combat operations in 1944–45. In addition, Grigoriy Timofeyevich received three silver combat medals: two 'For Valour' for bravery on the battlefield and also the prestigious 'Order of the Red

Banner', a silver, numbered medal. He wears these Soviet medals on every 9 May Victory celebration and on other official occasions. He will pass them on to our son, Fyodor, so that he never forgets the terrible sacrifices the Red Army and Soviet citizens made in confronting the German army and preserving our country, our land and our freedom."

"Enough of the past – we must look to the future now," said Grigoriy. "Let us refill our glasses. *Davai*."

Grigoriy's long exposition of the horrors of the Great Patriotic War and the impact they had wrought on the Soviet state and people had darkened the mood of the small gathering. It was a raw memory for him, for his wife and for his assistant Nina Petrovna. The war had irredeemably impacted the lives of every Soviet citizen. Will had never grasped before the lasting damage inflicted on the southern region of the USSR.

Trying to lighten the mood and thanking Grigoriy for taking the time to explain what had happened thirty years ago in the region, Will changed the subject. "Grigoriy Timofeyevich, could you kindly inform me about the progress in improving Soviet citizens' livelihoods since the war? I am informed that the grain harvest in this region this year will surpass the 1974 level. Is that correct?"

Grigoriy, calling for another round of vodka shots and a toast to the Red Army, took some more food and responded, "You know, Vill," Grigoriy pronounced in authoritative, terms, "the weather, above all, determines the size of the grain harvest in the USSR and in Krasnodar Krai. We cannot combat nature. We can only take measures to mitigate the consequences of bad weather and defend our crops to some degree. Winter wheat this year was better than in 1972 but the weather is now too dry for a record summer crop. We need some more moisture quite quickly if we are to have satisfactory yields this year. Rain is not currently forecast."

Will interjected, "Yes but official Party organs, newspapers, are reporting the prospect of a record harvest this year, as much if not greater than in 1973. Are they right?"

"I am aware of these official statements. We work, as managers, to deliver a good harvest outcome. I know my land and the land of my neighbours. We plan for high yields but without rainfall at the right time, in sufficient quantity in the right place, the crop will be affected. The next two weeks will be very important. I showed you today how the growth of our wheat and barley are being held back. This will extend to other crops soon."

The evening lightened up after this exchange, anecdotes and jokes being exchanged and toasts multiplying. By the time fruit and coffee had been digested Will and Tolya were lightheaded and in an increasingly fragile shape. Grigoriy was about to open another bottle of cognac when they both decided it was time to call a halt to proceedings and retire for the evening. They said farewell, thanking Grigoriy, his wife and his colleagues profusely for their generous hospitality. Their driver, sleeping soundly in the car, was abruptly woken by their return, shook off his slumber and started the ignition for the return to Krasnodar.

As Will stumbled to the right-side passenger door Grigoriy took him by the arm and whispered, "It was good to meet you. Honestly speaking I have worries about this year. *Vsyo* – that's it. Have a good journey back to Krasnodar. *Vsevo dobrovo* – all the best."

EIGHTEEN

Rail Journey to Nowhere

The train journey next day from Krasnodar to Cherkasy, a town of some 225,000 people in central Ukraine, via Rostov-on-Don, took over twenty-four hours, including two changes of train en route. Early in the morning, the carriage that Will and Tolya were travelling in became detached from the rest of the train and was shunted into a railway siding. A few passengers alighted to have a smoke. It was a strange feeling of total abandonment. Will wondered when a locomotive would return to recover their wagon. Had they been forgotten? He descended the steep carriage steps to stand amongst wheat fields extending as far as the eye could see. As he walked up and down the railway track smoking a cigarette, he amused himself by thinking about the scandal that would have been created at home if British Rail had deposited a railway carriage full of passengers in a siding with no habitation in sight. The tabloid press would have had a field day.

Strange and bizarre though the situation was – a British graduate student becalmed in a railway wagon by a wheat field in the middle of Ukraine – Will didn't feel the slightest bit concerned. Or even isolated for that matter. He felt quite content and pleased that he had coped with six months' living in the USSR. He only had a few months of his studentship to go and in the time remaining he had a date with Valya to look forward to. No point in getting steamed up: the Soviet railway authorities would eventually figure out that there was a railcar with people on board that had gone missing and send out a search party with an 'all hands on deck' summons –*avral* – to sort the situation out. An engine would show up later rather than sooner. He and Tolya, who was increasingly surly and embarrassed by this mishap, had enough food and drink to share between them.

Sure enough, an ancient-looking steam locomotive arrived three hours later to pick up the railcar and they subsequently arrived at their destination, tired, hot and dishevelled.

During visits to farms the next day Will was briefed on the high quality of agricultural land in this part of the vast black earth region that provided much of the USSR's staple grain products – wheat, barley, maize and sunflowers. But, as in his previous stop in Krasnodar, Will realised that there had been no rain at all, and temperatures were steadily increasing above thirty degrees centigrade in the daytime. Conversations with managers and workers confirmed that moisture was essential to ensure adequate crop growth and yields. Nobody appeared overly concerned at this point but, as Grigoriy had stated earlier at the Oktyabraskii *kolkhoz*, another two weeks of hot sunshine, increasing temperatures and no rain would start to make big inroads into yields and seriously affect this year's harvest outcome.

NINETEEN

Return to Moscow

Will was glad to be back in Moscow after his trip to the south. It felt like returning home. Tolya had been a pleasant and harmless enough companion and had not held him back or interfered with what he wanted to ask or do, but now he wanted some time on his own without having his every move closely observed and noted.

The morning after his arrival back in the academy Svetlana Antolevna knocked on his door and entered without waiting for Will's reply. Ever ready to engage in conversation, she proceeded to ask Will about his trip south and thanked him for delivering her parcel to her sister Masha. She had spoken with Masha since by telephone and recounted her sister's favourable impression of Will, his modesty, his friendliness, his good looks and his good command of Russian.

"You made a fine impression there," said Svetlana teasingly.

"Masha was very thankful to you for sending the large parcel. She sent you and Valya her very best wishes. I enjoyed meeting her and hearing about Krasnodar and the black earth region," replied Will.

"Ah, *Bozhe moi*, I should see Masha more often. Our circumstances prevent us from meeting more regularly. Our lives are so busy. I hope we will see each other soon in happy circumstances," sighed Svetlana in reply.

"And how is Valya?" asked Will. "I haven't seen her for some time. I hope she is well."

"Oh, I almost forgot," exclaimed Svetlana. "Valya wanted to speak to you about your trip to the south. She will call you soon. But now I must get on with my work, excuse me," and with that Svetlana scuttled unsteadily out of the room, straw broom in hand, to begin her daily chores of sweeping and cleaning the living quarters of the academy's visitors.

By the following Friday, there was still no phone call from Valya, so Will decided to catch up with Tristan in the British Embassy bar. The atmosphere was subdued until Tristan arrived in an inebriated state, smoking profusely and drawing disapproving looks as he demanded a double shot of whisky from the barman.

"How was the trip?" he asked Will as he surveyed the room for what he inelegantly described as quality diplomatic 'crumpet'.

Will, cognisant that Tristan's mind was elsewhere and that he was not in the slightest bit interested in hearing about his trip south, replied briefly before noticing the presence of Wendell and Stephanie in a dark corner of the room away from the immediate vicinity of the bar. Tristan went off in the other direction brazenly in pursuit of a new date and soon raucous noise and laughter could be heard from that part of the room. Turning towards the bar, Will met the glance of Wendell, who was replenishing a round of drinks.

"Well, well, if it isn't our blue-blooded Billy boy Brit," he blurted out, "back from the wild south of Russia, huh? How was it?" Wendell asked, not looking at Will but focusing his attention instead on the barman, who poured out a glass of Jack Daniel's on the rocks for him and a dry white wine for Stephanie.

"Do you have time right now?" responded Will, conscious that Wendell was occupied with Stephanie.

"Not really," retorted Wendell, flicking his head towards the waiting Stephanie. "Duty first. But, hey, Billy boy, I gotta proposition for you. Come next Monday to Spaso House, the US Ambassador's residence, where we are hosting an evening reception for a high-level delegation of US grain traders including my uncle. You might learn something about what successful American go-getting capitalism is all about! I'll put you on the guest list. Lawrence is your last name, isn't it? 6pm. Don't be late."

"That would be interesting," said Will, thinking that he would get good food and drink at the US Embassy. "I will be there."

TWENTY

Speeches at Spaso House

As the guests settled and the hubbub died down at the US grain traders' reception at Spaso House, the Deputy Head of the US Mission (DCM) and acting Chargé d'Affaires Thomas Ryan, a career State Department official, took to the podium. After tapping the microphone to ensure it was switched on, he began reading from some notecards in heavily American-accented Russian.

"Deputy Minister Katanov, esteemed guests from the Soviet Union and the US, *damy* i *gospoda*, ladies and gentlemen, I'm pleased to welcome you here to Spaso House for tonight's reception. Ambassador Powell, who has been called to Washington for urgent consultations, very much regrets not being able to host tonight's important event, and has asked me, as Chargé, to convey to you a warm welcome to this historic house.

"We are especially honoured to have with us tonight forty senior representatives and managers from the US Grain Traders Association, who have come from Chicago, Washington DC and New York to visit the USSR to meet with their Soviet counterparts here in Moscow. They have a full two-day programme, the highlight of which will be the meeting with the Soviet Minister of Agriculture tomorrow.

"We meet at a time when US-Russian trade ties and economic cooperation have been growing steadily. Our countries have also been working to achieve a successful outcome to the Conference on Security and Cooperation in Europe in Helsinki in August to provide enhanced political and economic stability in Europe. Important and welcome though these developments are, I am sure we can all agree that there is substantial, untapped potential to further strengthen business between our countries. So let me encourage our Soviet and American guests to use the opportunity this evening to forge new and lasting relationships for the future benefit of our two great nations."

The Deputy Head of Mission then invited the Deputy Minister of Agriculture, Mikhail Sergeevitch Katanov, to address the gathering with the aid of an interpreter.

"Deputy Head of Mission Ryan, President Angell of Grain Growers, esteemed *kollegi*, my ministry and colleagues from other Soviet departments sincerely welcome the opportunity to meet with our visiting American guests today. The Soviet Union highly values cooperation with Western countries, based on mutual understanding and respect, in accordance with the policies of the Communist Party of the USSR and its General Secretary, Leonid Ilyich Brezhnev. Business development will bring mutual prosperity to our two nations. Although US-Soviet agricultural trade will be small this year – due to the record Soviet harvest of over two hundred million tons of grain which will provide for all our needs and provide a surplus for export – there is long-term potential to strengthen cooperation. So let me welcome our American visitors to Moscow and thank Chargé d'Affaires Ryan for hosting this reception. *Spasibo bolshoye! Za vashe zdoroviye* – thank you and to your health," concluded Comrade Katanov, raising his glass of red wine and draining the contents in one gulp.

"And finally," DCM Ryan said, "let me now turn over the podium to President Angell of the US Grain Traders Association for a few words. Mike, the floor is yours."

Angell, a tall, big-hearted, rotund mid-Western American with a booming drawl and foghorn of a voice began.

"Mah sincere thanks, Tom and Mikhail Gayevitch Kaytyanov, for your kind words of welcome. We, grain traders and farmers, come here in friendship. We want to develop new, mutually profitable business opportunities with y'all. As men forged from working the land and trading its bounties we understand what quality grain, corn, wheat, oats, oilseeds look like – you name it and we, in the US, can produce and trade it. The last few years, though, have seen great harvests in the Soviet Union here – congratulations to y'all for results. 1975 is also going to be a great year for Soviet agriculture.

"But even in harvest-rich years of plenty, you gonna need to import some feed grain – US-sourced, ah hope! – to nourish your expanding livestock population. If the Soviet Union wants to achieve its goal of matching US per capita meat consumption y'all gonna have to raise the number of cattle on your Soviet ranches" – laughter – "oops, ah, ah mean on your socialised communistic farms. We in the US have silos full of high-quality grain. And, as y'all just heard, we have a US government willing to support trade in agriculture with the USSR.

"So, as we say in the mid-West of the You'nited States, let's get down to business in the cowshed when we can" – ripple of laughter. "Ah raise mah glass to y'all – *Nah zdro viy eye*, ah think you say here in Moscôw."

Glasses were raised and clinked, with Russian speakers cringing at Angell's excruciatingly bad accent but recognising his well-meaning attempt at formulating a toast in Russian.

Speeches mercifully over, there was a stampede towards the buffet at the other opposite side of the chandelier room, which was laden with quality hors d'oeuvres, a choice of main course of chicken supreme or baked creamy salmon with rice and a selection of desserts, fruit and cheese. Choice Californian red and white wine *'au choix'* were readily available from waiters circulating around the room with trays full of wine glasses and tumblers of water, still and sparkling.

Will noticed that Kuznetsov, with whom he had conversed with earlier, lost no time in squeezing everything from the buffet onto his plate, forming a pyramidal mound of jumbled up food – meat, fish, hors d'oeuvres, rice, salad, cheese – which he proceeded to tuck into with relish, washed down with a few additional glasses of red wine.

As he stood in the food line Will observed that Counsellor Wendell Randall III had joined Kuznetsov's table and that the two were engaged in animated conversation.

Will, who didn't know anyone else in the reception, moved with his plate to an upright table covered with an impeccably ironed white tablecloth close to Kuznetsov and Wendell. He listened with half an ear to snatches of his neighbours' conversation, easy to follow in Wendell's case due to his loud, booming voice.

Wendell: "...you are... planner in the ministry?"

Kuznetsov: "Our department works... new tenth five-year plan 1976–80 beginning next year... increase agricultural output... overtake US levels... the Party has prioritised agriculture..."

Wendell: "You advise your authorities on... choices for the USSR?"

Kuznetsov: "...modest... role... Party decides... As the Deputy Minister said... a record grain harvest in 1975... no need for American imports..."

Wendell: "Ah... here's my uncle Tom Randall, who is part of the grain traders' delegation..." said Wendell, leaving Kuznetsov momentarily and guiding Tom by the arm over to his table.

Kuznetsov: "Pleased to meet... Mr Randall," as he exchanged business cards. "And this is..."

Tom: "Likewise... so, Alexei, how is your grain harvest... this year?"

Kuznetsov: "...USSR state policy... officials cannot discuss harvest details... but... for certain it will be a record..."

Tom: "...when will the USSR say publicly what the harvest will be this year?"

Kuznetsov: "...harvest information when we know all the facts... investments, the weather, storage... and other factors..."

Tom: "But you... make assumptions..."

Kuznetsov: "Yes, of course..."

Tom, manifestly disappointed at his failure to elicit any useful information from Kuznetsov, bid him goodbye in a typically affable American way, implying that he was the most important person he had ever met.

As he walked past Will's table with his back turned he quietly said to Wendell, "...other grain traders here have sources... better than ours... up the game..."

Will looked around carefully from his vantage point, having finished the remaining food on his plate. Neither Kuznetsov nor Wendell were anywhere to be seen. Already the reception was winding down with guests drifting away into the night. Only a few stragglers remained. Embassy staff were busily and noisily clearing away used crockery and glasses scattered throughout the chandelier room, transmitting the message, unsubtly, that it was time for remaining guests to leave. Will took one last swig from his glass of chilled white Californian wine and headed towards the exit.

It had been a curious, not uneventful evening. Will pondered Katanov and Kuznetsov's rhetoric about the stellar Soviet harvest prospects in 1975, which did not match what he had seen and heard during his trip to the south. Was this just the typical Party propaganda line for the outside world or did the Soviets really believe it? Wendell and his uncle also appeared anxious to ascertain the facts about the harvest. Did they believe what they were being told by the two Ks?

TWENTY-ONE

Valya's Call

Returning to his room in the *obshezhitye* on Listvennichnaya Alleia a little lightheaded after four glasses of excellent wine at the US Spaso House reception, Will changed into some casual clothes and was relaxing on his bed when the phone rang outside in the corridor. *Not for me*, he thought, but to his surprise there was a knock at his door and his ubiquitous nosy neighbour, Lyudmila, told him the call was indeed for him. Will left his room and picked up the receiver.

"It's Valya," was the first thing Will heard, followed by silence.

It took a few moments for this announcement to sink in, but Will quickly came to, "Valya? How are you? I met your aunt Masha in Krasnodar some weeks ago, a very nice lady. She sent her very best wishes to you."

"Yes, I heard this from Mama," responded Valya, *sotto voce*.

Something was bothering her. Evidently, she wanted Will to lead the conversation and take the initiative.

"How about meeting up soon for a drink or a meal one evening to catch up? I would like to hear your news and see you again," suggested Will.

"That would be nice, Will. There are a number of things I need to speak to you about as soon as possible," replied Valya.

"How about next Tuesday evening then? Shall we meet in town?" asked Will.

"Tuesday I cannot do. Wednesday, perhaps? By the Bolshoi theatre at 5pm?"

"*Soglasno* – agreed," replied Will. "I look forward to it."

"Until Wednesday," Valya said, terminating the phone call.

Will returned to his room somewhat perplexed. Valya had made no contact with him after his return from the south, and she had to all intents and purposes avoided him. The message was confusing.

What did he, Will, really think of her? He did find her attractive, yes, but being the daughter of his omnipresent cleaning lady was awkward. He hadn't been able to find out more about what made her tick. Her reserve, caution and care in not saying anything which could be misconstrued meant that she was still unknown to him. What did she really believe in? That she was very caring and protective towards her mother, Svetlana Antolevna, was obvious. This bedrock relationship in many ways appeared to define the contours of her life. Beyond that he was very much in the dark.

Would he find out more in a few days' time?

TWENTY-TWO

Kuzmenov's Wisdom

Will arranged a short meeting with his academic supervisor Professor Kuzmenov after returning from the south.

Kuzmenov's office was situated at the far end of Listvennichnaya Alleia in a corner of a series of buildings making up a half-moon crescent. Will was asked to wait by his secretary, a small, diminutive woman with her hair tied in a grey bun, who must have been well into her seventies. She must have witnessed the entire Soviet period – the 1917 Revolution, Lenin, the liberal New Economic Programme of the 1920, Stalin, collectivisation of agriculture, the purges, victory in the Great Patriotic War, the death of Stalin, Khrushchev, the denunciation of Stalin in 1956, Yuri Gagarin's historic space flight, Khrushchev's demise and now Brezhnev. She was quietly typing away on an old Underwood Cyrillic typewriter. Will asked her where it was from. "The USA," she replied. How long had she had it in her possession? "Since the war," she responded.

There was a buzz on the secretary's desk, and she indicated quietly that Will could now enter to see Kuzmenov.

Professor Kuzmenov welcomed Will into his cavernous office. His prematurely greying hair suggested he was older than he looked but Will estimated that he was probably in his mid-fifties. An austere, serious agronomist and economist, Kuzmenov shook Will's hand and invited him to sit down on the chair in front of his desk. Will thanked him for arranging his trip to the south which had been fascinating, most notably the visit to the Oktyabr *Kolkhoz*. Kuzmenov, it turned out, knew Grigoriy well and pronounced him to be a fine professional manager and comrade.

Will wanted to broach the delicate subject of the harvest. "Professor Kuzmenov, permit me to raise one issue which is puzzling me. During my discussions in the southern black earth districts of your country I gained the impression that too much dry weather and lack of moisture would adversely affect this year's grain harvest. Is my impression correct?"

Kuzmenov shifted uneasily on his seat before replying. "It is too early to determine the outcome of this year's harvest and the extent to which national investments in grain production and storage will bear fruit. The ninth Five-Year Plan provides for a harvest in excess of two hundred million tonnes. I am confident it will be attained," said Kuzmenov unconvincingly.

Will shifted to a different tack. "Professor, if, for whatever reason, there was a shortfall, what would the USSR do to ensure adequate supplies of grain in the country and to guarantee that Soviet citizens are well fed and provided for?"

"In this purely hypothetical case, which of course will not occur, the Party would consider options to import grain or draw down the USSR's reserves or both. Requirements would be determined by the highest Party and state organs. Many state ministries and bodies would be involved. Such decisions would not be made lightly. In 1972, due to a very bad harvest, we were obliged to import large volumes of grain from the US. When the US government discovered that the USSR had concluded substantial contracts with US grain traders at favourable prices, they put in place surveillance measures to prevent this happening again," replied Kuzmenov matter-of-factly.

"What would be the timing of Soviet grain purchases from Western countries if they did prove to be necessary?" asked Will.

"By late July – or early August – the situation would be fairly clear. First import contracts could be expected to be placed by then," said Kuzmenov.

"Quite soon, in other words," said Will.

"Indeed," said Kuzmenov matter-of-factly.

They conversed a bit more before Will got up to leave.

"Do not worry about the USSR," said Kuzmenov, smiling. "We will survive. We have strong leaders, a lot of hard currency in reserve, a top Western credit rating and we are reliable traders. In the highly unlikely event that we have to go to world grain markets to supplement our domestic supplies we will do so. And Western traders and banks, as always, will be falling over themselves to do business with the USSR, a prestigious and reliable client. Profit always prevails over principle in capitalist countries. We, in the Soviet Union, understand this fully."

TWENTY-THREE

Bolshoi Steps

Will arrived early from the Lenin Library for the 5pm Wednesday afternoon rendezvous with Valya, a bit nervous as to what to expect. He wandered round the exterior colonnades of the Bolshoi theatre and glanced at the upcoming programme of opera and ballet. He noted that the Bolshoi's spectacular show, Yuri Grigorovich's *Spartak*, with top Soviet national artists Vladimir Vasiliev and Ekaterina Maximova dancing the main roles, was due to be performed at the end of the month. Will approached the *kassa* with some hesitation to enquire about tickets for the show.

"*Vam povezlo* – you are lucky," said the saleslady in the cubicle. "Two tickets have just been returned."

"How much are they?" asked Will.

"*Dva bileta* – twelve roubles," she replied.

"I'll take them," said Will boldly, aware that tickets for this ballet were widely sought after and that further opportunities to purchase them would, in all likelihood, not arise. He would ask Valya if she would like to come.

Transaction completed, he returned to the colonnade and saw Valya quietly waiting for him at the far end, looking away. From a distance she was wearing a plain blue dress with a handbag hanging loosely on her shoulder. In the space of just a few weeks the seasons had changed in Moscow and early summer had now arrived. The atmosphere in the city was jollier and lighter as Moscovites celebrated warmer weather, shed their functional heavy winter clothing and enjoyed trips outside Moscow to the countryside and, if they possessed them, to their dachas. The small plot growing season was now in full swing.

"Greetings, Valya," said Will as he approached her.

"Oh, Will, gallant Englishman," replied Valya, putting her arms around his neck and kissing him on both cheeks, the warmth of her greeting suprising him after the froideur of their telephone call.

"Let's walk a bit," said Valya, and they headed off in the direction of Red Square.

After a short time, they reached and ambled across the vast, imposing, cobble-stoned Square chatting amiably without paying any attention to who or what was in the immediate vicinity. Will recounted his trip to the south and his impressions.

"There is something I don't understand, Valya," Will said. "Everywhere in the south there are signs of the grain harvest being negatively impacted by excessively hot weather and no moisture. Yet I heard the Deputy Minister of Agriculture and Director Kuznetsov at a US Embassy reception the other day saying it will be a record harvest. Who is right?"

"Oh, let's not talk business or harvests or grain or Soviet economy, Will. The weather is beautiful. Let's enjoy it," replied Valya, deflecting the conversation and tightening her hold on Will's arm as they walked through Red Square and approached the Moscow River. Some newly married couples were having their pictures taken by St Basil's Cathedral. Will noticed how young the newlyweds were; the brides, in their white wedding dresses, barely looked twenty years old.

Will continued, "Seriously Valya, I want to understand things. I'm perplexed. Confused. Is it because the USSR doesn't want to admit publicly to harvest shortfalls or is it just that I am wrong?"

"Will, I don't want to discuss this. The harvest will be what the harvest will be. Why do you go on like this? *Za chem?*"

"Well, sorry, Valya, but I don't want to talk about trivial things. I am a serious person," replied Will.

"I have bigger concerns," said Valya, irritated, raising her voice. "Family matters. My mother is very unwell. I must find some money to pay for the medical operation she badly needs. She has chronic arthritis in both knees and is in constant pain. She cannot do physical work anymore. I have to find ways to support her."

"I thought the USSR provided free medical services for its citizens," said Will.

"A middle-aged cleaning lady with no influence or money cannot easily get access to state medical services when she needs them. I am trying to see if something can be done through my ministry. But I need money. Not roubles but dollars to pay the surgeon, the anaesthetist, and the hospital and nursing charges. Without hard currency she will not be treated in the foreseeable future. Her case is not considered urgent," intoned Valya. "I have to get some dollars."

Was Valya appealing to him for money? Will wondered. *He didn't have any dollars.*

They continued walking slowly towards the Moscow River before descending the steps by the Bolshoi Moskvoretsky bridge to continue their promenade along the south side of the Kremlin walls.

"Valya, I would like to help you and your mother, but I don't have access to any hard currency, I'm afraid. I am a bit shocked that you have to pay for medical operations at all," asserted Will.

"I am not asking you for money, Will," said Valya, becoming emotional. "Please believe me, I am not. Never. I'm upset if I made you think this – my bad expressions and language. I am not trying to borrow from you. No. But my mother... she has given me everything, everything, without any help – she has done her best but has struggled to make ends meet without support... she has sacrificed her life for me, her only daughter. I have to help her. Though she never says it, she is suffering and in pain. She needs to retire... she cannot work anymore..." Valya was now visibly upset; she took out a handkerchief from her bag to dry her eyes.

"I'm sorry," said Will weakly, "it was not my intention to make you unhappy."

"You don't understand our country, Will. Everything in Soviet Russia is *po blatu*," she continued. "You get things done through contacts, through influence and with Western money – dollars. My mother and I have none of these. We are just ordinary citizens. Nobodies. Proletarians in the eyes of the nomenklatura."

The mood had become sombre.

"And your father?" asked Will sheepishly.

"Father?" said Valya, spitting out the words disgustedly. "I do not have contact with my father. I do not know him, and I don't want to know him. He abandoned my mother when I was a very young child, leaving her to struggle alone while he pursued his career. And other women. No hope from that quarter," replied Valya dismissively.

"If I can help in any way, Valya, within my means I would be pleased to do," Will offered. "By the way, over there," said Will, pointing across the river, "is the British Embassy building. Beautiful, isn't it?"

Valya was distracted. She was mulling something over.

"How many dollars do you need?" asked Will.

"I don't know. Many. Two thousand, perhaps," said Valya.

"Two thousand?" replied Will incredulously. "That is a very large sum."

"Yes, not just for Mama's surgical operation but to keep her in safety and comfort in the future," replied Valya without looking at Will. "She cannot possibly live on her meagre Soviet state pension. She must have more money to live on and be secure. My salary is small. Sometimes people sell valuable items and keepsakes to pay for emergencies. We don't have such things. We have always lived very modestly. I don't see a solution," said Valya.

"You know, Valya, I could sell the information I obtained about Soviet harvest prospects when I was in the south of Russia. Grain traders are always sniffing around for information to get a jump on their competitors. But I don't want to do this," said Will. Before Valya responded Will added, "By the way, that American diplomat we met when we went to the Metropol Hotel, Wendell Randall, he was once a grain and gold trader."

They walked on in silence. Valya broke it by saying, "I could never contemplate selling state information or secrets to the Americans or to anyone. But I cannot exclude that other operators would do it... in this country everyone is on the make, seeking extra money, getting privileged access to goods and services without which you cannot live normally. It is a never-ending struggle."

"Wouldn't that be rather dangerous? I mean, if they were caught, they would surely be in big trouble with the Soviet authorities? Wouldn't it be considered treasonous to sell information to Western capitalist interests?" asked Will.

"Yes, it would. But, who knows, some may be desperate or greedy enough to run the risk," Valya replied. "Such is the state of our country."

They had reached the north-west corner of the Kremlin and now turned right, back towards their starting point, walking through the Kremlin gardens, past the Central Exhibition Hall and skirting the imposing red-brick wall on the northern side of the Kremlin complex.

"*Ladno* – clear enough," said Valya, smiling, having regained her composure. "Let us buy a drink and sit in the Kremlin gardens for a while."

They found a stall selling lemonade and sat down in a quiet spot.

"Valya, I just bought some tickets for *Spartak* at the Bolshoi for the last Sunday in the month. Vasiliev is dancing the role of Spartak. Would you like to come?"

"Oh, Will, certainly, that's a wonderful invitation. I have always wanted to see this famous ballet. Thank you so much," replied

Valya, kissing him on the cheek. "Maybe we can have dinner somewhere before or afterwards," she added.

"Agreed," said Will, thinking that her response sounded encouraging. He would have to locate a decent, not too expensive restaurant near the Bolshoi. Maybe he was beginning to make some headway.

"Please forget about what I said earlier about *mamochka*, Will," said Valya. "I was just talking to myself. It's of no consequence. It's my responsibility as her only child to find a solution. I must and I will."

Valya announced suddenly that she had to return to the office to do some extra work on a special document she was preparing.

"That's a shame, Valya. I have been enjoying our time together. On what?" asked Will absentmindedly.

"Forecasts. But never mind, we will see each other again soon. In the meantime..." Valya playfully sidled up to Will and kissed him.

After a while Valya got up to leave for her ministry. Though it was late Will didn't ask about what work she had to do. It was better to separate her professional obligations from his personal feelings towards her.

"Until our next meeting, Valya," said Will, giving her one final kiss. Chancing his arm, he added, "If you like I could instead cook something for us at my residence after the ballet."

"You! Cook! Not many Soviet men do that, I can tell you! Dear Will, I accept your exceptional offer! An English dinner for two it is after the death of the heroic slave *Spartak!* So be it!" and with that Valya headed off towards the metro station smiling to herself.

Will stayed in the Kremlin gardens. His relationship with Valya was now on a more promising path. Maybe if things went well the relationship would develop further. Will felt more confident that his last months in the USSR were going to pass by more agreeably.

TWENTY-FOUR

Mixed Messages

Some days later Will received a wake-up call from Valya.

"I cannot come to the Bolshoi theatre," said Valya. "I apologise."

"Oh, I am really sorry to hear that," replied Will disappointedly. "Weren't you looking forward to *Spartak?* And an English supper? What is up?"

"Work obligations," replied Valya curtly, once again in her matter-of-fact perfunctory tone on the telephone that contrasted so markedly with the warmth of their parting two days before. *This lady is capricious*, thought Will, *and subject to big mood swings*. He thought he knew where he stood with her but now, not for the first time, he was not so sure.

"On a Sunday? Communist construction never waits," said Will sarcastically but immediately regretted it. "Would you like to meet another time, Valya, or shall we leave it for now if you are busy?" asked Will.

"Late Saturday afternoon is possible," replied Valya.

Will, trying to hide his consternation at the change of arrangements but wanting to see Valya, despite her flighty manner, replied, "Valya, that is fine in principle. But I have a slight problem.

I have already arranged to meet a friend of mine – Tristan – that afternoon at 5pm at Moscow University. I will bring him along too if you have no objections. I am sure he would be delighted to meet you."

Following a short silence, Valya replied, "If unavoidable, Will, I understand. So, let's meet at 6pm on Saturday. There is a popular café near the bend in the Moscow River. It is not too far from Moscow State University. Everyone knows it. Until then goodbye."

Lacking focus, Valya seemed jumpy. Taking Tristan along was a risk and not his preferred option: Will hoped he would behave himself and leave his boorish side behind him for once, but he was volatile and unpredictable. On the other side it would be useful to have Tristan's considered view of Valya, the only young lady he had met in Russia whom he had found attractive and who had shown any interest in him, albeit fleeting and highly erratic.

TWENTY-FIVE

By the Moscow River

Saturday came round. Will met with Tristan as planned at the entrance of Moscow University around 5pm. The late afternoon was very humid and debilitatingly hot. They slowly headed towards the Moscow River and the planned rendezvous with Valya. Tristan knew exactly where the café was – about thirty minutes from the university. Halfway there, they decided to seek some temporary shade under a female poplar tree shedding its "fluff" – known locally as *pukh* – prior to arriving at the café.

Brushing some tufts of white *pukh* from his clothing, Tristan said, "This *pukh* fluff stuff drives me crazy. It gets everywhere and can even cause fires. Brilliant Soviet planning – they planted female gender Balsam poplar trees instead of the male version. Wrong sex at the wrong time if you take my meaning…!"

Will ignored the innuendo and decided to broach the delicate subject of Valya: "Tristan, about Valya, whom we will meet. She's a nervous, shy, retiring sort of girl, so let's be gentle with her, please. I am not suggesting you are *not* gentle with women, but she is edgy and withdrawn. She is not yet my girlfriend, I hasten to add, just the friendly daughter of our cleaning lady. So, let's go easy, OK?" said Will.

"Understood, old boy," responded Tristan. "I'll take my lead from you. Stiff upper lip, best behaviour, British reserve, and decorum and all that. My liege..." said Tristan, bowing before Will exaggeratedly.

Ten minutes later the friends arrived at the café and bought two beers to quench their thirst. It was six on the dot. No sign of Valya. The rundown, sweaty café was frequented by mainly young people, students from the university mostly, and it was crowded and boisterous. Will and Tristan found a bench outside near the entrance and sat down to await Valya's arrival.

"She won't appear before 6.30pm earliest," opined Tristan after ten minutes. "Time for another beer," and he headed off in the direction of the *kassa* to get a chit to replenish their supply from the barman.

The time passed slowly and after forty-five minutes of waiting both Will and Tristan were getting exasperated.

"Typical Russian girl," blurted out Tristan, now onto his third beer, "keeping us waiting indefinitely."

"I don't know if it's so typically Russian," said Will. "I once went out with a girl in England, and she kept me waiting seventy minutes on our first and only date. A difficult start with that one, though I might actually look her up when I get back to England."

Still no sign of Valya after nearly an hour of waiting, and the patience of Will and Tristan was now approaching breaking point.

"Sod it, Will, it's just plain insulting to keep the two of us waiting this long. Fuck it – let's go for a stroll in the hills by the river after I've had a leak," and with that Tristan headed for the rudimentary hole-in-the-ground latrines to relieve himself.

Will sat and reflected, very disappointed at the turn of events. He felt let down and messed about by Valya. What was her problem? Treating him in this way was not reasonable. She had proposed the revised meeting time and place and had failed to show up.

The sun was slowly beginning to set when Tristan returned, and they set off for a stroll on the path in the Lenin Hills overlooking the river. It was still a balmy, hot evening as they meandered along. They passed some other casual strollers on the way: no-one seemed in a hurry. Flies buzzed lazily in small swarms. The number of people on the path gradually thinned out as they walked further away from Moscow University. The path became rougher and less even. Turning back towards the riverside bar after chatting and walking for a good hour, they rested for a few minutes to drink some water before continuing. It was now well after eight in the evening and getting darker.

They walked on, uphill now, and turned round a bend. Will saw, against the gathering hazy dusk, what looked like a pair of poles sticking out from behind a scruffy bush. He and Tristan glanced at each other, unsure of what exactly it was in their view.

"Funny place to put your walking sticks," said Tristan.

"More likely legs," replied Will. He assumed that if legs they were then they were engaged in some sexual activity behind the cover of scrub and dusk. They did not stop but continued walking. Fifty yards further on Tristan reduced his pace and asked Will if he had seen the legs – if that was what they were – move at all.

"No," responded Will, "and just as well too as their owner might otherwise have found herself viewed by voyeurs in in an embarrassing situation."

Tristan was not satisfied. "It is a bit bizarre," he said. "The legs were seemingly straight out, motionless, at an angle to the ground." He hypothesised that something might be amiss.

"Forget it," answered Will. "Let's not go back."

They walked on a few metres and Tristan, headstrong and determined as always, decided he was going to go back after all to take a look. Will strongly advised against it. Reluctantly, he followed on some metres behind Tristan, fearful that they might land themselves in an awkward situation. Disturbing lovers 'in flagrante' was not the surefire way to enhance Anglo-Soviet relations.

As they reached the bend they once again saw, in the gathering gloom, the two elongated legs that had not moved from the position they had earlier observed. Tristan began clambering up the incline and slowly approached the large bush. He reached it and looked at it intently through the gloom.

"What's there?" asked Will.

"I can't see properly," shouted Tristan.

A few moments passed. Tristan called out in Russian, "Is anyone there? I don't mean to disturb you, but is everything alright?"

No answer. Some moments passed.

Tristan slowly inched forward, not wishing to give the figure masked by the bush any cause for alarm. Tristan turned to Will, who was some metres behind him: "Will, come here. I need some light to look at what's going on. Do you have a light?"

Will had a box of matches on him. He scrambled up the bank and lit the first match. What they then saw shocked them to their core and they receded backwards in horror. It was a scene Will would never forget.

"Oh my God," said Will.

"Jesus Christ," uttered Tristan.

At their feet was a partially clothed, dark-haired young woman in her late teens or early twenties, her skirt in folds around her middle, her legs bedraggled, stiff and pointing horizontally beyond the bush, and her hair completely dishevelled. They examined her head, which was to the side. There appeared to be several blue-black bruise marks on her neck. It was a horrendous sight; there was no sign of life in her at all. Tristan tried her pulse on both wrists and gently shook her. Nothing. Her body still had some residual warmth but there was absolutely no indication of any of her vital organs functioning. There were no signs of any gunshot or knife wounds. There was no trace of blood on the young lady or nearby. She had obviously not been there that long. It looked as if her body may have been brought there somehow and dumped behind the bush.

Tristan and Will began to panic in the half light.

"What the hell should we do?" Tristan said.

Will, numb with shock, lit another match and peered more closely at her face before recoiling in horror.

"It's Valya, Jesus Christ, it's Valya, Tristan. Valya. I don't believe it." Will stood stunned by Valya's lifeless body, thoughts racing through his mind, wondering what on earth had happened and why this innocent young woman's body was lying there motionless when she was supposed to have been meeting them. She appeared to have been brutally assaulted.

"Are you sure, Will?" said Tristan.

"Absolutely sure," replied Will, moments before clutching his knees while he retched uncontrollably into an adjoining bush. He was absolutely poleaxed by what he had seen; his legs were like jelly, his stomach hurting, his mind was scrambled and he couldn't think straight. He fell onto his knees with his head in his hands.

Tristan, clearheadedly, saw the need to act quickly and came to his senses. "We need to contact the Moscow Militsiya – the police – but also the embassy and explain what has happened. And get the hell out of here now. We can't afford to be seen anywhere near the body or goodness knows what the police might think. Get up, Will – we've got to go now," said Tristan urgently, endeavouring to lift Will under his shoulders and help him up.

Will, barely taking in what Tristan had suggested, stumbled to his feet and started to walk away from the corpse to look at how Valya might have been brought to the spot where they had found her. He followed a track perpendicular to the river for some fifty metres looking for signs of footprints or tyre marks. There were some footprints on the dusty track but no evidence of Valya's body or her feet having been dragged along uneven ground to the place where it was unceremoniously dumped behind the bushes. *At least two people must have moved her body there*, he concluded. Will searched around briefly in the twilight in the environs for anything else which could provide a clue to what had happened. He found no bag, no papers, no personal items – in short, absolutely nothing.

Tristan, rightly getting increasingly nervous that their presence at the crime scene would be noticed by someone, urged Will once again to leave. "For Christ's sake, Will, let's get the fuck out of here right now," he screamed.

Will took a last look at Valya as she lay there. His head was bowed and he was gasping for air. "My God, this is just unbelievable. She was just twenty-four. Our age. Jesus Christ," murmured Will. "Nothing can justify or explain this. Her mother... Svetlana... her mother will never survive this catastrophe..."

Tristan pulled Will down the slope, where they rejoined the path they had just taken. They headed towards the centre of Moscow, numbed and distraught, picking up speed as they fled further from the crime scene. They agreed that once they had found a Militsiya officer Tristan, who possessed the better-spoken Russian, would explain what they had found, while Will would head towards the British Embassy compound to inform the diplomatic staff there and seek help. He had vomited at the site of the crime so he would have a great deal of explaining to do.

TWENTY-SIX

Moscow City Militsiya Headquarters

The discovery of Valya's body meant that a senior Militsiya inspector would be summoned to lead the inquiry into the unexplained circumstances of her death and to determine what had had happened at the crime scene. Upon arrival at the Moscow City Militsiya headquarters at 10pm that evening, Will and Tristan, accompanied by Charles Fosdyke, the second secretary from the British Embassy whom they had met at Stephanie's party some weeks before, were informed that Nikolay Borisovitch Isakov, a chief inspector of the Criminal Investigations Department of the Moscow City Militsiya ('*Moskovskii Ugolovni Rozysk*') would be in charge of the inquiry into Valya's death and that they would be required immediately to submit themselves to preliminary questioning. Fosdyke was told brusquely that his presence at the interrogation would not be permitted: the two students were not diplomats and were not covered by the 1961 Vienna Convention on diplomatic relations and privileges. Consequently they would be required to speak with the police authorities unaccompanied by embassy staff. This caused consternation for Will and Tristan. The students were, *de facto*, on their own in the hands of Soviet Militsiya investigators and Soviet justice.

Isakov, a balding, large man of medium height and ample girth, was wearing a crisply pressed militsiya uniform. Folds of flesh accumulated under his chin while his eyes were sunken in their sockets and bordered by lined eyelids and sagging skin underneath. He was seriously overweight and had a tired, deadweight look about him, the consequence of having to deal with and solve a multiplicity of civilian crimes over his thirty-year career. He adjusted his thick, black-rimmed, rectangular-shaped glasses, raised his large oval-shaped head and looked the students over carefully. He shuffled a few papers on his desk and opened a new cardboard dossier. There were procedures to follow in investigations into unexplained deaths and Isakov knew them by heart. The first step was the opening of a preliminary investigation to establish the facts and circumstances of the case.

Isakov abruptly put his pen down on his desk. Staring directly into Will and Tristan's eyes, he addressed the two students in a gruff, loud voice, exuding authority while simultaneously conveying that he was a man of great experience who had seen everything that Moscow had to offer in terms of serious crime.

"This is a most unusual case," he began. "I've seen a lot of murders in my time but dead bodies do not turn up frequently behind shrubbery in the Lenin hills near the Moscow river, the centre of the capital of world socialism, let alone the body of a young woman discovered by two British students. We are investigating the crime scene now and will then remove the body for a detailed forensic examination."

Leaning over to eyeball the two students facing him across his desk, he said, "I want to know exactly the sequence of events that led you to find the body, step by step with the approximate times of each development. Why were you near the river? What were you doing there? How long had you been there? What did you observe in and around the path? In detail. Leave nothing out."

Will and Tristan went laboriously through the sequence of events leading up to the discovery of Valya's body in the undergrowth. They were pressed to recall whom they had seen at the café, whom they had passed on the path and specify anything suspicious they had observed.

Isakov was remorseless, demanding again and again that facts were confirmed, pointing to any minor discrepancies in the students' testimonies. They were challenged to repeat their observations. At around 4am Will and Tristan were destabilised by Isakov's announcement that henceforth they would be questioned separately.

A typical divide and rule tactic, thought Will, who continued to be interrogated by Isakov while Tristan was moved to another room to be interrogated by his deputy. Now the questioning was focused on Will's relationship with Valya. How long had he known her? When had they dated? What did they do when they went to the concert at the conservatory? Were they lovers? Did Valya have a jealous lover? Why had she cancelled their rendezvous and the planned ballet at the Bolshoi on Sunday? The endless questioning went on until 7am without a break. Will was hungry, thirsty, ragged and exhausted, his head spinning from the catastrophic sequence of events which had engulfed him, and he had a belting headache.

"Gospodin Lawrence," said Isakov, beginning to show signs of weariness himself after a night of relentless questioning and challenges to Will's testimony. "I am not satisfied with the information you have given me. Not satisfied at all. I want to know more about your relationship with the deceased. For now, however, you may return home. You will report to the Timiravskaya Militsiya Station every day at 10am, beginning tomorrow, and you will inform them of your scheduled whereabouts each day in detail. You will be summoned back here for more questioning in a few days' time. That is all."

"Chief Inspector Isakov," replied Will, struggling to express himself clearly in Russian, "I am devastated by the murder of this young woman. Her mother, the cleaning lady in the residence where

I live, will be utterly distraught. I will follow your instructions and report regularly to your authorities."

With this Will was escorted out of the Central Militsiya premises. Regaining the fresh air, there was no sign of Tristan. Will returned by 87 bus to his hall of residence, grabbing a pirozhki a meat pie from a small stall on route, and crashed out on his bed.

He did not awake until 4pm, when Fosdyke rang to find out how he was and what was going on. Will outlined the lengthy interrogation and his instructions to report to the local militsiya daily. Fosdyke advised him to follow these requirements scrupulously and not give the militsiya any excuse to allege procedural violations which could open the door to other formal interrogatory measures. Tristan, it seemed, had been told to do the same.

Fosdyke added, "Just to let you know that we are in touch with the Foreign Ministry (MID), who said they can't intervene as this is a criminal investigation under the responsibility of the Moscow Militsiya. We will continue to press MID for your exclusion from this investigation as it is obvious you are innocent. Our chargé d'affaires is seeing the Deputy Minister of Foreign Affairs tomorrow and we will raise our concerns with him. We don't want any adverse propaganda being conjured up by the Soviets around this matter at what is a sensitive time, politically, so rest assured we will carefully follow the case and, given our consular responsibilities towards UK citizens, we won't hesitate to make firm diplomatic representations as and when required. You have my telephone number: don't hesitate to call if you need any assistance."

Shortly thereafter Tristan called wondering how Will was after the ordeal.

"Shell-shocked, to be honest, my friend," replied Will. "I can't believe what has happened. I'm exhausted. Numbed and in shock. I got grilled for four hours about my relationship with Valya. How about you?"

"Got out at 5am after we got split up. Contacted Fosdyke immediately and woke the bugger up – poncy prick, wasn't too

111

pleased; sod him. According to what's written in my passport he's here to assist British citizens, of which I am one. Hope the embassy have got our backs covered. Don't want to be the sacrificial lamb in this grizzly affair. Bollocks to the lot of them," ended Tristan on a habitually upbeat and defiant note.

*

Two days later Will and Tristan were told to report back to Central Militsiya headquarters for further joint questioning.

It was immediately apparent that the issue of most concern to Isakov was Tristan's fingerprints: they were on the dead woman's wrists. Had he molested and strangled her? No matter what Tristan explained – that he had tested her pulse for signs of life and, finding none, had left with Will to seek help – Isakov remained suspicious.

"And I now want to pursue another line of inquiry," Isakov interjected suddenly. "You knew who this woman was. But we found no trace of her identity, nor any handbag or any documents. No Soviet internal passport either. Did you see anything on or nearby the deceased? Did you remove anything – her bag, her documents – from the crime scene, and if so, why?"

Will was dumbfounded at this question. "Chief Inspector, why would we have removed documents? In any event we saw no documents or bags, not that we were looking for them. We were in total shock – we couldn't believe what we had just witnessed. It was a gruesome scene."

Tristan weighed in. "Why would either of us want to harm this young woman, Chief Inspector? For what motive?" he argued. "We are students visiting your country, not killers. I never met her alive in any case. Will met her just a few times. We had arranged to meet her at the riverside café for a drink and she didn't show up. Why? Because someone fucking killed her. There's no more to it than that. What you have ascertained from the crime scene and why do you believe she was killed?"

"Revealing details of the investigation would be highly irregular," replied Isakov. "It is my business to analyse the evidence, determine who is guilty and prepare the prosecution for the State Prosecutor's Office. Experienced forensic investigators on the site have combed through the surrounding terrain and have not found anything materially useful to the case. Some beer bottles, cigarette stubs, used condoms and other detritus and rubbish were in the nearby undergrowth plus Lawrence's vomit but no murder weapon. I believe the victim Valentina Michaelevna had been strangled, maybe with a scarf or such like (there were some cotton fibres on her skin) or by sustained pressure from the hands of a strong man or men. There had been a struggle, but overwhelming force had prevailed. It seems likely her body was dumped there. It had all the hallmarks of a professional job – a contract killing, perhaps. The young woman had had no chance to survive this violence. The investigation continues. Follow instructions and report to your local militsiya stations daily. You are free to go now."

"Has her mother been informed?" asked Will plaintively.

"Yes," said Isakov.

Will was still stunned. What could possibly be the motive for violently assaulting and killing this innocent young woman? It didn't make any sense.

As he left with Tristan he realised that he would have to convey his deepest condolences to Svetlana Antolevna, Valya's mother. This was going to be one of the hardest things he had ever done in his life. It would have to wait until the next day – he was in no condition to speak to her today.

TWENTY-SEVEN

Svetlana's Grief

Will set off the following day to convey his condolences and pay his respects to Svetlana Antolevna.

She lived about thirty minutes away from Will's residence to the north-east of Moscow. After changing buses at a main junction and proceeding northwards for eight stops Will arrived at a vast, soulless, high-rise housing estate. He asked a number of people before he identified the location of Dom 2, Corpus 1, Kvartira 7A, the apartment where Svetlana lived. He entered the building, took the lift to her apartment on the seventh floor and rang the doorbell. After a while the door opened and a woman he did not know opened the door.

"Is this the home of Svetlana Antolevna?" Will tentatively asked.

"Yes, but she is not receiving visitors now," said the woman abruptly, and moved to close the door.

Will reacted quickly. "Please tell her that Will, the Englishman, from the hall of residence in the Timiryazev Academy where she works, has come to pay his respects to her and offer condolences for her loss."

The woman returned after a minute or so and beckoned Will to come in. *"Pozhaluysta, prikhoditye"* she said.

Will entered slowly, with trepidation and reverence, dreading the harrowing scene he was about to witness.

In the kitchen he saw Svetlana standing in a dark headscarf, wearing a peasant-type smock and jacket, her eyes red and moist with tears streaked widely across her cheeks. They were close to flowing again. She greeted Will solemnly and took his hands in her much smaller ones, the palms rendered rough through hard manual labour over many years. Her sad demeanour spoke of one thing – why, she was pleading, why has such a misfortune fallen on me, an unassuming lady just trying to live a quiet life and support my daughter?

The small apartment had bouquets of flowers of condolences in vases and pots scattered around the kitchen. Two neighbours were present. It was a wretched, pitiful scene. A simple, kind Soviet mother's life had been brutally upended by the violent loss of her daughter. Will had the impression, just looking at her, that the essence of her being, all her hopes and aspirations had just been extinguished. He dared not imagine how much worse this was going to get for Svetlana when she found out from Chief Inspector Isakov that Valya had been strangled. The demise of her daughter in this way would haunt the poor woman forever and Will doubted she would ever recover from it. Her sister Masha had said as much when they had met in Krasnodar. Valya had been Svetlana's life work.

Will plucked up the courage to express his heartfelt condolences to Svetlana for the loss of her daughter.

"Svetlana Antolevna," Will said solemnly, "I am deeply devastated and shocked by the loss of your daughter Valya whom I was due to meet the evening she died. My deepest and heartfelt condolences to you and to Masha and to your family and friends."

She nodded her head, thanked him for coming and invited him to drink a *stakanchik* of tea, which he accepted. Will and her neighbours sat around the stove and drank tea in silence while the poor distressed lady suffered. At various moments one or other of those present would hug and try to comfort her. Her head bowed, Svetlana was utterly distraught and quite incapable of absorbing comforting words of sympathy. She was clutching a small silver icon on which there was an image of the Holy Mother and Infant.

"I am helping the Militsiya with their enquiries," offered Will, to break the silence. "The lead investigator is very thorough. I will do what I can to help."

Svetlana nodded. But they were just empty words. Nothing could bring her Valya back.

Will made to leave, having drunk his tea, and went slowly towards the door.

Svetlana accompanied him. She was not moving easily; her knees were as swollen as Valya had told him a few days before. Before Will reached the outside door she pulled a small passport-sized photograph of Valya and an A4 sized envelope from the inside pocket of her overcoat and handed them to Will.

"Take it, please," said Svetlana, pointing at the envelope. "Valya said if anything happened to her it was for you. I want you to have it," said Svetlana with tears in her eyes.

Will thanked Svetlana, took the envelope and hugged her tightly before taking his leave. *It just doesn't get any worse than this*, he thought, as he descended the seven flights of stairs of the building to the ground-floor entrance. Stepping outside he stopped and, resting upright and, leaning against the ground-floor brickwork of the building, breathed in multiple gulps of balmy summer air before lighting a cigarette and inhaling the smoke powerfully. Children were playing in a nearby playground, whooping and laughing, while their onlooking parents and *babushki* stood chatting idly nearby.

Will would never forget the moment he encountered Svetlana Antolevna in her home. He stubbed out the butt of his cigarette and headed slowly towards the bus stop, head down, reflecting on a grim, unforgiving day.

Arriving home emotionally drained, Will swigged down two bottles of beer and collapsed onto his bed. He had barely had time to take in what had happened and was totally confused and disorientated. He didn't even have the energy to open the envelope given to him by Svetlana, which he just flung to one side on his table.

Instead, he took the small picture of Valya given to him by Svetlana from his wallet and looked intently at this young, attractive, mysterious and fragile young woman he had got to know only superficially but of whom he had become increasingly fond, despite her capriciousness. She had touched his life fleetingly but then was no more. It seemed barely credible that she had now ceased to exist as a person. All her hopes, aspirations and dreams had been destroyed in a frenzy of gratuitous violence. It was beyond his comprehension that anyone could end a defenceless young woman's life in this way.

Will was starting to feel scared. His hopes of spending an agreeable last few weeks in the USSR with Valya had vanished. He was now embroiled in a murky and grisly affair.

Will felt claustrophobic sitting in his room alone; things were totally out of control and his head was spinning. He jumped up and headed out of his building to get some fresh air. He headed along Listvennichnaya Alleia to the park where he had passed a few agreeable moments with Valya prior to leaving for the south. Resting on a bench with his head held tightly in his hands, he wept at the fate that had befallen Valya and her mother. Two ordinary people with no privileges, no favours, just trying to navigate and make their way in a harsh and brutal world. 'Little', disposable, inconsequential people about whom few cared. *Who is responsible for this tragedy?* he asked himself. *Who is guilty?*

Will sat up on the bench, resting his arms by his side. A light rain was beginning to fall but he took no notice of it. With a clarity that had been lacking, Will realised that the tragedy he had witnessed had brought him to a fork in the road. The path he now took would determine his future. Was he going to allow external events to overwhelm him or was he going to take a stand and influence them?

Will committed himself there and then to find out the truth about what had happened to Valya. How had she spent her last days, hours, minutes on the earth? What had she done – or not done – to cause her to lose her life? Who had done this? Who was guilty? Would they be held accountable?

Pursuing this uncharacteristically risky course was necessary not just for his own peace of mind. He owed it also to Svetlana, who had been crushed by her loss. And above all to Valya.

His mind was made up.

He was not going to be a bystander.

He was going to act.

TWENTY-EIGHT

French Bastille Day Reception, 14 July 1975, Moscow

Some days later, Florian, a cheery French agronomist in his thirties from Lyon University who was spending three months at Will's academy and who occupied a room along the corridor of his *obshezhitye* residence, reminded Will early in the morning of the Bastille Day reception being held at the French Embassy to which he had been invited. Florian said, in his franglais, that Will should wear a '*costume*', which puzzled him until he realised that he meant a suit. Will did not have a suit (or a costume) in Russia, just a crumpled jacket, shirt and tie. This kit, which had been worn by him at the Spaso House reception, was now a bit worse for wear. It would have to do.

Will was still reeling from Valya's murder and had spent a succession of sleepless nights trying to imagine what could possibly have happened to her. He had lost his appetite and had eaten little. He felt as if he had taken a pummelling. Though in a very dark and sombre mood, an excursion to a diplomatic reception and some decent food and drink might help him take his mind off the traumatic events of recent days, at least for a few hours.

Together Florian and Will set off for the embassy on Bolshaya Yakimanka Street, south of the Moscow River.

The French reception, he was informed, was always one of the best events of the diplomatic season, with a gourmet buffet and real French champagne and wine.

Arriving at the ambassador's residence there was already a large crowd of people both inside the building and in the garden. Feeding stations and bars outside were a buzz of activity. Florian and Will got in one of the buffet lines to fill their plates. At the other side of the garden Will noticed that Kuznetsov, the Ministry of Agriculture official whom he had met at the US reception at Spaso House some weeks earlier, was reactivating his pyramid technique of cramming as much food as possible onto his plate. As they moved towards the centre of the reception Florian hailed Kuznetsov, whom he had met during his stay, with a hearty '*Bonjour et bonne fête*' greeting.

Kuznetsov, struggling to recall who this guy was, replied in French: *Bonjour.* Florian introduced Will (who recalled to Kuznetsov that they had met before at the US Spaso House reception) and the three of them got chatting in Russian about the economy, the harvest and fulfilment of the five-year plan. Florian was most interested in how the French government could develop the provision of phytosanitary and agro-engineering services to the Soviet government.

Will recalled again that two months before he had been in the Kuban and Ukraine and that there were concerns about the weather impacting the harvest. Will asked, "Gospodin Kuznetsov, has there been any change in the harvest prognosis for this year? Any rainfall in the last month or are the main grain growing districts still facing drought conditions?" *That sounded like a competent and expert series of questions*, thought Will to himself as he awaited Kuznetsov's reply.

After taking a gulp of white wine and arranging his thoughts, Kuznetsov replied, "The harvest outlook is excellent – as sound, if not sounder, than I said before. There will be a record grain tonnage reflecting the planned investment practices of the USSR which are now yielding consistent results. Ill-informed Westerners should cease provocatively speculating about our scientific, socialist grain targets – they will be more than fully met," said Kuznetsov assertively.

Will was just about to ask again how there could be no impact on yields when the weather in the south had been so unfavourable in the early and middle part of the growing season when Wendell Randall III, from the US Embassy, announced his arrival by deftly manoeuvring himself into the gathering from the side and then positioning himself between Will and Kuznetsov, preventing Will from taking any further part in the conversation. By this time Florian had drifted off to speak to a French diplomat.

"Alexei Vladimorovitch, we need to talk. Privately," said Wendell in English.

The reception was now very crowded. Wendell coaxed the Soviet official away from the centre of the reception for a one-on-one talk, leaving Will marooned in the middle of the reception, underdressed compared to other guests, not knowing anyone and feeling awkward.

There was only one thing for it, Will decided: another glass of *vin blanc*. Objective defined, he headed towards the nearest bar, where white-jacketed bartenders were busily dispensing a chilled, crisp Mâcon-Villages in generous quantities from dozens of open bottles nestling in transparent bowls of crushed ice. Will drank a couple of generous glasses and headed to a quieter corner of the reception where small fruit tartlets and crème fraiche were being served for dessert.

Will noticed from his vantage point that Wendell had succeeded in isolating Kuznetsov on the fringes of the reception and that he was engaged in a very animated conversation with him, finger-wagging, arm-waving and gesticulating. Kuznetsov threw up his hands at one point, seemingly communicating to

Wendell words to the effect of, "...and what the hell do you expect me to do? ...I'm not responsible..." No-one was within earshot of them.

Will wandered around the reception for a while, but it was hot; there was little shade. *No point in hanging about,* he thought. Will made a move towards the exit, deciding to make a pit stop at the *Messieurs* on his way out before leaving. Kuznetsov walked briskly out of the toilets as Will entered, brushing past him in a hurry and ignoring him. Relieving himself, Will turned his head round to see Wendell exit another cubicle.

Preparing to leave the reception himself a minute or so later Will observed Wendell thanking the French Deputy Head of Mission for inviting him. Will was marginally behind Wendell now. Reaching the pavement outside the embassy he decided to have a quick smoke before heading home.

Wendell was pacing around by the entrance of the French residence searching for the US Embassy car to take him back to his office.

"God damnit, where is my driver? Useless airhead Boris, late as always," Wendell exclaimed, looking for his chauffeured vehicle in the general mêlée of cars and drivers queuing, manoeuvring and shoving one another in the vicinity of the French Embassy residence, looking to pick up their respective diplomatic charges. "Totally unacceptable to wait: I have urgent political matters to attend to," he continued.

Will, who overheard his remark, interjected, "Well, at least you have a car and chauffeur, Wendell. It's a bus, metro or tram for me."

Wendell said he had never taken, nor did he ever intend to take, public transport in Moscow.

After taking a lengthy drag on his cigarette, Will said, "That Soviet agricultural guy Kuznetsov. Very odd what he was saying about the harvest."

Wendell became slightly more attentive while still looking for his chauffeur. "What was he saying?"

"Well," Will replied, "when I was in the south two months ago there was no rainfall at all. It was obvious that there were local concerns about damage to harvest grain yields. Yet today, at the reception, Kuznetsov still persisted that the forecasts were still very good – record harvest levels to be expected and so on. He was even more upbeat than a few months ago. It doesn't add up."

Wendell: "Even if there may be some minor crop damage, on which there are no facts, would you seriously expect a proud Soviet official to admit anything different to a greenhorn student from a capitalist country, Billy boy? Get real, man! There will be a record harvest, believe me."

"A record harvest is at variance with the facts. There must be an adverse effect on crop yields from the excessive summer heat." Will retorted.

Wendell was not listening and had moved down the pavement in search of Boris and his car. He returned after a few minutes in a volcanic temper, still having failed to locate his driver.

Will decided to broach the subject of Valya. "You remember the young lady Valya who came with us to the Metropol Hotel whose telephone number you asked me for?"

"Sure. You mean Val, how is she?" said Wendell, his gaze remaining elsewhere.

"She's dead," blurted out Will.

"Dead?" replied Wendell, clearly startled and thrown off balance. "Dead? Are you serious? From what?"

"Murdered," replied Will. "My friend and I found her body in the foothills by the Moscow River two weeks ago, after we had failed to find her at a planned meeting place. The Moscow Militsiya are investigating how and why she was killed."

"Don't shit me, man. Murdered? What for?" asked Wendell, clearly disorientated.

"I thought you would want to know," responded Will.

"Christ, it wasn't long ago that I was talking about her when I was having a drink at the National with Kuznetsov and his colleague. A smart, pretty girl. I was looking forward to seeing her again. One on one. I don't believe it… can't internalise it…" said Wendell, for once, seemingly, sincerely.

"Who do you think might have killed her?" asked Will.

"You expect me to answer that?" Wendell boomed hot-headedly in reply. "With no information at my fingertips? I deal in facts, Billy boy. Facts. God alone knows. Maybe a jealous date or something," offered Wendell unconvincingly.

"Maybe. Or maybe she was involved in some murky schemes," said Will.

"Murky schemes? What does that bullshit mean? I'm shocked. That's all I can say. What a crap day," said Wendell, working himself up into a lather while simultaneously searching for Boris, who had at last come into view. He seemed genuinely disturbed.

Boris eventually succeeded in manoeuvring Wendell's clunky, oversized Buick to a pickup spot near the French Embassy residence and opened the right-hand rear door to enable the American diplomat to get in. Instead of doing so, Wendell subjected his chauffeur to a volley of invective and abuse in front of all the waiting diplomats and drivers for being late and threatened to fire him on the spot. He left without as much as a cursory *'au revoir'* to Will.

Arrogant, obnoxious, pig-headed prick, Will thought to himself. *What the hell was he talking to Kuznetsov about anyway?*

Will walked from the French Embassy down the wide Bolshaya Yakimaka boulevard towards the Kremlin. As he reached a fork in the road he noticed on his right-hand side the yellow, fading former residence of Prince Nashchokin, set back from the street, in some disrepair. *That place would make a good diplomatic residence one day*, he thought to himself. He could imagine living in a place like that.

Will continued walking and crossed the Moscow River. He decided on the spur of the moment that he would drop into the National Hotel, situated on the far side of a vast open area facing the north wall of the Kremlin on the corner of Ulitsa Gorkogo. He wanted to follow up on what Wendell had just revealed, to see if any staff member there remembered Wendell's meeting with Kuznetsov and who was present at it.

TWENTY-NINE

National Hotel

Will entered the hotel, one of Moscow's most famous given its superlative location and generous high-ceilinged rooms, and approached the reception desk. A young man and a powder-blonde woman receptionist kitted out in dark blue Hotel National uniforms manned the reception area, each busy with registers, paperwork and an abacus used for making monetary calculations. Neither bothered to look up when Will arrived at the desk, concluding, most probably, that he was not an actual or a potential hotel guest.

"*Vam shto* – what do you want?" asked the woman without looking up.

"Yes, thank you, I was due to meet a friend here some days ago and, unfortunately, I was late. I was wondering if she might have left a message with one of your staff?" said Will.

"No, she did not," said the woman without looking up.

"Ahem," continued Will, "I'm sorry to insist but it is a matter of importance. Could I possibly speak with your staff members who were on duty and might have seen her? I would appreciate it."

"Go and ask in the bar then," snapped the receptionist. "It's not my business. This is a hotel not a police station."

Chastened, Will walked up a flight of stairs to the bar area situated on the first floor. He bought himself an expensive beer for four roubles. When it arrived he took out of his pocket Valya's picture and asked the barman if he had by any chance seen this young lady recently. He said no. Will, quickly realising that some roubles would be necessary to encourage further deep mining of his and other staff members' memories, thrust a three-rouble note into the barman's hand together with Valya's picture and asked if he could ask his colleagues if anyone had seen her. The waiter pocketed the money and disappeared behind some swing doors.

Will looked out from the window of the bar towards the imposing light brown brickwork of the northern walls of the Kremlin, a sight probably unchanged over many centuries. He had sipped half his beer when another employee, tall, slim, slicked-back fair hair with moustache, wearing the same dark blue Hotel National uniform, approached him carrying Valya's photograph in his hand.

"Was it you who was asking about this girl?" he asked.

"Yes," replied Will. "Do you remember seeing her here?"

"I think I remember her," said the man, deliberately vaguely. "I need to reflect."

Will, took out another three roubles from his wallet, smoothed the note gently between the thumb and forefinger of his right hand, regretting that he was about to say goodbye to it, and asked, "Would this perhaps jog your memory?"

"Thank you. Always helps to activate the brain cells," replied the man, smiling, sliding the banknote into his waistcoat pocket and returning Valya's picture to Will. He sat down beside him. "Listen, I can confirm this girl was here. With three other people. Around 6pm – some days ago on my evening shift. I remember because they were by the window facing onto Ulitsa Gorkogo and one of them was not Russian. He only spoke English, so everything had to be translated. They stayed for about an hour but the foreigner kept getting up and down suggesting he might leave at any moment. They drank champagne. The girl was the quiet one of the four," said the man.

"And the other men?" asked Will.

"Russians," said the man. One was middle-aged, overweight. Smoked a lot. The other taller, fitter, square-jawed, harder. Military, security type or whatever – I'd recognise him again. Plus the foreigner – American, I think."

"Anything else you noticed?" asked Will.

"The foreigner was picked up by a driver. I saw that from the window facing the Kremlin when I was clearing up a table."

Will, trying with a longshot, asked, "Did you by any chance overhear or pick up anything they were talking about?"

The man reflected further before answering. "It was quite an intense discussion. About a business matter. I wasn't listening, of course – my job is to be a waiter. I remember hearing words like 'business' and 'deal' a few times. And 'dollars'. I didn't really pay attention. I am not a *stukach* – an informer or a stool pigeon."

"Do you remember who paid for the drinks?" asked Will.

"Oh yes, the foreigner, because he gave me $50 from a large wad of banknotes in his wallet and said he didn't want the change back. Russians would never do this. It was a very healthy tip," said the waiter, smirking with satisfaction.

"And then the foreigner left on his own?"

"No, the girl followed him. To be honest, I didn't pay that much attention – for me it was just a normal, regular pickup of a young tart organised by a couple of Russian pimps. Foreigners like pretty, young, well-proportioned Russian girls," the waiter added, winking crudely, "and they're cheap by Western standards."

Disgusted by the waiter's insinuations, Will nonetheless pressed on. "Anything else you recall?"

"Not really. The two men stayed awhile finishing their drinks, talking animatedly. They seemed pleased with themselves. They then ordered another bottle of champagne. No tip this time, though. Typical Russian generosity! Then they became quieter. After about an hour and a half they left suddenly in a hurry."

"You have been very helpful," said Will. "It will assist me in tracing the girl."

Will made his way out of the hotel and walked towards the 87 bus stop by the Bolshoi theatre for his ride home.

Wendell had been lying. He had met with both Valya and Kuznetsov at the National. And with one other person too.

Will was fuming.

THIRTY

Pavel Yeremevich

Unknown to Will Pavel, the shadowy third member of the Russian triumvirate seeking to conclude a deal with the American Randall, was a long-time friend and comrade of Kuznetsov. They had shared a common childhood including completing primary and secondary school education together in Leningrad after the war. They had been young Soviet *Oktyabryonki* and Pioneers at school and knew and trusted each other instinctively like brothers. Both had followed promising career paths in state service and had initially advanced swiftly, but their hopes of attaining top positions had not been realised and their careers had plateaued. They were, in their different ways, frustrated. The system had conspired against them: it had not rewarded loyalty, engagement and hard work. They now understood that connections, family ties and providing services to the Party were far more valuable in terms of getting ahead than dedicated service.

There never had been any doubt where Pavel's career path would take him. Guided by his father, a NKVD retiree who, according to unconfirmed rumours, had played a prominent part in preparing the Article 58 counter-revolutionary cases against

Kyrgyzstan political leaders in 1938, Pavel was always headed towards the secret intelligence services of the USSR. Hopeless at languages, he orientated towards the Fifth Directorate of the KGB, the successor agency to the NKVD. Every Soviet citizen knew about the 'Fifth' – it was instantly recognised as the department dealing with censorship and internal security against artistic, religious and political dissidents. Pavel initially showed himself adept at this work and proved to be a rigorous and tough interrogator with a fearsome reputation. He brooked no dissent. If rough methods – including torture – had to be used to extract confessions, our Pavel was up for it. He was a loyal hatchet man.

Pavel was quickly appointed to Principal Interrogator, Class 2, in the fifth department of the KGB. But then, unexpectedly, his professional advancement stalled. By failing to take account of the prevailing winds of reform during the Khrushchev period, the emptying of the Gulag camps and the more tolerant atmosphere in the USSR which endured for a short period, Pavel found himself out of sync with his authorities. An interrogator of the 'old school', lacking any subtlety or sensitivity, his skill set was suddenly less in demand. His superiors suggested that he move to another department, which he duly did, by taking a mid-level post in the Seventh KGB Directorate responsible for surveillance of Soviet nationals and foreigners. He had stayed in this post for twelve years without a promotion.

Pavel was bored, frustrated and angry that many comrades from his yearly intake into the KGB had progressed not just to higher posts but also in more prestigious directorates, whereas he had been limping along consigned to a lesser department whose output – surveillance material – was merely fodder for the more substantive security work of the Bureau. He had not been given managerial responsibilities. His requests for a reassignment back to the Fifth Directorate and a long-merited promotion had fallen on deaf ears.

Around this time in the late 1960s and early 1970s Pavel began to observe that some of his comrades were availing themselves of opportunities to enrich themselves 'on the side', using their connections to higher-level cadres in the Soviet state machine. This type of activity was tolerated to a degree by the Soviet authorities provided that the spoils were shared out amongst all those in the chain of command. Pavel made himself available to provide freelance 'security and intelligence services' to schemes organised by comrades. He saw himself as a hired hand but not the instigator of nefarious activities.

Nothing much turned up apart from one or two minor bribery and extortion opportunities. One evening in June 1975 he met his old pal Alexei Vladimirovich Kuznetsov at his modest dacha – not much bigger than an outside shed – just outside Moscow.

The two pals commiserated with one another about their stalled careers.

"I'm not going anywhere, Alexei. Why? I'm stuck in the basement. Boring, footslogging work. I can't get another opportunity matching my skills. Things were so much easier in the old days," moaned Pavel.

"Likewise, my friend. The Ministry of Agriculture is a giant monolith. My work is the same, year in year out. I have no access to the elite *Buro Propuskov* shops for the nomenklatura and high-ranking Soviet officials," said Kuznetsov.

They downed some Extra vodka shots in a contemplative, and unhappy mood. After their fifth shot Kuznetsov, who was less good at holding his drink, said, "My only hope is to materialise a business proposition that has come my way. But it's risky."

Pavel, his curiosity aroused, immediately responded, "Business proposition? I'm all ears, Alexei. Let's hear it."

"It's about selling some confidential statistics on the USSR harvest and other matters to an American diplomat I met at a reception at Spaso House, the residence of the US Ambassador, earlier this month," expounded Alexei. "The American is demanding and aggressive, though – he wants a lot of information for an absolute minimum outlay in dollars."

"Did you say dollars?" Pavel's face lit up when he heard this magic word. "How many?"

"He's offering two thousand," replied Kuznetsov.

"Two?" said Pavel incredulously. "Just two? Are you crazy? I can't believe you are so naïve, Alexei. Not serious. Don't touch it. Not nearly enough."

"What do you think would be a reasonable price then?" asked Kuznetsov naïvely.

"Not less than $10,000 cash – absolute minimum," replied Pavel. "Look, Alexei, this capitalist American will exploit this information and make big money. And you run all the risks of putting it together, wheedling it out illicitly from under the noses of state authorities and then get paid virtually nothing as a reward! Let's tell him $10,000 cash or forget it. And in used notes," advised Pavel, sounding assured, experienced and in charge, before even being invited to participate. "Have you got the information the American wants?"

"Not yet," replied Kuznetsov. "And there is the problem. I need the help of a young woman in the economics-statistics department of my ministry to get the key harvest forecast data."

"Who is she? Is she willing to assist?" asked Pavel.

"Yes, in principle. Her mother is ill. Needs a medical operation on her knees or something and needs money. The young woman knows about the American and has met him. But she's young, nervous and naïve. Unstable. I'm not sure about her reliability for such a sensitive, confidential business transaction," summarised Kuznetsov.

"Did you discuss payouts with her?" asked Pavel.

"Well, I suggested fifty-fifty of the smaller amount, but that was before I consulted you. She seemed content with that," said Kuznetsov.

"Listen, comrade," said Pavel, pouring out another round of vodka shots, drawing closer to and linking arms with Kuznetsov, "bring me on board. I'll professionalise the operation and ensure its full success. I know my business. We can make this deal work. For both of us. Let's offer the girl $5,000 – that should help her put her qualms aside and provide the information we need. Leave the 'persuasive side' of the operation to me – I'm an expert at that. Now, let's drink to success. *Davai* – down the hatch," and the two friends knocked back two more full vodka shots.

*

Kuznetsov and Pavel met again a few days later at a café-bar near the Ministry of Agriculture, where they discussed the details of the forthcoming transaction. They agreed that Valya would be instructed to prepare a dossier consisting of three elements – the harvest forecast for grain, to which she had access, and the planned monthly schedule for Soviet grain imports, which Kuznetsov could get hold of. More problematic in terms of access was getting information on Soviet plans for offloading Soviet gold onto the Zurich gold market to pay for the imports. This could only be obtained from the Central Bank of the USSR, from the Soviet Foreign Trade Bank or from Wozchod Handelsbank, the Soviet trading bank in Zurich. The Ministry of Agriculture would not have this information. Pavel, whose contribution so far had amounted to bluff and bluster, offered to take this task in hand. However, he warned Kuznetsov that he would have to pay to get hold of this secret financial information. They agreed to proceed in this way.

Pavel knew how to get hold of the Zurich gold sales information. An old comrade of his, Misha, a carpet crawler-type known in the KGB as the 'worm', a man constantly on the make, was working in the Sixth Directorate responsible for economic counterintelligence and industrial security. For an appropriate one-off fee he felt sure his former comrade could get access to and supply the data on gold shipments. Sure enough, Misha, when approached, was entirely amenable to supplying the information required. However, he demanded payment of $1,000 in cash from Pavel, a very large sum. Pavel had $1,100 in cash stashed away at his home from previous 'off-piste' freelancing operations and could, in principle, use most of this to pay Misha, but he was uncomfortable doing so as this sum would virtually wipe out his entire hard currency savings. On the other hand, the potential profit from the deal with the American – four hundred per cent – was significant.

Of course, Pavel had no intention whatsoever of paying the girl Valentina fifty per cent of the business deal. $5,000? *How idiotic can you get?!* She would get $500 max if she was lucky, provided she delivered all the information to his entire satisfaction and kept her mouth firmly shut. To ensure that was the case, she would be told, in the clearest terms, that if she pressed for any more of the payout, she would be reported to KGB internal security services for stealing state secrets with the intention of selling them to capitalist enemies of the USSR. The prospect of twenty years in a labour camp in Northern Siberia should encourage her to remain silent. The fact that Alexei had naïvely made a promise to pay her a great deal more was irrelevant, as was the medical condition of her mother. He didn't care a monkeys about some clapped out old baba's knees. Nothing was set in writing. There was no contract. He would just bully her in the thuggish manner that had served him so well in the past. And it would leave Kuznetsov and himself to share out a handsome $8,500 (a large sum even after his pre-payment of $1,000 to Misha was factored into the settlement). The prospect of such a promising return, four times more than his initial investment, was worth taking a risk for. *Lucrative business opportunities like this*, he surmised, *do not come along every day.*

THIRTY-ONE

Negotiations

The idea that he could supplement his meagre Ministry of Agriculture salary by making some hard currency on the side had only really struck Kuznetsov when he met the American diplomat Wendell Randall at the US Embassy reception at Spaso House at the beginning of June. Subconsciously, though, he had been on the lookout for ways to improve his lot for some time. Not only was he was frustrated with his job and the lack of any realistic promotion prospects; he was also fed up with the paucity of his material possessions and his lousy living conditions in a block of flats located in the outer southern suburbs of Moscow; he was also exasperated at the constant carping and whingeing of his wife, Olga, who wanted more clothes, shoes, cosmetics, expensive meals and a better life for herself, as well as enhanced prospects for her idle teenage son, Yuri, from a previous marriage. That required cash. It was the American diplomat, together with his uncle, the Chicago grain trader, who had peppered him with questions about his knowledge of Soviet grain harvest projections for 1975. That discussion led to ideas being exchanged with the capitalist diplomat and consolidation of the framework for today's promising 'cash for information' business deal.

Getting the dossier together for the American had been no mean feat. He himself had provided the planned schedule of imported grain, mainly from US grain stocks, since, in his capacity as director for forward planning of Soviet agricultural product supplies in the ministry, he had access to such data. Valya Michaelevna worked on collating forecasts of the grain harvest drawn from all agricultural districts of the USSR. Pavel was able to get his hands on planned Soviet gold sales to fund the imports through his contacts, though he had to pay handsomely for this information. Together the three elements constituted exactly what the American wanted.

Their meeting in the National Hotel to finalise the deal with the American was carefully choreographed. Pavel Yeremevich, who spoke no English, would remain silent and would not intervene. Valya also spoke little English so she too would remain an onlooker. However, she would act as the courier and make the exchange. Kuznetsov instructed her to put on her best dress and be radiant, smiling, friendly and encouraging. Kuznetsov himself would handle the final negotiations, having previously drawn up a negotiating strategy with Pavel.

They pre-ordered a table in the corner of the hotel bar area overlooking Ulitsa Gorkogo, the Gorky Street side of the hotel. After they had ordered a bottle of champagne Kuznetsov got down to business.

"So, Mr Randall, are you ready to pursue the mutual exchange? Of material products?" said Kuznetsov, smiling and speaking in the most general way.

"You bet," said Wendell curtly. "What's the process? How do I get the data? The documents. When?"

"First, we need to reach a mutual business understanding. Agree a price for this information," responded Kuznetsov. "We can then move forward to the handover arrangements."

"$2,000 is the deal, right?" replied Wendell in a deadpan voice, reaching for his inside jacket pocket to produce the cash.

He was cut short by Kuznetsov's next comment. "Mr Randall, permit me to say that this sum was purely the initial, indicative price." He continued, "Getting this information together has been far more difficult and costly than foreseen. So, the final price has had to be adjusted upwards – to $15,000," stated Kuznetsov with a straight face, knowing full well that this figure, a more than seven-fold increase on Wendell's proposal, was ridiculously high and would not be acceptable to the American. He added, "This is an exceptionally low price given the efforts and resources we have deployed to procure the information you are looking for."

Wendell was outraged. "$15k? Are you out of your mind? No deal," he replied. Wendell had no intention of being taken for a ride by this unscrupulous racketeering threesome and got up to leave.

Kuznetsov swiftly interjected. "We are prepared to negotiate, Mr Randall. Within strict limits," said Kuznetsov, who had anticipated some theatrics from the American. "However, $2,000 is far, far too low."

After much gamesmanship, to-ing and fro-ing, concocted drama, phony wounded pride and fake threats of walkouts, they agreed and shook hands on a compromise sum of $10,000. Wendell, who had given a lot of ground in the negotiations, had been ready for this Russian manoeuvre to reopen the deal: the original price of $2,000, he had to admit, was an out-and-out steal. And when all things were said and done, Wendell knew that $10k could be recuperated on the Chicago Board of Trade wheat exchange in the blink of an eye. So he did not complain overly aggressively at the Russians' inflated demands.

"OK. $10k is the deal. So where is the document?" asked Wendell.

"The document is in the ministry for safekeeping. We propose that you accompany Valentina Michaelevna Dontsova to get the dossier after our meeting," replied Kuznetsov, confident that things were now on the right track and that this arrangement would suit the American. "You will give her $10,000 in used dollar bills which she will count before handing the document over to you."

Valya smiled.

"By car?" asked Wendell.

"If you like," said Kuznetsov.

"Mine?" responded Wendell.

"Why not?" said Kuznetsov.

"It's got US diplomatic plates," said Wendell.

"I don't think anyone will notice in the hustle and bustle outside the hotel – they'll probably just see it as a young woman joining a man for the evening," replied Kuznetsov, smiling, assuming Valya would not understand what was being said. "It happens all the time round here, as I am sure you are aware."

"OK," said the American.

They finished their drinks with a toast to their successfully concluded business arrangement and the American paid the bill with a $50 note. Wendell left slightly in advance of Valya, who followed after getting final instructions from Kuznetsov and Pavel. Once she had secured the money she was to return immediately to the National Hotel, where they would be waiting. The dollars would then be discreetly divided out between them. It seemed straightforward enough.

V principye. In principle.

THIRTY-TWO

The American Dealmaker

After his initial contact with Kuznetsov at the US grain traders' reception at Spaso House in June Wendell had met him again by prior arrangement at the British Embassy's reception to honour the Queen's official birthday a few weeks later. They agreed to enter into a business arrangement and to finalise its terms at the National Hotel some days after that.

Wendell didn't agree to this transaction lightly. He had done the calculations one would expect of a sophisticated risk-taker. As a top market operator he was proud of his cold, calculating and careful evaluation of risks and rewards under pressure. And of his gut instinct in assessing potential business opportunities and partners. He was not in any way reckless. He would not gamble everything in pursuit of high reward: what counted was the calibration of risk against potential gain. And sound commercial judgement.

In this case, the risk-reward equation and the acquisition of valuable insider information met his criteria for full engagement. Nominally, of course, his loyalties lay with the US State Department, his current employer, but, in practice, private business and personal gain – money – were what motivated him. He saw no real conflict in interest between his proposed course of action and US global priorities, provided the matter was kept discreet and under the table. He was in no doubt that if this guy Kuznetsov delivered what he had promised then the information would be invaluable insider market intelligence for his uncle. A ticklish secondary issue, which did preoccupy him, was how to get the procured dossier to Chicago. He couldn't use US Embassy cable traffic or Soviet telephones. Fortunately, he would be visiting West Berlin soon for the semi-annual regional conference of US political counsellors. So, he could either meet his uncle there or, alternatively, send or wire the dossier to him directly from the West German capital. All was seemingly set fair.

Once his uncle's trading brokerage received the dossier, the information in it could be deployed immediately to make highly profitable trades on spot and forward grain and gold markets in conjunction with the brokerage's business associates in Chicago and Zurich. The Randall family firm would be ahead of the trading curve, a step in front of its competitors and in possession of detailed and time-sensitive knowledge of Soviet buying and selling intentions on two key international commodity markets – grain and gold. Wendell looked forward to enjoying his share of the spoils from the substantial trading profits that would come his way once he returned to the US for good after completion of his Moscow posting in about six months' time.

A factor of modest concern was how Wendell could be certain that the dossier would contain what his Russian partners promised. Here, to a large extent, he was in their hands since his Russian language skills were rudimentary. He could read numbers, though, and, all in all, trusted himself to determine the authenticity of what he would be purchasing. He had to acknowledge, however, that there was a residual risk element here. It was not as if he would be buying blank sheets of paper, though.

Upon leaving the National Hotel, Wendell waited for Valya, who followed a few minutes later. Initially she made out as if she would get into his Buick car, the same one she had ridden in with Will and Stephanie after the February concert, but then she hesitated. There were a lot of people milling around the entrance to the hotel and some of them appeared to be looking at her. *Am I not courting potential trouble?* she said to herself. An informer would spot her getting into an official diplomatic car. It wasn't worth taking the risk.

"Mr Wendell, meet you and me," said Valya, pointing to herself and Wendell. "*V Ministyerstvye. Ya, na metro*," said Valya, smiling.

Wendell, bemused, failed to comprehend the message. "Don't understand," said Wendell.

"*Ya, na metro*," said Valya. "*Metro*." She tried to describe with hand signals what it was like travelling underground.

"Oh, OK. Meet at ministry?" said Wendell, trying to figure out what Valya was trying to communicate.

"*Da*," said Valya. "*Cherez Chas.*"

"*Chas?* You mean in one hour," said Wendell, pointing to his watch and indicating to her one hour forward at 7.30pm.

"*Pravilno* – correct." Valya smiled.

"Where?" asked Wendell.

"*V Vkhode*," said Valya.

"Entrance?" replied Wendell, indicating with his right hand a movement towards a nearby building.

Valya nodded.

Wendell asked his driver if he knew where the Ministry of Agriculture was, to which he replied affirmatively. Valya set off for the metro. They went their separate ways to the ministry.

Wendell instructed his driver Boris to approach the Ministry of Agriculture building on Orlikov Pereulok slowly and park in a nearby side road to be as inconspicuous as possible, a challenge given his vehicle's diplomatic number plates.

Boris duly located a suitable side road nearby the ministry and parked the Buick under a tree.

Wendell had thirty minutes to kill. He walked aimlessly around the environs of the Ministry of Agriculture thinking about the information he was about to acquire and how useful it would be to his uncle. And about how his own bank balance would, in due course, balloon when his cut was paid.

As the hour for the meeting approached Wendell positioned himself nearby the ministry looking at the main entrance. He waited to see signs of Valya emerging with the document file. He reminded himself that he had presumptively reserved and paid for a hotel room at the Hotel Bucharest which he planned to use later that evening in the company of Valya. Chilled Russian champagne had been ordered. The prospect of a steamy evening with this pretty young lady to celebrate the conclusion of a successful business transaction was enticing. He had no doubt that his proven charm and prowess with women would prove irresistible to the naïve Valya and he was confident that she would succumb to his advances. Purring with anticipation, he looked forward to a highly enjoyable evening to reward his outstanding business acumen.

His mind refocused again on the planned exchange. It was now thirty minutes after the scheduled meeting time. No sign of Valya. Wendell returned to the car, where Boris was snoozing.

"Boris, did you see the young lady Valya walk by?" asked Wendell.

"No, sir," he replied.

Well, he wouldn't have done, would he? thought Wendell, as he was sound asleep.

Another twenty minutes went by, and Wendell was beginning to get very impatient. He idled around the ministry building for a few more minutes before wandering slowly back to his car again.

"Boris, ask the guards at the ministry building if they have seen Miss Dontsova, Valentina Michaelevna, arrive and ask them to call her in her office. Tell them that the person she is due to meet has been waiting outside for nearly an hour," instructed Wendell.

"Yes, sir," replied Boris. He got out of the driver's seat and headed towards the ministry entrance. He returned a few minutes later with surprising news.

"Miss Dontsova was not in the office today, sir, the Okhrana guard said. He checked with reception and the ministry's register and called her office number. She is not there and has not been seen in the office today, sir," reported Boris.

"Goddammit," said Wendell, and swore under his breath. *What the hell is the stupid bitch up to?* He waited a few minutes longer before abandoning the rendezvous. Almost an hour and a half had passed. It was clear Valya was not going to show up. No sex either. *Shit.*

"Home. Now," Wendell barked out furiously to Boris.

THIRTY-THREE

Tristan

A day after the French Embassy reception Will met Tristan in town, headed for the nearest Pivo bar and ordered some Soviet beer. For all his bluff, bluster and seeming insouciance, Will observed that Tristan had been disoriented and unnerved by Valya's death and that his behaviour was becoming even more careless, risky and rash.

"Bollocks to them," said Tristan. "Bloody outrageous that these Soviet cops are trying to insinuate that we're implicated in or responsible for the murder of Valya. Does Isakov really think we removed items from the crime scene? We're just innocent bystanders. Giant cock-up in the fragrant garden of socialism if you ask me. Not my problem," and with that Tristan went in search of a bottle of Green Label vodka which habitually could be bought with a suitable backhander given to the barman.

Will looked around at the bunch of grizzled middle-aged male drinkers hovering by the bar, some of them gesticulating, noisy and drunk. This was not the sort of place that Will would choose to frequent, but he was being guided by Tristan, who reappeared with a bottle of Extra vodka and two small glasses.

Pouring out two full shots, Tristan exclaimed, "Down the hatch, Will. To hell with the Moscow Militsiya, Lenin, Stalin, Brezhnev and the whole fucking lot of them," Tristan exclaimed in a such a loud voice that some of the other standing patrons propping up the bar turned to look at him quizzically as Tristan poured the forty per cent proof transparent liquid down his throat and refilled their glasses. Will's own glass was still half full; he sipped vodka rather than drinking it in shots. He could not keep up with Tristan's elevated rate of alcohol consumption.

"Tristan, pipe down. You're bloody crazy. Why take these risks? We'll get arrested for insulting Soviet leaders. The investigations are worrying. But keep cool, man. We know the truth, we know we are innocent, we have credible alibis and the British Embassy are watching out for us, so why are you so destabilised and nervous? Was it what we saw – Valya's body – the fear of incarceration in the USSR or what?" Will asked.

"You're more upset than me, Will – me, I didn't even know the girl. Have another drink," replied Tristan, replenishing their glasses again and taking out his umpteenth cigarette of the day. Tristan's index and middle finger on his right hand bore traces of ingrained orange-brown nicotine stains and his teeth were yellowing. Both needed a good clean.

"Tristan, as your friend, let me say bluntly you are jeopardising your health by playing so hard, smoking like a chimney and drinking too much hard liquor. It's what many Russians do so recklessly. You are slipping inexorably into bad local habits. You don't look well at all, your skin is pale, you have a rasping cough from smoking too much and you seem disturbed if not unhinged. Get a grip, my friend. What is bothering you?"

Instead of reacting strongly to Will's admonition, Tristan, in an unusually reflective mood, spoke quietly, almost whispering. "I'm trying to cope... failed relationships, family break-up... already been dried out once... parents divorced when I was fourteen... mother left for Switzerland with my sister. Hardly seen either of them since. Would I even recognise them in the street or them me? Don't get on with Dad... came here to get away from stifling bourgeois England to feel free... in the USSR. Imagine that! Freedom in the world's most repressive state! Better than being at home, though."

"I'm sorry, Tristan, about all this... but you've got to get a handle on things, man... it's getting out of control. You're taking too many risks, your health is deteriorating, I can see it with my own eyes, you're young—" urged Will.

"Not so easy to change course, old mate," said Tristan, coughing and spluttering before expectorating into a grubby blue handkerchief. "People drink excessively here... to escape communist reality and the numbing cold in winter... am also sucked into this drinking culture... don't fucking care anymore where it all ends up for me, I really don't... I've lost any sense of perspective and hopes for the future, except that I don't want to spend twenty years in a Soviet Gulag for a crime I didn't commit. That really gives me the shivers..."

"Well, at least deep down, Tristan, you seem to care about your own self-preservation. Listen, we both only have a few more weeks to go here before our studentships end. Why don't you apply for an exit visa now? Leave. Go home. I have some research to finish but you can go now. Think about it. This place is not doing you any good," suggested Will.

"It's OK for you, Will. Where is my home?" said Tristan after a pause. "England? Switzerland? The USSR? Anyway, need to finish my research on my Bolshevik Kentilovsky. Can't go now. That old agitator would miss me. So, comrade, let's bury this bottle. Last hurrah of a serial drunkard, hah. Let's drink to better times when we return to wherever we belong," and with that Tristan sunk another full shot of vodka.

Tristan was not going to do the sensible thing and leave the USSR. It was against his risk-taking, live-for-now reckless approach to life. Will was getting seriously alarmed that Tristan was drinking himself into oblivion. His health and well-being were deteriorating at an alarming rate. Tristan's mournfulness, his fatalism and his tangled past suggested he lacked the willpower to change course.

THIRTY-FOUR

A Russian Funeral

After the autopsy had been completed by the militsiya some days later confirming the cause of Valya's death as strangulation, Valya's body was released to her mother Svetlana Antolevna for burial. It laid in her home for three days. After the wake, family and friends gathered at a funeral parlour near Svetlana's home to participate in the funeral obsequies. A priest was present to conduct Russian Orthodox funeral rituals.

Will and Tristan joined the line to walk round Valya's open coffin anticlockwise, in accordance with Russian Orthodox traditions, to pay their respects to the deceased. Valya was dressed in a white dress buttoned up to her neck. Will observed a marble-like pale pallor to her skin. She looked serene in her coffin, her body partially draped in a white shroud. A white band of cloth was placed on her forehead. Her hands were resting together on the shroud holding an Orthodox cross. The coffin was bedecked in flowers brought by distressed mourners. Will laid the small bouquet of flowers that he and Tristan had bought at a corner of the catafalque. Svetlana Antolevna and Masha sat near the end of the coffin, where Valya's head lay on a cream pillow. The two sisters were dressed in black, supporting each other with whispered words, their hands touching the side of the coffin. Svetlana leant over regularly to kiss her deceased daughter's face as if to comfort her, her grief profound, desperate and moving.

As the line of people slowly made its way round the coffin, Will and Tristan touched its side as others did before them. There was a deep sense of respect and reverence for Valya, and the only sounds were of shoes softly shuffling on the wooden floor and Svetlana's inaudible words and tears. Will was moved by this simple yet profound ritualistic ceremony honouring the deceased Valya. Glancing at Tristan following behind him, Will was surprised to see that his friend's cheeks were flecked with tears; he was deeply upset, breathing heavily, and unevenly.

"You OK?" Will whispered.

Tristan barely nodded.

They reached the side of the coffin where Svetlana and Masha were seated. Will took Svetlana's hand briefly and conveyed his sadness and condolences. He nodded to Masha. Distraught though they both were, they acknowledged his presence.

Around fifty people had gathered for the funeral. Glancing around, having walked around the circumference of the coffin, Will noticed Kuznetsov, the director from the Ministry of Agriculture who was speaking to some people whom Will took to be Valya's work colleagues. Will hesitated to introduce himself again but an opportunity arose when Kuznetsov turned towards him.

"Mr Kuznetsov," Will began, "we met a few times at embassy receptions. A very tragic, untimely death."

Kuznetsov, struggling to remember who Will was, replied, "Yes, tragic."

"Did you work with Valentina Michaelevna in your ministry?" asked Will.

"I am director in a parallel department," replied Kuznetsov.

"My friend and I discovered Valentina Michaelevna's body by chance. We were totally shocked. Such a beautiful young lady. Brutally and pointlessly murdered," said Will.

Kuznetsov, manifestly surprised by this revelation and momentarily caught off guard, swiftly recovered his composure. "You found her? Are you sure she was murdered?"

"Yes. Strangled. We haven't recovered from the shock," said Will.

The conversation was interrupted because at this point an Orthodox priest initiated the more formal part of the ceremony, pulling the white shroud fully over Valya's face prior to the closure of the coffin and its removal to the burial site and the burial itself. The austere and mournful gathering, young and old, stood with heads bowed in profound respect for the deceased as the committal ceremony proceeded.

Will and Tristan stayed a while but left quietly as close relatives and friends of Valya gathered round the coffin to say their last goodbyes. They were not part of Svetlana's inner circle and did not want to be seen to intrude at a time of maximum sorrow and mourning.

"What moved you so deeply?" said Will to Tristan as they exited the gates of the funeral home.

"God... that was grim... if we dedicated as much attention to taking care of the living as we do to ensuring the peace and tranquility of the departed... things in this world might be better... life just hangs by a gossamer thread... there is no rhyme or reason why this poor young girl deserved this. Mother destroyed. Family and friends distraught. Pitiful..." whispered Tristan.

"There's a lesson for all of us in this tragedy, you are right there," said Will. "The fragility of our existence should make us more attentive and focus on what is really important."

"You know me, Will," Tristan murmured. "...don't play by the rules, push out the boundaries, take chances, abuse my body, yet I survive... probably don't deserve to, still just about standing...

how many people would come to my funeral if I died so young? ...
fewer than here, for sure... wonder if my mother would even turn
up..."

Tristan was deeply troubled and preoccupied by Valya's death.
Will realised how damaged and hurt he had been by the upheavals
in his teenage years. In contrast to the deceased Valya, he lacked
stable moorings and an anchor. There was no solidity in his life;
he was itinerant, a traveller with no home abode, tossed about in
choppy waters, and indulging in wild, hedonistic pursuits.

Endeavouring to change the gloomy atmosphere, Will said,
"We'll drink a toast to Valya next time we meet. We won't forget
her."

And with that they headed to their respective homes, chastened
and upset. Will felt, spiritually, a little more at ease. Tristan not at all.

THIRTY-FIVE

The Envelope

Will finally got round one evening to opening the envelope that Svetlana had given to him. Removing the dossier from the sealed buff envelope the first thing that Will noticed was that the cover of the file was marked 'Ministry of Agriculture – Secret'. Intrigued, Will wondered why he should be in receipt of such a file. Opening the front cardboard cover he discovered that there were about five sheets of thin paper pinned in the top left-hand corner by a brass clip. The first two pages consisted of rows and columns of statistics under a Ministry of Agriculture heading.

Will began to disentangle these data and work out what he had in front of him. It didn't take him long to realise that the statistics were the latest forecasts for the USSR grain harvest in 1975 compared to yearly results from 1970–74, broken down by main agricultural region, by product (wheat, barley and other grains) and by date.

Having perused the numbers superficially Will looked more carefully at data for the Krasnodar oblast that he had visited in May. Sure enough, just as he had observed when he was there and picked up from discussions with Grigoriy at the collective farm Oktyabr, grain yields were forecast to be substantially down. Indeed, the document foresaw yields dropping by at least thirty-five per cent and by even more in the northern farms of the Krasnodar Krai region. The national picture, set out on the second page, was of a forecast decline in grain production of twenty-five to thirty per cent compared to 1974, an outcome which, if confirmed, threatened fulfilment of the USSR's ninth five-year plan finishing at the end of 1975. This would be a major blow to Soviet prestige.

Will then turned to the other three sheets of paper in the file.

The first one was an official document from the Ministries of Trade and Agriculture in the form of a memorandum. Reading through the two-page document Will saw that it set out, in detail, the USSR's grain import requirements for the remaining months of 1975 and for 1976, with comparisons for the 1974/5 period, including details from where such grains were to be sourced and when. The foremost supplier was to be the US, which was earmarked to provide eighty per cent of the imported grain, with France and Canada selected as secondary suppliers. The proposed supply schedule envisaged the USSR's first and most significant purchases to be made in early August 1975 followed by regular monthly deliveries thereafter. Soviet ships were expected to transport fifty per cent of the imported grain.

The final one-page document was a memorandum from the Soviet Ministry of Trade, endorsed by the Ministry of Finance and the Central Bank, setting out a schedule of gold sales to be made in Zurich through the Soviet Wozchod Handelsbank to finance the grain purchases. Two banks from the Zurich gold pool were earmarked to market the gold in strict sequence and in accordance with a predetermined monthly timetable, beginning in August with precise amounts in tonnes assigned to each sale and each bank.

Holy smokes, exclaimed Will. Assuming the five pages were authentic he had in his possession a highly valuable, commercially sensitive document whose contents were politically explosive.

He recalled that both the US Embassy, in the form of Wendell Randall, and Kuznetsov from the Ministry of Agriculture, were both arguing, at least in public, that the Soviet grain harvest was set for bumper levels in 1975. These assertions flew in the face of the information he now had in front of him. Who stood to gain from the pretence of fictitious high grain yields in the USSR? Why had Valya left this document for him? Or had she? Maybe Svetlana had just wanted to get it out of her home. Perhaps Svetlana was muddled because of her grief and had wrongly given it to him.

Will was confused. He would have to ask Svetlana Antolevna about the background to all this. An opportunity would arise tomorrow because he had been invited to the nine-day commemoration of Valya's passing at which, by Russian orthodox tradition, family and friends would gather for a *pominki* to remember her. Her spirit would not have left the earth after nine days but would be restlessly flitting between the outer world and earth. The nine-day remembrance gathering would mourn her passing while sharing memories and stories of her. Will hoped he would have an opportunity to have a quiet word with Svetlana about why Valya had wanted him to have the documents – assuming, that is, she had indeed insisted on this.

THIRTY-SIX

Pominki

In Svetlana's kitchen, where everyone had gathered for the *pominki*, Will and Tristan's attention was drawn to the table full of traditional Russian dishes served at such gatherings including *koliva* or *kutya* (a dish made of rice and raisins) and *blini* (pancakes). People were talking quietly, respectfully and reverentially, everyone's concern being the welfare of the diminutive Svetlana and how they could support her through her ordeal.

Tristan, who was on his best behaviour, asked an invitee, "Could you kindly explain the significance of the towel and the cup of water that have been placed on the window sill in the kitchen? Is it for a special purpose?"

Masha, Svetlana's sister, who overheard the question, replied, "This is a tradition followed by families in some parts of Russia. When our mother died during the war we followed the same ritual. The towel and the water here are for Valya in case her soul wishes to return home in the forty-day period after her death, to seek refreshment or to take a rest before her spirit leaves us forever. They will be removed from the sill on the fortieth day after her passing and cast away."

"That is moving… so the family takes care of Valya's spirit until she leaves you forever," said Tristan, thanking Masha for the explanation. It had taken Valya's tragic death for this sensitive trait of Tristan's personality to reveal itself. This was far removed from his public image of a booze-soaked bore.

At this point a bearded priest in a black robe brought the gathering to silence and began reciting and chanting some Orthodox prayers. Some women and men crossed themselves in the Orthodox manner at various points during the recitals and joined in the chanting and prayers. It ended with Svetlana, and those present, being blessed by the priest. This was the signal to begin sampling the sumptuous and delicious *pominki* buffet that had been prepared. Will and Tristan hovered at the rear of the queue, not wishing to be prominent in the gathering.

"Oh, shit," whispered Will quietly to Tristan. "That oily creep Kuznetsov is here too."

"The guy at the funeral?" asked Tristan.

Will felt a tap on his shoulder from Kuznetsov, the same man who had batted his questions away and treated him so disdainfully at the embassy receptions.

"You told me you discovered the body of Valentina," said Kuznetsov, drawing closer to Will, "but how did she appear when you found her? What condition was she in?"

Will and Tristan, the latter having overheard the questions, glanced at each other, taken aback by the maladroit and heavy-handed nature of Kuznetsov's crude intervention at a poignant moment in the *pominki* proceedings.

Deciding to parry the question, Will replied, "I do not recall very much. Our primary concern was to alert the Moscow militsiya authorities about the incident."

"But you must remember something," Kuznetsov countered. "Was her body in an unnatural position? Were her possessions strewn around the crime scene? Was she fully clothed? Was her handbag nearby? Were there any papers, documents lying around?"

These questions matched the ones that Chief Inspector Isakov had put to Will and Tristan at their last interrogation.

"As I already said, Gospodin Kuznetsov," replied Will firmly, now struggling to keep his irritation in check, "we were greatly shocked. Neither of us had ever seen a dead body before, let alone the corpse of a murdered young woman. In such circumstances your mind freezes. You are numbed by horror. You don't take everything in. We have informed the militsiya of our observations."

"Yes, yes, but items, bags, a briefcase, paper – did you see any of these?" Kuznetsov insistently enquired.

"There were none," replied Will curtly.

At this point Tristan intervened. "Why are you asking these questions, Comrade Kuznetsov? We are in mourning. We stumbled upon a shocking crime scene. We are not discussing this matter further. We want to grieve quietly with Svetlana Antolevna and the rest of Valentina's family and friends."

Kuznetsov, rebuffed and surly at not getting the information he wanted, sidled off to another part of the kitchen to get some food.

"Well-spoken indeed, Tristan, old mate, you really nailed the nosey bugger there. Let's go and taste the food and pay our respects to Svetlana Antolevna," said Will.

Will and Tristan filled their plates, took a small glass of Hungarian white wine, and slowly ate the *koliva*, *blini* and other *zakuski*. Masha came over to them and they discussed Valya for a while and how she had supported her mother.

"I am very worried about Svetlana," said Masha. "She is not young and cannot work much longer. She never complains, but she has a bad back and, worst of all, badly swollen knees caused by arthritis. Valya's support would have enabled her to retire soon and be a *babushka* once Valya had children. She would have been a wonderful grandmother. She has lost everything. What is to become of her? She will struggle to manage financially. I am thinking maybe I have to come to Moscow to live with her or she has to return to her birthplace in Krasnodar. I don't think she will want to come south, though – she is a true *Moskvichka* now."

Will and Tristan mumbled their recognition of Masha and Svetlana's dilemma and expressed their sincere sympathies. Guests were huddled around and craning their necks to hear Svetlana, who was sitting on a chair by the kitchen table and barely visible as she spoke softly and reverentially about her beloved daughter.

Will feared he would be unable to grab a word with her alone, but just at that moment she got up to go to the bathroom: he would try to speak with her before she returned to the kitchen, where everyone was gathered. Kuznetsov, meanwhile, was hovering about, not far away, keeping a watchful eye on Will and Tristan.

"Tristan, I need you to occupy Kuznetsov for a few minutes as I have to talk with Svetlana alone. Can you do that for me?" asked Will.

"Just told him to piss off and now you want me to butter him up! He's going to appreciate that. What can I say to him?" replied Tristan.

"Offer him a fag – here, take my ciggies," said Will, handing over a red Rothmans tin with a statue of Nelson in Trafalgar Square on the front. "He's probably partial to a good smoke. Take one yourself. Get him off my back for a few minutes."

Tristan proceeded to block Kuznetsov accessing the corridor leading to the bathroom and the outer door of the apartment by engaging him in a conversation about ice hockey and soccer. He offered him a Rothmans, which he accepted. Tristan then deliberately fiddled about clumsily with a matchbox before eventually offering Kuznetsov a light. Svetlana was taking an inordinate amount of time in the bathroom. Eventually she emerged and Will seized the opportunity to speak with her with his back to Kuznetsov some eight metres away.

"Svetlana Antolevna, thank you for kindly inviting us to this ceremony to honour and commemorate Valya and for your kind hospitality. I find Russian traditions moving and sincere. Tristan and I will be heading off soon to leave you with your family and close friends, but I have one question. Why did you give an envelope to me the other day? Was it meant for someone else, perhaps? I just want to be sure it was really meant for me," Will said quietly.

"I am pleased that you and your friend came today. It was important that those who saw Valya closest to her life's end were present today at the *pominki*. The envelope was for you. Valya brought it home just before she died. When I asked her about it she insisted that, if anything happened to her, I must give it to you. To no-one else," Svetlana responded.

"And may I ask you, who is this man Kuznetsov?" asked Will, glancing over his shoulder to see the man himself endeavouring to survey what was going on while Tristan had raised his knee and put his thigh horizontally across the entrance to the corridor from the kitchen to bar his way.

At this question Svetlana hesitated and glanced around. She was, manifestly, uneasy. "He is a director at the ministry, or so I understand," replied Svetlana. "A *grubi nyepriyatni* – rough and unpleasant – man," she added quietly.

"Did Valya work with him?" asked Will.

"Not directly," replied Svetlana.

Will didn't push for more information as he sensed that Svetlana wanted to get back to the *pominki* gathering. Meantime, Tristan, who had spread his slender body across the door frame, was being hard pressed keeping the inquisitive Kuznetsov at bay.

"Well, thank you again, Svetlana Antolevna, for the invitation to this *pominki*. I will always remember Valya fondly," Will said, signalling to Tristan by a jerk of his head towards the door that it was time to hit the road. Kuznetsov shot Will a parting unfriendly glance and the students made their exit.

Once outside they each lit up a Rothmans and took a few drags before Tristan spoke: "That guy Kuznetsov. Rough diamond… spoke as if I was under interrogation. Where do we come from, where are we studying, when did we last see Valya, did we pick up any of her things, papers… and so on… Nosy sod… too many questions…"

"Thanks for occupying the smarmy pillock for a while," said Will.

They wandered on a bit before Will said, "You know, Tristan, the contents of the envelope Valya passed on to me via her mother are politically and commercially highly sensitive. It could interest a lot of people, in particular Western grain and gold traders. It's a treasure trove of information. When we meet tomorrow at the British Embassy bar, if I bring the dossier, could you put it in your trunk or hide it somewhere in your room in MGU for safekeeping? I have a feeling it would be safer with you than me."

"No problem," replied Tristan, not really paying much attention. His gaze had fixed on a shapely Russian *blondinka* in a short miniskirt on the other side of the street. "Man, what sleek, sexy legs, Will, take a look at that Russian beauty in all her elongated glory," exclaimed Tristan wistfully. "Absolutely gorgeous."

It hadn't taken long for Tristan to revert to type.

They continued towards the nearest bus stop and onward to their respective journeys home.

"*Do zavtra tovarisch* – see you tomorrow, comrade," said Will to Tristan as he boarded the bus back towards his academy.

THIRTY-SEVEN

The Investigation Stalls

Plans for Tristan and Will to meet at the British Embassy bar were interrupted by a third summons to Moscow Militsiya Headquarters. *What on earth awaits us now?* pondered Will, as Isakov strode into the interrogation room with several files under his arm.

"There are currently no new developments in the case," he began, "but I want you to sign these documents, which are summaries of your previous interrogations."

Like a coiled jack-in-the-box, Tristan reacted immediately. "Mr Chief Inspector, we have read Russian and Soviet history, and I know all about the history of 'confessions' extracted from innocent people, especially in the 1930s. I will not sign anything until I have read and understood it and I agree with it. I am sure my friend Will would concur."

"This is a factual record of your witness statements," replied Isakov. "Nothing more. You may take the time to read it over if you so wish. In the meantime, I can confirm that neither of you are prime suspects in this case."

"We are relieved about that but surprised it took you so long to come to that conclusion," retorted Will.

Isakov continued, "We believe that the girl was killed in another place and dragged there along the path leading from a road nearby. The killing certainly took place before twilight."

Neither Will nor Tristan found this information very revelatory. There was no indication of any motive.

Trying his luck, Tristan said, "Mr Chief Inspector, what motive have you discovered for this senseless killing? Money, sex, family feud, blackmail, violence for its own sake or what?"

"No motive has been established," replied Isakov curtly. "None whatsoever. You will need to sign your statements in the next twenty-four hours. You no longer need to register daily with your local militsiya departments. Finally, a word of warning. This investigation is confidential. You are not free to talk to anyone about it. Should you do so sanctions could be applied."

"What sanctions, Chief Inspector?" asked Tristan.

"Appropriate measures," replied Isakov.

And with that Will and Tristan left and headed for the British Embassy bar. Before he forgot, Will handed over to Tristan the dossier given to him by Svetlana and asked him to put it somewhere safe. Tristan shoved it carelessly into his blue canvas briefcase, which he left casually by the side of the bar before plunging into a group of vivacious young secretaries from English-speaking embassies, on the prowl once again for a new female conquest.

Will and Tristan agreed to meet again in a bar near MGU in a week's time.

THIRTY-EIGHT

Next Steps of the Two Comrades

A few days later Kuznetsov reported back to Pavel on his failed attempts to locate the missing dossier at the *pominki* commemoration and the students' persistent attempts to rebuff his enquiries and keep him at bay. The two Russian conspirators were at an impasse.

"Our business transaction can still work out if we can locate the dossier quickly," said Pavel confidently. "The girl's mother had no knowledge of it, you say, when you put the question to her at the funeral. The students must know something. We are not going to be thwarted in our business endeavour by a couple of Western student spies who shouldn't even be admitted to the land of socialism."

Kuznetsov was exasperated. "Why the hell Valentina Michaelevna pulled out of the deal is beyond me. I always felt she was capricious, unstable and unreliable, and so it proved to be. If she had just handed over the dossier and taken receipt of the money from the American everything would have been fine. She could have washed her hands of the whole affair and disappeared for ever into the Urals if she had wanted to."

"Regrettably she had to be neutralised," replied Pavel matter-of-factly. "And was. Without fuss. By some reliable comrades. Our only issue was the location of the dossier, of which she had the only copy. It could not be found in her ministry. She was warned multiple times to come clean and hand it over for her own good and for the sake of her mother. She categorically refused to tell us where it was and then pretended it had been destroyed along with my $1,000 investment. Which just had to be a lie. So, my comrades picked her up before her meeting with the students, at which she would have revealed everything to them. Generously, they gave her one final opportunity to honour her contractual obligations. She refused to cooperate. 'Nyet,' she said. 'Nyet, nyet, nyet.' Slava, Mika and Volya had no option but to implement my instructions and execute measures of a terminal nature. She knew too much and could have landed us all in big shit. Seriously, Alexei, I mean, how can the USSR function properly when naïve fantasists fail to honour their commitments and refuse to accept responsibility for their actions?"

Pavel's chilling exposé of what had happened to Valya unnerved Kuznetsov; his consternation was manifested in a furrowed brow and an expression of deep concern. He was not Valya's killer, but he was irrevocably implicated in this affair by association.

Pavel Yeremevich, detecting Alexei's unease, sought to put his mind at rest. "Don't worry, Alexei. Things don't always go smoothly in the world of government and business. Sometimes reactive countermeasures have to be implemented. Take it from me, my friend, you will have completely forgotten the victim after a while. As Comrade Stalin used to say, '…no person… no problem.'"

Kuznetsov remained silent as he digested the violent attack on Valentina Michaelevna. He never dreamed that things would turn out this way. His project had been to make a quick financial gain. Instead he was complicit in the murder of a colleague. Not only had the whole scheme unravelled but, even worse, it had been hijacked wholesale by Pavel. Matters were now completely out of Kuznetsov's control. While he was feeling increasingly ill at ease at the direction that events were taking, Pavel, by contrast, appeared to be in his element.

Speaking authoritatively, he stated, "We will now put in place a two-pronged offensive strategy to recuperate the dossier: firstly, my authorities will instruct that sleepy, sluggard Chief Inspector Isakov in the Moscow Militsiya to wake up and pressure the students to reveal where the file is. He should apply forceful tactics immediately. That dumb, dopey goon will be reminded that state secrets are in play which, in the hands of capitalists, could embarrass our Socialist Motherland. And if he doesn't find the dossier quickly there will be a price to pay by him personally. He's close to retirement – his pension can be removed at the stroke of a pen by my authorities. He needs to be galvanised into swift action."

"And what's the second prong?" said Kuznetsov.

"We need to apply some enhanced surveillance techniques on the students and, at an appropriate moment, threaten them with some mild physical pressure. Frighten them a bit. Time is critical. The American is not going to wait for the file. We need prompt action if we are to save this promising business deal," replied Pavel, confident that his new strategy would remove all obstacles impeding the successful conclusion of the transaction.

Kuznetsov did not want to be implicated in any more rough methods that were bread and butter to Pavel and his associates. Indeed, he was now regretting allowing his friend to muscle his way into the deal in the first place. If he had been on his own, he, Kuznetsov, might already have thrown in the towel. Now he was implicated up to his neck in everything that had transpired and in whatever would happen next.

"Pavel Yeremevich, we are old comrades. We go back a long way. We understand one another," said Kuznetsov, trying a softer approach. "I don't object to stirring things up a bit with the students, but please, no more violence."

"Violence? Who spoke of violence?" replied Pavel with a straight face. "Mild physical pressure is not violence. You should know that! Our methods are far more subtle than that. No, my dear friend, I have in mind no more than level one persuasion techniques, as per our KGB state-certified operating manual. Gentle, baby pressure methods to make the students see rationality and common sense."

"Which student do you have in mind?" asked Kuznetsov.

"The drinker. De Fallières. He's the weaker one. We'll have a friendly discussion with him and tell him to cooperate with us and hand the file over. He'll get the message!" replied Pavel confidently.

"And Lawrence? He's the one who knew Valya Michaelevna," Kuznetsov said.

"One step at a time, my friend. We can deal with him later, but in the meantime, we can conduct a search of his belongings," said Pavel, in charge of all operational matters. "Once de Fallières has understood that he needs to cooperate with us we'll get the dossier, don't worry. Pavel will deliver the kasha. And then we'll have our prize, $10,000, a worthy reward for our labours. And now there's a bonus: we don't even have to pay a share to that idiot girl Dontsova now! Comrade Alexei, my friend, just think of the riches and pleasures those dollars will bring to us, to our wives and to our girlfriends!"

"I leave it to you, my old friend," said Kuznetsov, seeking to absolve himself from any responsibility for the 'mild' techniques about to be perpetrated on the weaker British student. However, he feared the worst: Pavel was ruthless and utterly determined to bring the transaction to a successful conclusion. If violence was necessary to seal matters, then violence there would be. The risks were multiplying as each day passed.

As for Pavel, he was getting worried about Kuznetsov's flakiness and diminishing commitment to the project. His character was weak; he was a follower, not a leader, unwilling to take the rough with the smooth.

Time is of the essence now, Pavel reasoned. *Swift action was needed.*

THIRTY-NINE

Upheaval

Will returned home after an exhaustingly hot day spent at the Lenin Library, interrupted by a short excursion outside at midday to search for some bread and cheese for supper. Turning into the short walkway leading up to his *obshezhitye* residence after alighting from the 87 bus and looking towards his building, he had the sense that his omnipresent trade union neighbours, Lyudmila or her husband Valery or both, were looking out for him behind their net curtains. Will opened the front door and walked down the drab, green-painted corridor on the ground floor towards his room, the last one on the right. As he got out his keys to open the door, he saw immediately that the lock had been forced and that the door was already partially open. Once inside his room he could scarcely believe his eyes.

His possessions had been ransacked and the room completely turned upside down. The two mattresses were slashed, his two suitcases ripped open, his clothes tossed about and his papers and books strewn across the floor. His cupboard for kitchen utensils had been smashed and, in a corner of the room, the floorboards forced open. It was a complete mess, a wrecking-ball job. He was stunned.

The perpetrators had evidently come looking for something – presumably Valya's document – and had been prepared to trash the room and rifle through his possessions in a desperate search to get what they were after.

Will's sense of shock soon gave way to anger. *How on earth did this happen in plain daylight?* he asked himself. Someone down the corridor must have seen and heard what was going on – a wholesale upending of a room by slashing furniture items and flinging everything on the floor cannot have been done in silence, even by trained professionals.

Will knocked on the door of the trade union couple Valery and Lyudmila, three doors down the corridor on the right. Lyudmila answered the door. "Oh, Will, I did not know you were back, how are you?" asked Lyudmila.

This is hardly an auspicious start, thought Will, *and a blatant untruth.*

"My room has been smashed up and wrecked. Come and have a look," said Will, ushering Lyudmila towards his room.

"*Bozhe moi*," Lyudmila uttered upon seeing the devastation in Will's room. "Who could have done that? Terrible – *uzhasno*."

"Did you or Valery see or hear anything?" Will asked. "The destruction must have occurred in daytime, between me leaving for the centre of Moscow at 9am and returning just now. You must have seen or heard something," insisted Will.

"Absolutely nothing, I'm afraid," replied Lyudmila. "Valery left early this morning and me too. We were not in the building all day. Try asking the others in the corridor," she suggested, not very helpfully.

Will doubted she was being truthful as she rarely left the building in the morning. More likely she just opened the front door to let the intruders in, looked the other way, closed her door and let them get on with it. *No point in getting caught up in something risky*, she would have thought to herself. Keep your nose clean was the safest course of action.

The obsequiousness shown by Soviet citizens towards officialdom was a common feature of life in this totalitarian state. Virtually no-one, except for a few brave, brutally repressed and marginalised dissidents, dared challenge the omnipotent governing authorities. To do so was a one-way ticket to land you in trouble. So Lyudmila's reaction was understandable in a Soviet context and true to form. But it irked Will.

Will surmised that, most probably, some official types had barged in, waved some identity documents in Lyudmila's face and told her – if she needed telling at all – to disappear from sight for her own good. The break-in was most unlikely to have been aimed at stealing his student property, which was worthless. The perpetrators were after something else. The secret dossier.

"Can you ask Valery, please, if he saw anything?" Will requested.

Valery, sitting in front of a noisy, black and white, crackly TV, responded disinterestedly in the negative to Lyudmila's question, intimating that he didn't want to be troubled by such trivia, all the more so as he was watching a Spartak Moscow football game and his team, for once, were winning.

"Sorry not to be able to help more," said Lyudmila, beating a retreat by slowly edging backwards towards the door of her room. "Try the others in the building – perhaps they saw or heard something."

Will duly knocked on all doors down the corridor. No-one had seen or heard anything. Svetlana was not working so she could not help either.

Not content with not pursuing the matter further, he went in search of Zina and Natalia. Maybe their connection to the Komsomol could help. He knocked on the door of their room. Natalia answered it.

"I am sorry to disturb you, but something unpleasant has happened to me. My room has been ransacked and my possessions trashed," blurted out Will.

"Well, I never," Natalia replied, appearing taken aback. "What happened?"

They walked over to Will's room. Natalia was aghast when she saw the wreckage in the room and the mess scattered over the floor.

"It must be thieves," Natalia said with some certainty. "This has happened before but not to a foreign guest in my experience. We must alert the security officer of the academy." With this Natalia went to the phone outside Will's room and requested the security officer on duty to come immediately.

"This is very strange, Will. What things do you think the thieves were looking for?"

"I have no idea," replied Will innocently, knowing full well that Valya's dossier would have been the object of their search.

Shortly afterwards a well-built security guard arrived to inspect the damage and make a report. "What happened? Is anything missing, citizen?" he asked gruffly, looking at the room with studied indifference, intimating that he might well have been prior informed about the planned search of Will's room.

Will was tempted to react strongly to this gormless question but held back. "I don't know yet as I haven't started to sort out this appalling mess," he replied.

"You need to work out what items have been taken and make a list, citizen. Then make out a *spravka* – a request for assistance. Only then can I make a report to my authorities," said the guard, not in the slightest bit sympathetic or interested in investigating the incident. Rather it was clear from his attitude that his summons to action by Natalia had disturbed his normal routine and this investigation was nothing other than a bloody nuisance.

"Well, that is a huge help," said Will sarcastically. "I will do that in due course. What about my door lock?"

"We'll send someone to fix it," said the guard as he exited the room.

"When?" Will asked.

"Soon," the guard replied unhelpfully, turning to leave the room.

"That was not much use, Natalia," said Will. "I'll have to sort things out now and tidy up. But thank you for coming round."

Will declined Natalia's offer to help him get things in order, probably wrongly, but he was now suspicious of everyone round him.

Will now knew what he was up against. People involved in the conspiracy were desperate to get their hands on Valya's file. The risks and the stakes were getting higher. He called Tristan; he needed to see him urgently.

FORTY

Last Orders

Will arrived at the Comrades Bar near Moscow University in time for his planned rendezvous with Tristan. On the route there by 87 bus and by metro Will tried to observe, amateurishly, if he was being followed, but he failed to notice anything unusual.

Tristan turned up ten minutes late, fag in hand and distinctly hungover. They ordered a round of beers.

"Look, Tristan, it seems obvious that Svetlana's dossier was the object of the upending of my room. Everything in it was ransacked from top to bottom. A professional job and a total mess. We are in possession of a very hot dossier whose contents are strongly sought after. I don't understand how Valya came to possess all this information and why she asked her mother to pass it on to me. *Za chem* – for what?" said Will.

The beer was helping Tristan to gather his thoughts together. "Who stands to gain from knowledge of this agricultural forecast information, Will? And from the planned schedule of imports and gold sales? What about money – is there money exchanging hands here? If so, who is paying whom and how much? Let's analyse it from these standpoints, my old mate," said Tristan, introducing new elements of chicanery into the discussion. "And how does this all fit with Valya's murder? What was her role?"

"These are valid points, Tristan. I don't have answers. But, in the meantime, let's keep the dossier safe. Where did you put it, by the way?" asked Will.

"There is a small crack between the window protruding inwards in my room on the twenty-first floor of my block and the ceiling. The dossier fits perfectly there. It cannot be seen. It's safe," replied Tristan.

"Well, I'm glad it is hidden away, so thanks for that. But take more precautions – I am getting alarmed about how we are getting dragged into something dangerous, violent and beyond our control," responded Will.

"No problem. Don't worry about me. Old Tristan can smell danger – and opportunity – miles away. I've gone 'neutral', Will: focus now is on Finnish ice maiden, Karita. An absolute blonde stunner. Reserved, though. Making slow progress thawing her out, warming her up – my God, the Nordics… massive time and investment needed! More to follow, Will. Now, let's have a final beer before closing time to wet our whistles," said Tristan cheerily. Will went off in search of two bottles of the local brew, which they drank before parting in good spirits around 11pm.

"See you soon, old mate. *Do vstrechi* – until we meet again," said Tristan, slapping Will's back in friendship and waving as he set off towards MGU along the dark tree-lined boulevard, seemingly without a care in the world, intent on furthering his pursuit of the charms of Karita.

FORTY-ONE

Smoke and Dust

It was now well into July and Will had less than a month left of his studentship in the USSR. He wanted to spend his last week in Leningrad before heading home on the SS *Baltika* to London Tilbury via Helsinki. The aim was to visit the Winter Palace and the Hermitage, Tsarskii Selo, the Tsar's Summer Palace and St Catherine's Palace, and to experience the special atmosphere of historic St Petersburg in the summer months.

In Moscow, the weather was now very hot, sultry and humid with daily temperatures of more than thirty degrees centigrade. People walked slowly and deliberately on the pavements, seeking shade wherever possible to avoid the sweltering heat and becoming sweaty and uncomfortable. The atmosphere was made worse by thick blue smoke drifting over the city from spontaneously combusting peat bogs in the marshes and forests outside Moscow which created a yellowish-blue haze and made breathing difficult, especially for asthmatics. These *dimkas* occurred when rainfall was inadequate, as had been the case for much of this year's summer. Small tankers selling *kvass*, a refreshing and nutritious drink made from rye bread, also appeared on the streets during the summer months and Will regularly bought a cup for a few kopecks to quench his thirst.

Walking along the dusty streets by the Lenin Library Will felt mentally and physically exhausted and ready to return home. Notwithstanding the tragedy of Valya's death, living in the USSR had been a fascinating experience and had matured him. But he longed for a return to a familiar pattern of life on his home turf in England.

Arriving back that evening at his residence he passed Lyudmila, his neighbour, in the corridor, who told him Inspector Isakov had called for him. No message had been left.

Sod him, thought Will.

Will slumped onto his new mattress, supplied by the academy after the other ones in his room had been slashed open. His belongings were strewn around and he couldn't be bothered to rearrange everything neatly and tidily as before.

As anticipated, the security authorities of the academy had been useless in tracking down those who had illicitly entered his room and smashed it up. Will had concluded they had probably been forewarned about the search and instructed not to undertake any meaningful investigation. His neighbours were tight-lipped ostriches with heads in the sand who hadn't seen or heard anything. Will toyed with the idea of informing the British Embassy of his misfortune, but to what purpose? They couldn't do anything other than alert the local militsiya and that line of enquiry would go nowhere.

He was just preparing an omelette with cheese and rye bread for his supper when Isakov called again.

"Isakov here. You must come down to Central Moscow Militsia Headquarters immediately for further interrogation. There are important developments."

"Inspector Isakov," replied Will wearily, "I have just returned home after a long hot day in town. May I come tomorrow morning?"

"No," replied Isahov sternly. "I expect you here before 10pm this evening."

This is becoming utterly intolerable, thought Will. He had told Isakov everything he knew. Why the urgency? He finished his omelette, refreshed himself with a warm shower – for once the hot water was functioning in the building – and headed off downtown once again, expecting another lengthy interview with the bombastic and bullying Chief Inspector who was clearly under pressure to solve the Valya Dontseeva case.

FORTY-TWO

Searching for Evidence

Will arrived at Central Moscow Militsia HQ around 10pm. He was told to wait by a burly officer manning the reception area, who thereafter ignored him, having told him that Chief Inspector Isakov was busy. Tired, Will waited, head in hands, uncomfortable in the steamy, sweaty, smelly building in the height of summer, trying to imagine what on earth was the purpose of this unexpected summons late at night. Furthermore, he wondered where the hell Tristan was. Why hadn't he been ordered to appear before Isakov as well?

Isakov eventually appeared flanked by two younger officers and beckoned Will to follow him. They went up a flight of stairs and along a wide corridor before turning into an interrogation room with just a table and four chairs. Nothing else. Isakov settled himself into a seat opposite Will with the two juniors occupying seats to his right and left along the other sides of the rectangular metal table.

"You are probably wondering why we have summoned you here at this late hour," began Isakov. "The reason is that there have been developments and I need to ask you more questions. Urgently."

"Well, that is fine," said Will. "But couldn't it have waited? Why the urgency? And why just me?"

"There are two reasons. Firstly, Soviet investigating authorities have ascertained that the deceased, Valentina Michaelevna Dontsova, stole some secret documents, including agricultural harvest forecasts for the USSR, from her ministry with a view to selling them to capitalist interests for thousands of dollars. Such behaviour, if it had been discovered when she was alive, would have resulted in her serving a twenty-year criminal sentence in a penal colony in Siberia with hard labour. Betraying the Motherland is one of the worst crimes a Soviet citizen can commit. My authorities want to find this document. Where have you put it?"

"Gospodin Chief Inspector, I have no such document in my possession," said Will truthfully.

"Are you aware of any such document or papers?" asked Isakov.

"I already told you multiple times that we found nothing by Valentina Michaelevna's body," said Will, answering carefully, hovering on the borderline between truth and lies. "And that leads me to another point. My room in the academy was ransacked two days ago by person or persons unknown, presumably your officers. Perhaps I now understand why. Instead of upending my possessions and smashing things up, implying that I have been hiding secret Soviet documents, you could have had the courtesy to have conducted the search in my presence," stated Will, endeavouring to turn the conversation round to his advantage.

Isakov, however, was a wily operator and was not going to fall for this diversionary ruse. "I have no knowledge of what you are talking about. It is irrelevant, in any case. Answer my question. Are you aware of any missing documents?"

"I am not studying here in the USSR to traffic in missing Soviet state secrets," replied Will, now entering risky territory. "Why don't you ask Valentina Michaelevna's friends, acquaintances and family where the mystery documents are? I met the girl only a few times, for God's sake. So, no. I am not aware of where any such documents might be located," replied Will, sticking with his precarious strategy of riposte and counterthrust.

"Very well. And how about your friend Tristan de Fallières? Has he got the documents?" pressed Isakov.

"You will have to ask him that question, Chief Inspector. And on the subject of Tristan, I am surprised that you have singled me out for interrogation here alone when we discovered the body of Valentina together," replied Will.

"I want to know where those documents are," said Isakov menacingly. "My authorities are very concerned. Let me ask you again. Where are they?"

"I am sorry, Chief Inspector. You can ask the same question any way and any number of times you like. I do not have the documents and I can only suggest you look elsewhere. Perhaps now, at this late hour, you will now allow me to go home. I am tired," answered Will.

Isakov shuffled on his chair and changed position. The two junior officers remained upright and still. There was an atmosphere of increasing froideur and tension in the room. No-one moved.

After a long silence Isakov flicked intently though some papers in his dossier in preparation for his next move.

"Before you leave, we have to address another issue of relevance to you," said Isakov slowly and deliberately.

"And what is that, Chief Inspector?" replied Will.

Isakov stared at Will intently. Speaking slowly and with deliberation he said: "It concerns your British friend, Gospodin Tristan de Fallières. He is not here because he was found drowned in the Moscow River this afternoon not far from the place where Valentina Michaelevna Dontsova was murdered."

FORTY-THREE

Moscow State University

Early the next morning, at the conclusion of an all-night interrogation, Will was told he would have to accompany Isakov and an officer to Moscow University to inspect Tristan's room in the tower block where he had lived. Word had evidently got around that Tristan was missing and his fellow students on the twenty-first floor, mostly foreign, were quietly chatting in small groups near the door of his shared twin quarters, whispering to each other when Will, Isakov and another officer arrived and stepped out of the lift. There was a reverential, reflective and concerned air amongst the students, who were milling around aimlessly.

Isakov ordered the *dezhurnaya*, or floor attendant, to immediately open the door of Tristan's shared apartment. They entered the small entrance, which led to two long, thin, parallel student rooms. Tristan's room was on the right of the twin room ensemble and stank of stale cigarette smoke and beer. There were bottles of various descriptions scattered around the room – vodka, beer, wine, cognac – on his side table, on his desk and in his wastepaper basket. In his closet, jumbled about, were his clothes, shoes and a selection of female items – nylon tights, jeans, lipstick, cosmetics – which he no doubt planned to sell to fund his wild lifestyle.

Will stared disbelievingly into the small, compact, empty space of his friend's room, struggling to comprehend that he was no longer alive. Isakov ordered the accompanying militsia officer to begin searching the room, a job he performed in a heavy-handed, slipshod and slapdash manner, turning out drawers, rifling through Tristan's research notes, feeling around the mattress before reporting that there was nothing unusual and there was nothing of interest to be found in the room.

"Are you aware of your friend hiding any secret documents here?" asked Isakov.

Will, his mind elsewhere, cast a quick glance at the gap between the large window and the top of the wall. He replied casually, "Not at all, Inspector. I only ever came here briefly once. We used to meet outside at different places. The room looks as I would have expected it. Tristan lived hard, especially at night, and the mess here reflects his lifestyle. It is another tragedy. He had just turned twenty-four with his whole life in front of him. Like Valentina Michaelevna, I am just devastated."

Isakov looked nonchalantly around the room a bit more before calling an end to the search. "I don't think we'll find anything here," he said to the officer accompanying him, "regarding the whereabouts of the missing document or about what happened to the deceased. I need to go back to the office and get the pathology report. Lawrence: report again tomorrow to our headquarters," and with those concluding words Isakov and his sidekick exited the room and headed towards the lift. On the way out he instructed the *dezhurnaya* to pack up the deceased's belongings and arrange for them to be brought round to the Militsiya HQ for further inspection later that day without fail.

Will hung around until Isakov was descending in the lift before turning to speak with the gaggle of bemused onlooking students.

"Did anyone see Tristan the evening before last?" Will asked.

Evan, a fellow British student, whom Will had seen little of since they had set off from London together last November, said he had seen Tristan leave the floor by lift at around nine-ish two days ago in the evening but there had been no sign of him since.

A Russian student agreed. Tristan had not returned to his room since then but this was not unusual as he was often out gallivanting around the campus night spots, living it up, boozing and chasing women.

What exactly happened to him, they asked?

"He was found drowned in the Moscow River," Will said. That produced a collective gasp of shock.

"Are you serious?" Evan asked incredulously.

"Yes, regrettably, I am," answered Will. "He's dead. Am I right then that no-one saw him that night after 9pm?" asked Will.

The students murmured in agreement. Evan asked if there was anything he could do to help. Will, thinking on his feet, quickly replied, "It's OK for now, Evan, but thanks all the same. As his close friend, allow me though to pass a few moments of quiet reflection in his room alone. I am going to have to talk to his parents in the next few days. I want to be able to relay to them how he lived out his last days." The students dispersed whispering amongst themselves while Will headed into Tristan's room. He shut and quietly locked the door.

Will had engineered a few minutes in Tristan's room to try to find the secret dossier. He quickly manoeuvred the table closer to the long, rectangular window and clambered onto it with a view to being able to search the cracks between the window, which jutted out into the room, and the ceiling. He tried the left side first.

No joy.

Carefully he pulled the table to the right side of the window, got up on it again and stuck his fingers into the crack. He felt something immediately but couldn't get enough purchase on it to extract it. He jumped down and got a kitchen knife lying around Tristan's unwashed dishes. By shoving the knife into the crack and digging it into the dossier with as much pressure as he could muster, he succeeded in levering the file out from the crack and recuperating it intact. He took a quick glance at it to confirm that the dossier was the same one he had given Tristan a few days before. It was. He then shoved it into his briefcase and returned the table to its normal position.

"Good old Tristan," he murmured to himself under his breath. "More reliable than he would like us to have believed."

Overcome by the whirlwind of events that had engulfed him in the last twelve hours, Will sat down on Tristan's unkempt bed. He lowered his throbbing head into his hands. Only then did he begin to come to terms with the disaster that had befallen Tristan. He broke down and sobbed at the tragedy of his friend's passing at the age of just twenty-four. Will felt responsible and guilty for what had happened. After all, was it not he, Will, who had invited Tristan along to the aborted meeting with Valya? The events that unravelled thereafter were a direct consequence of that evening. Yet it was Tristan, a forthright, daring and uncompromising risk-taker, who had insisted that they turn back to examine the bushes on the embankment which had led to the discovery of Valya's body. His instincts had been right, but his decision had led to catastrophic and unforeseeable consequences. If they had just meandered further along the path in the Lenin hills neither he nor Tristan would have found Valya's dead body nor become enmeshed in a conspiracy whose scale remained unclear.

Devastated though he was by the turn of events, Will had always sensed that Tristan was living on borrowed time. Everything he did was on the edge, excessive and, at times, bordering on the totally reckless, not least his drinking, smoking and womanising. Tristan knew this himself, but he was unable or unwilling to exercise any self-restraint. Will had warned him repeatedly of his concerns. Tristan had ignored him and lived life to the full, his way for sure, but it had ended, almost inevitably, in tragedy. Yet Tristan had been a loyal friend. Will had learnt a lot from him and would miss him terribly.

There remained the mystery as to what had happened to Tristan after they parted the night before last. Will had to try and piece together the puzzle of these events for his own peace of mind. He had not one but now two deaths to come to terms with.

In the meantime, Will had back in his possession the file he had entrusted to Tristan. He had to decide what to do quickly; he did not want to be caught in possession of the dossier under any circumstances. *I'm best shot of it*, he told himself. Leaving MGU he retraced the route that Tristan would likely have followed from the bar at which they had had their last meeting. Somewhere between there and the university he felt sure that Tristan had been intercepted by people seeking the secret dossier and threatened if he didn't hand it over. It was dark and he could have been attacked without anyone observing an assault on him.

Will walked down towards the river and then along the towpath towards the city. He passed some moored boats and hypothesised that Tristan's body might have been ensnared with the ropes of the anchor of one of them, as Isakov had stated.

He took out the folded five-page document from his pocket, now separated from its cardboard cover, and he read it once again carefully to ensure he had absorbed the main gist of it. He was on the point of ripping it up into the smallest shreds he could and tossing them into the Moscow River.

But then he hesitated.

No. He was going to need the bait of the document to unravel the catastrophic sequence of events that had led to the premature deaths of his friends. He decided on a riskier course: he would keep the file after all and deposit it temporarily in a locker in the Lenin Library. It would be safe there, at least for a short while.

FORTY-FOUR

Alone in Moscow

Twelve hours earlier, in the late evening at Central Militsiya HQ, Will had emitted a stunned gasp and cry of, "What? It is not possible. I don't believe it," when Isakov had broken the devastating news of Tristan's death to him.

Will was devastated. The blood drained from his face. He just couldn't take it in. He felt nauseous.

Isakov carefully observed Will's reaction to the news he had bluntly conveyed. His junior colleagues maintained their sentry-like stillness at the table, showing no emotion whatsoever.

"I-I… don't know what to say. My God," said Will, desperately trying to hold himself together. "How do you know it was Tristan de Fallières?"

"By the documents on the corpse, his *propusk* and his identity document from Moscow University which, although suffering water damage, still enabled us to identify the deceased individual," answered Isakov. "There is no doubt that the body is Gospodin Tristan de Fallières."

Stunned, Will sat in silence, his head resting in his hands, his eyes watering.

"Have you informed the British Embassy?" Will said after a while. "His family must be told what has happened."

"This is being done as we speak by the Ministry of Foreign Affairs," replied Isakov. "They know what to do and will make appropriate arrangements."

After another pause, Isakov spoke. "When did you last see him?"

"Yesterday evening. We had a beer and finished up at around 11pm. I then took the bus home," replied Will, who was trembling, unable to control nervous, jerky movements in his arms.

"Which bar? Where is it located?"

"The Comrades Bar not far from Moscow University."

"How far is the bar from the Moscow River?" asked Isakov.

"It is not that close. Maybe two kilometres away. I can only presume that Tristan decided to go for a walk by the river and slipped," surmised Will, not believing this story for a moment.

"Why would he do that? Was he going to meet someone, perhaps? A meeting? Was he in a hurry to leave you?" continued Isakov.

"No, we parted amicably. Neither of us was in a rush. He never mentioned anything about seeing someone else or going down to the river," responded Will. "Moscow University is fifteen to twenty minutes away from the bar. An easy walk along a quiet boulevard, though it is quite dark at night. I had no reason to suspect anything. I assumed Tristan would just walk home. He said he was going to have a quiet night after some hard partying the previous days."

"Did you see anyone in the bar or outside who looked unusual or suspicious?"

"No."

The chief inspector, diligent as usual, continued probing for some time, looking for clues as to what Tristan may have got up to after he left the bar. Will was unable to help. Upon leaving Tristan he had headed for the metro, the start of his journey home. He had observed nothing unusual.

"You say, chief inspector, that he drowned. Are you sure of that? Were there any outward signs on his body of a struggle?" asked Will.

"We are undertaking forensic tests on the corpse. For the moment we think he just drowned. A typical case," replied Isakov.

"A typical case of what?" asked Will, raising his voice.

"The death of a drunk. By accident. Happens all year round. In winter we call them snowdrops," replied Isakov.

"I insist he was not drunk. Furthermore, while the Moscow River is wide it is not particularly fast-flowing and I know that Tristan could swim well. So, I am puzzled, to say the least, chief inspector, how he could have drowned," Will said firmly. "I don't think this can be the full story for one minute."

Leaning over the table to emphasise his next remarks, Isakov said in a cold, calculating and authoritative manner, "Listen, young man. I have been a militsiya inspector for a very long time – much longer than you have been on this planet. And during my career I have investigated many deaths – murders, manslaughters, criminal killings, lovers' revenge, settling of scores amongst thieves, currency traders and drug dealers, robbers and so on. You name it. I have seen them all. There is nothing per se unusual in your friend's death at all. Nothing. Such incidents – or accidents – happen all the time here in Moscow. For me it is a simple case, just another statistic in Moscow's death figures. The only novelty here is that your friend was a British citizen, not a Soviet one. Otherwise, for us, it's just another corpse to be investigated and disposed of."

Isakov's soulless 'it's just my job' monologue – expressed without a shred of feeling or emotion – shocked Will. For the chief inspector all that mattered were the interests of the State. The honour, prestige and image of the USSR. Expired human life was nothing more than a simple Soviet statistic. The chief inspector's task was to solve, categorise and archive the case quickly and get it out of the way. After that – well, as far as Isakov was concerned, it was the family's problem, not his. Case closed. Goodbye. Will wondered if this man Isakov was capable of showing any emotion at all for the murder victims he had investigated whose lives had been cut tragically short.

"Well, chief inspector," replied Will, "that just sums up a big difference between us. This guy was my best friend here and I'm concerned that conclusions appear to have been drawn about the circumstances of his death already before a proper investigation has taken place. And what about the link with Valentina Michaelevna's murder?"

"There is no link. You should desist from engaging in such cheap, ill-informed speculation. In the USSR we implement socialist protocols on investigations; we establish facts, and we apply the law of the people. The two cases are entirely separate and will be treated as such by the militsiya," responded Isakov forcefully.

As far as Isakov was concerned that was the end of the matter. He got up from his chair. "It is late. After a break for an hour – return to the waiting room by the reception – you will accompany me to the deceased's room in MGU to identify his belongings," barked Isakov, and headed off out of the room.

FORTY-FIVE

Militsiya Conclusions

The next day Will was contacted by telephone at his *obshezhitye* residence by the British Council representative in Moscow and requested to go to the British Embassy at 3pm to meet with the ambassador and with Tristan's father, who had arrived overnight from London to identify his son and repatriate his body. Will could hardly refuse such a summons, but he was dreading the occasion, the more so as it was the second time in less than a month that he had been called upon to express condolences to the parent of a twenty-four-year-old who had died in mysterious circumstances.

Earlier that morning he had reported again to Central Militsiya HQ for a further interview with Chief Inspector Isakov following the visit to Tristan's room at MGU.

Isakov began by asking if Will had any further information regarding the missing secret dossier, to which he replied negatively. *Well*, thought Will, *it's more than clear now what the priorities are for the militsiya: not the investigations of the deaths of Valya and Tristan.*

"We have searched the belongings of de Fallières. Nothing useful to the investigation was found. The forensic department is completing their examination of the body. They have identified a fracture and severe bruising on the left side of the deceased's skull, so he must have hit his head on something hard before or after he tumbled into the Moscow River. The pathologists have already confirmed that he had a very high alcohol content in his blood and that he had taken several painkillers. The case is clear: hooligan behaviour by the deceased, who was paralytically drunk. He banged his head accidentally on a sharp object and subsequently drowned," stated Isakov in a matter-of-fact way, seemingly satisfied that the case would soon be off his hands. Tristan would then be accounted for in the Moscow accidental death statistics.

"Well, Chief Inspector," replied Will, "I am very surprised by your conclusions. I repeat: Tristan was not drunk when he left me that evening. No-one seems to have seen him after our parting. You appear to have dismissed the possibility that he was accosted and hit with a sharp object and his body dumped in the river, without any proper investigation. How do you know he was not dead before he entered the water?"

Isakov replied testily, "Tests have been undertaken on the approximate date of death. Around midnight is the estimate. His corpse was in the water for about twelve hours before he was spotted by a passer-by on the Moscow River towpath. Everything fits," replied Isakov confidently and assertively, "and for this reason the file and casework will be passed on today to the Ministry of Foreign Affairs (MID), who will make arrangements with the British Embassy to repatriate the body to England."

"Well, your conclusions are wrong," retorted Will, convinced that the Moscow Militsiya were under pressure to close the case as soon as possible. "Furthermore, how can you conclude your investigation of the case before all remaining examinations are completed?"

"They will have no material effect on the case. This interview is terminated," said Isakov abruptly. "All further enquiries about the deceased should be addressed to Ministry of Foreign Affairs, consular section," said Isakov, as he raised himself quickly from his chair, folded his dossier and headed out of the room. Will was escorted off the premises by a junior officer.

Gathering his thoughts outside the Militsiya HQ, Will was both perplexed and angry. Isakov clearly wasn't going to expend any resources getting to the bottom of Tristan's unexplained death. By contrast the search for the toxic dossier was unceasing. Was there a money link, as Tristan had speculated? As he was mulling this over he made his way over to the British Embassy and his meeting with Tristan's father.

FORTY-SIX

Repatriation

Will arrived at the embassy compound opposite the Kremlin and noticed several cars in the forecourt including the ambassador's black Rolls-Royce with its Union Jack hanging limply on its small flagpole on the front right wing of the vehicle. He made his way to the chancery and told the receptionist he had been requested to visit to meet with the father of Tristan de Fallières. He was told to wait.

Some minutes later he was escorted to the ambassador's office on the first floor of the building where, two men were standing speaking quietly.

"Oh, hello, I'm Sir Archibald Mansfield, British Ambassador, and this is Peter de Fallières, father of Tristan," said the ambassador, offering his right hand to Will. "Let's sit down over here, shall we?" he said, pointing to the three deep-cushioned fawn settees arranged as three sides of a rectangle.

"Dreadful business about Tristan," the ambassador began.

"Ambassador, Mr de Fallières, I regret having to meet under these terrible circumstances," said Will diplomatically, adding quickly, "Mr de Fallières, my deepest condolences to you and your family at the loss of Tristan. I am totally shocked. As you must be too."

Tristan's father, immaculately dressed in a black suit, white shirt and black tie, with swept-back grey hair overlapping his collar, projected an image of a suave Mayfair antiques trader. He acknowledged Will's remarks by nodding. He was older than Will's own father, maybe by ten years, and was keeping himself together well. He was showing no visible emotion at the death of his only son. Will's first impression was that Tristan bore little resemblance to his father in terms of looks or demeanour.

An awkward silence ensued.

"Peter," interjected the ambassador, "Lawrence here was close friends with Tristan." Turning to Will, he added, "Perhaps he could fill you in with some details of his life here."

After a pause Tristan's father said, "Indeed, I would like that," in an impeccable Oxford English accent, the first words he had spoken so far at the meeting.

"We were indeed good friends," began Will, "though different characters from different backgrounds. Tristan was a very loyal companion and we met frequently around town, in bars and in cafés, and compared notes on life here in the USSR. Tristan spoke better Russian than me and I often relied on him to navigate my way round Moscow. He was a forthright character, lived life to the full, liked to have fun and to party, and had many acquaintances and friends. A true ladies' man as well." This raised an eyebrow from the ambassador but not from Peter de Fallières.

"Together, as you may already know, Tristan and I discovered, quite by accident, the body of a young Russian acquaintance of mine, a young woman, in the hills overlooking the Moscow River. We were both devastated by this. Tristan was profoundly affected and deeply upset by the utter pointlessness of the brutal murder of such a young woman. More recently, though, he seemed in better form and had reverted again to his old self. Yet here we are, a few days later, and he himself is another young victim. It's incomprehensible and tragic. I am just so sorry."

Another silence permeated the heavily draped room with its view over the embassy courtyard. *One's senses could be dulled permanently by these soporific surroundings*, thought Will.

Eventually Tristan's father spoke up. "Tristan was unsettled by my divorce from his mother nine years ago and went off in his own direction without, much to my regret, adequate parental support or guidance. He hadn't kept in regular touch with me in recent years. Or with his mother. Our family circumstances may have contributed indirectly to what happened to him…" A pause ensued as Mr de Fallières' emotions, hitherto kept in tight check, threatened momentarily to overcome him. His spectacles misted up and his eyes watered briefly. Was he was thinking of happier family times in the distant past?

Regaining his composure, he added, "One doesn't imagine, however, that anything like this can ever occur to one's family, does one… We are all too preoccupied with our routine daily lives to look out for others, even for our nearest and dearest… but, ironically, we do step forward to look after them in death."

Another pause ensued. Gathering himself, Peter asked, "What happens now, Ambassador?"

"Awful business. So very sorry, Peter. We are in touch with the Ministry of Foreign Affairs. The consular department will liaise with us to organise the return of Tristan's body to the UK. My understanding, this morning at least, was that the Moscow Militsiya – the police – had more or less completed their investigations into the circumstances of Tristan's death and had concluded that it was a tragic and simple case of accidental drowning. Once confirmed by their equivalent of a coroner – a proforma task – then we should be able to arrange for the transfer of Tristan's body to London speedily, by no later than the end of this week. In this sort of matter the Soviets are, in contrast to their normal obstructive behaviour in international matters, reasonably cooperative and effective," the ambassador said, suavely projecting an air of local knowledge, organisation and competence.

Will hesitated whether to give his version of events. He risked unsettling Tristan's father if he did so, but, he told himself, he couldn't just sit there and say nothing.

"Mr de Fallières, Ambassador. I would not want to let Tristan's tragic demise pass without at least mentioning to you both that I was with Tristan until 11pm on the night he went missing. We drank a couple of beers at a bar near Moscow University and he was fine and in good spirits when we parted. I want to emphasise that he was definitively not drunk when I left him – which is what the Moscow Militsiya are erroneously alleging. They say he was in the water for twelve hours before he was found at midday, which would mean he would have had to have drunk a massive amount of liquor between when I left him around 11 pm and midnight when he allegedly died. It doesn't add up. Tristan told me that he planned to return to his room in Moscow University and have, by his standards, a very quiet evening.

"Whatever happened between our parting and when he was found in the Moscow River is, for me, a total mystery. I think more investigations should be made of the facts and circumstances of his disappearance and whether, for example, he may have been the subject of an assault, which is what I suspect. The militsiya appear to be in an inordinate rush to close the case and hand it over to the Ministry of Foreign Affairs. It is all far too hasty and unexplained. In short, I don't believe he accidentally drowned," said Will.

The ambassador shuffled uneasily in his seat as Will outlined his version of events, clearing his throat at various points. De Fallières senior, by contrast, showed no reaction as Will spoke, quietly absorbing his devastating words.

Will was on the point of continuing when the ambassador interrupted. "Now, now, young man, I understand you're upset. It's a distressing time for the family and friends of Tristan. But one shouldn't resort to speculation and hearsay. Goodness me, it's bad enough for Mr de Fallières without things being made worse by the propagation of unsubstantiated, unproven theories bearing no relation to the facts," said the ambassador condescendingly.

Switching his gaze to Mr de Fallières senior, he continued, "Just to clarify, Peter: I was told this morning by Ambassador Boris Kurazin, the Soviet Deputy Minister of Foreign Affairs, that the matter is to all intents and purposes cut and dry. To be honest, and I don't mean this in a derogatory or unkind way at all, but your son's fairly... how can I put it delicately and diplomatically... 'risqué' comportment... in Moscow, was on our radar screen. Some of my staff were, frankly speaking, concerned by some of his hell-raising behaviour, drunkenness and wild escapades. It is, regrettably, not the first time that a British student behaves in this type of uncontrolled and loose manner in the USSR once shorn of parental shackles and liberated from British norms of correctness, convention and conduct. So, we were keeping an eye on your son. The fact that it has all ended so tragically is, of course, deeply shocking to us all. But taking risks in personal behaviour in a foreign country like the USSR rarely produces a positive outcome in my experience. I am frightfully sorry it has come to this for your family."

Peter de Fallières's mind was elsewhere, perhaps thinking of past times when Tristan was a child. He turned to Will. "Thank you for coming over, Lawrence. Here is my business card. Please contact me when you are back in London and we can have lunch at my club in Pall Mall. I would like to hear more from you about how Tristan lived here and spent his last days," said Peter.

"Very well then," intervened the ambassador. "Peter, let me arrange for a car to take you to your hotel – the Metropol, isn't it? We'll contact you as soon as we have more news tomorrow."

Will got up to leave, shook hands with the two men and made his exit from the ambassador's private apartment.

Correctness, convention and conduct. The pompous and condescending words of the ambassador rang in Will's ears as he walked towards Red Square and onward to take the 87 bus home.

No three words could be less apposite when applied to Tristan. Will could imagine how Tristan would have responded: with two nicotine-stained fingers pointed upwards in a V sign.

It had been another traumatic day.

FORTY-SEVEN

Visiting Svetlana

It had been over three weeks since the shocking discovery of Valya's body.

Will's life had been upended and changed forever during this period. He had been dragged unwittingly into a brutal world of score-settling, violence, unpredictability and ruthlessness. Nothing looked or felt the same.

Will was now intensely suspicious of all those with whom he was acquainted. He trusted no-one, not even the British authorities, who, as far as he was concerned, appeared anxious to get the Tristan 'affair' out of the limelight, done and dusted, lest it interfere with loftier diplomatic objectives. This Helsinki conference on security and cooperation in Europe in early August, whatever it was, seemed to have smothered any pretension of a normal investigation into Tristan's case. Will had no intention of letting things lie there, not least because of his loyalty to a close friend.

With these thoughts swirling in his mind, Will decided to take a chance and visit Valya's mother Svetlana again, unannounced, to try and tease out more information about the secret dossier. He arrived mid-morning and immediately saw Svetlana sitting alone on a wooden bench by the playground adjacent to her apartment looking forlornly into the distance.

"Svetlana Antolevna," called out Will. "Greetings. How are you?"

Svetlana looked up, surprised to hear her name, and immediately recognised Will. "Well, well, Vill. I am happy to see you. Sit down, please," said Svetlana, making space for him on the bench.

"I have brought a box of Soviet *confeti* – sweets – please, for you." Will handed over the colourfully wrapped sweets jumbled up in a flimsy cardboard box.

"It is kind of you – thank you. And how is your friend Tristan?" asked Svetlana.

"I am afraid I have bad news," replied Will.

Svetlana immediately grasped the red-patterned handkerchief she held in her hands, brought it to her mouth and uttered a plaintive, restrained exclamation. "Well, what now?" she asked.

"My friend Tristan is dead. He was found drowned in the Moscow River three days ago. I thought you should know," stated Will.

"*Bozhe moi*. It is beyond belief," whispered Svetlana, clasping her hands in front of her face. She stared in front of her for some time, genuinely shocked by Will's news. "Impossible to comprehend… Why is life so cruel? …My God, My God," she added, crossing herself in the Orthodox manner. "An accident?"

"So the militsiya believe," replied Will, not wishing to delve into what he believed had happened. "Tristan was a good friend. He lived and played hard. But he was honest and reliable. I will miss him."

After a further silence Svetlana said, "Let us walk a little."

She took Will's arm and they very slowly strolled along the paths through and around the vast, soulless Soviet housing estate where Svetlana lived. Will noticed how difficult and laboured Svetlana's movements were. He glanced at her knees, which were swollen, heavily bandaged and arthritic.

The housing estate was a faceless architectural monstrosity of multiple ten-storey tower blocks set out in corpuses of rectangles. An eyesore though they were, they did at least provide cheap and affordable housing for Soviet citizens. A small lake lay at the northern end of the complex and they slowly walked around it. Around the edges of the water proliferated a random cocktail of bottles, packaging, cartons and plastic wrapping dumped carelessly by those who couldn't be bothered to take their rubbish home with them. It was unseemly.

As they walked on, Will raised the question that was bothering him: "Svetlana Antolevna, I wanted to ask you something about Valya if I may."

She nodded. "Please."

"After I had returned from Krasnodar she kept changing the time of our second meeting. Something was affecting her, bothering her. We had agreed also to go to the Bolshoi Ballet but the next day she said she couldn't come after all. Do you know why she was so up and down, constantly changing her mind?"

Svetlana did not seem overly surprised by Will's questions. She was silent for a long while as they walked slowly around the lake.

"Valya was a secretive girl. She didn't tell me everything. But as a mother I observed things," said Svetlana. She continued, "She wanted to secure my future, to give me money so I could retire. I think she had made promises to some people that she could not keep."

"And you think this got her into trouble?" asked Will.

"Yes, I am sure of it."

"Was Kuznetsov one of the people she made promises to?"

"It is possible," said Svetlana.

Will decided to press further: "Svetlana, do you know what Valya had promised to do?"

Svetlana hesitated and looked around. No-one was nearby. "I think she was going to work with two people but then she decided against it. She changed her mind. That's when she began to get really nervous," said Svetlana.

"But why did she ask you to pass the dossier to me, someone whom she hardly knew? I don't understand why. Why not simply destroy it?" said Will.

"She said you would know what to do with it," suggested Svetlana.

That really surprised Will. *Why me?* he thought to himself. *What was Valya thinking of? Was she implying that I would put the information to good use, perhaps to foil the plans of those pressing her for it? Or to sell the dossier – perhaps to the British or the Americans?* He didn't really grasp what she had had in mind. Her motives were unclear.

"Do you know, Svetlana, why Valya decided to pull out of this 'transaction' with Kuznetsov?"

"No," said Svetlana. "Maybe she realised that what she was planning on doing was just wrong. I don't know. I brought her up alone as a good, honest Soviet citizen. All she wanted to do was to help me," said Svetlana tearfully. "Her motives were honest and pure. Must you die for trying to help your mother?"

Will hesitated before asking the next question. "I know this is impertinent of me, but was Valya at one time in a relationship with Kuznetsov?"

"I do not think so," said Svetlana. "But they say he was using her."

"You mentioned there were two people. Who was the second person, Svetlana?"

"I cannot say," said Svetlana, an imprecise phrase which could be interpreted as saying 'I don't know' or 'I know, but I don't want to say' or variations thereof. Svetlana was holding something back, perhaps through fear. Will refrained from pushing for an answer for fear of upsetting her further. They arrived back at Svetlana's apartment building.

"Thank you for answering my questions, Svetlana Antolevna. Things are a little bit clearer now," summarised Will. "It has been good to see you again, Svetlana Antolevna. Keep well. I think of you and Valya all the time." After a short embrace with the diminutive lady, Will headed off to the bus stop to return home.

FORTY-EIGHT

Document Trail

Will was far from forming a complete picture in his mind about the events impacting the fates of Valya and Tristan, the involvement of Kuznetsov and others, but intuitively he sensed that the two deaths had to be linked. Less clear was the role of Wendell, who had met with Kuznetsov, Valya and the third man at the National Hotel.

Svetlana had revealed a few nuggets but was holding back some information out of fear. He could not press her in the middle of the forty-day Russian Orthodox memorial period while mourning the loss of her daughter.

The British authorities, judging by his formal meeting with the ambassador and Tristan's father, were acting in a highly circumspect manner, reluctant to rock the boat with the USSR at this time.

The upshot was that Will was at an impasse. Something needed to move to trigger a reaction that would expose more of the circumstances that had led to the deaths of his two young friends. Regrettably, he lacked the ability to effect that movement.

It was against this backdrop that he received another call from Isakov instructing him to report to Central Militsiya HQ the next day at 11am. Will gathered his briefcase and headed downtown on the 87 bus to meet the chief inspector.

As per usual Will was kept waiting in the reception area of the Militsiya HQ, this time for twenty-five minutes. Bored and tired, he cast a glance at the guard in the reception area who was on duty. His hat was pushed back on his head, revealing a rather scruffy mop of unkempt, auburn-coloured, curly hair. His grey shirt was unbuttoned at the top and his red tie was hanging loosely. He appeared to have no official duties to undertake so he was reading the magazine *Sovietski Sport*, turning the pages over noisily every few minutes. On the one occasion the phone rang. Will listened to the briefest of conversations.

Officer: "*'Allo. 'Allo. Militsiya.*"

Officer: "*Shto vam?*" (What do you want?)

Officer: "*Nyet.*" (No.)

Officer: "*Nye rasresheno.*" (Not permitted.)

Officer: "*Nyet.*"

Officer: "*Nyet.*"

End of conversation, the officer slammed the phone receiver onto its cradle with a loud bang.

Officer: "*Sumashedshi durak.*" (Mad fool.)

Will wondered about the hapless individual at the other end of the line. Perhaps someone seeking information about a relative being held in custody. No information had been given to the caller. The officer returned to perusing his *Sovietski Sport* magazine, mumbling to himself, irate that his reading had been interrupted.

Ten minutes later the phone rang again. This time the officer was instructed to accompany Will to interrogation room B23 on the second floor. Emitting a sigh and a yawn at being interrupted for routine, trivial reasons – in this case the need to conduct a visitor to an interrogation elsewhere in the building – he motioned Will to follow him. He ushered Will into the interrogation room and departed immediately back to the reception area to resume perusing his magazine.

Isakov was already in the room seated at a table with two different junior officers when Will entered. This time, however, another person was seated at the back of the room. Plain-clothed, middle-aged with close-cropped hair, fit-looking and hardened, he observed Will closely with piercing eyes as he took his seat.

Isakov began, "You have been summoned here regarding further developments in the case of Valentina Mikhaelevna Dontsova."

"That is a surprise!" Will replied sarcastically. "But first could you tell me the names of your colleagues present in the room, please?"

"Two Militsiya officers are at the table and a special observer is sitting in the rear. No names will be disclosed. That would be against the laws of the USSR," replied Isakov.

"Who is this new person?" asked Will, pointing towards the non-uniformed individual in the shadows at the rear.

"I repeat: a special observer," Isakov said abruptly. "Let me remind you that I ask the questions here. I want to know again if, when you discovered the body of the deceased, or, subsequently in contacts with her family, secret official documents of the USSR came into your possession."

Will had been asked these questions before. He surmised that he was being asked them again so that the 'special observer' could hear the answers.

"Absolutely not," said Will definitively, a straightforward lie.

"I do not believe you," snapped Isakov. "Svetlana Antolevna Dontsova, the deceased's mother, has confirmed giving documents to you. So where are they?"

"Chief Inspector," Will replied in his politest voice, "we have had this discussion before. I have no Soviet State documents. As regards Svetlana Antolevna, she is, understandably, distraught at the death of her daughter. She is confused, upset, deeply unhappy and alone. She is in mourning. She never gave any documents to me," replied Will, making a tenuous distinction in his mind between a dossier and documents; he had no idea what Svetlana had said to the militsiya or whether Isakov was just using an old ruse to trap him. He suspected the latter.

"We have other evidence that you received these documents. Kuznetsov, Alexei Vladimorovitch, a Ministry of Agriculture official who was in attendance at Valentina Mikhaelevna's funeral, has confirmed in an official statement seeing these documents being passed over to you," insisted Isakov, growing in confidence that he was trapping Will.

"I believe I met this individual at some diplomatic receptions and at Svetlana Antolevna's home," said Will, playing for time and hoping to draw out more information from the insistent Isakov.

"He was at Valentina Dontsova's funeral. He saw you there and saw you receiving a package of documents," stated Isakov.

Kuznetsov had been present at both the funeral and at the *pominki* reception nine days after Valya's death, it was true, but he had not seen Svetlana hand over the documents to Will; they had been given to him when he visited her apartment alone some days before to present his condolences for her loss of Valya. Where was the proof? There wasn't any.

"Well, Chief Inspector, I think Kuznetsov is either confused, lying or stupid, or a combination of all three. Of course, there is one person who could have verified what I just told you – my friend Tristan de Fallières – but he too is dead, murdered by persons unknown," replied Will, promulgating a more offensive strategy to get Isakov off the scent. In doing so he glanced at the plain-clothed individual at the back of the room, who stared, stony-faced, back at Will, menacingly.

"Mr de Fallières was not murdered but drowned as a result of excess alcohol consumption. This has already been confirmed by Soviet state authorities. His body will be repatriated to Great Britain tomorrow. The Soviet Union has nothing further to say on this case and it is now closed."

"If you had spent as much time searching for the killers of Valentina and Tristan as you have chasing some non-existent secret dossier maybe you would be further forward in your investigations, chief inspector. Tristan was killed, in all probability by the same people who perpetrated the murder of Valentina Mikhaelevna. You've taken your eye off the ball, comrade," responded Will.

Isakov exploded in anger. "Such rank impertinence and arrogance will not be tolerated. You are at grave risk of being arrested for impeding a criminal murder investigation and insulting senior militsiya officers of the USSR. You have behaved with disdain for the legitimate interests of the investigative authorities of the Soviet Union. If you were not a foreigner, a Westerner, I would have you arrested on the spot. So, get out of here, go home and keep quiet. Any more mischief and you will be immediately arrested," said Isakov, furious that his latest effort to entrap Will had failed.

He got up, walked out and slammed the door behind him. The three other people in the room were silent. Not wishing to push his luck further, Will made to leave. One of the junior officers opened the door and accompanied him out of the room.

Will tried to engage the junior officer in conversation as he walked towards the entrance. "I wasn't aware that the militsiya had plain-clothed investigative officers present during interrogations," he said.

"We have to wear uniforms at all times. He's not from the militsiya," replied the officer.

"Oh, so which Soviet government service is he from then? The KGB?" asked Will.

The junior officer smiled disarmingly. They had reached the entrance of the building.

Well, that was revelatory by default, thought Will to himself as he exited the building.

FORTY-NINE

Draw of the Data

The one avenue of investigation Will hadn't explored was the involvement – or otherwise – of Wendell Randall III in the events which had led to the death of his two friends. Will had caught snatches of conversations at both the US and French Embassies that suggested that Wendell was actively on the hunt for information about the Soviet grain harvest, and he had observed Kuznetsov and Wendell engaged in a vigorous conversation at the French Embassy reception. Wendell had also met with Kuznetsov and Valya at the National Hotel. And it was Kuznetsov, as well as Isakov, who was pressing for information about the missing dossier.

Will remembered that he had Wendell's business card. Rummaging around his disorderly room, he eventually found it. The American had asked him to pass it on to Valya, but Will had never done so. He decided he would call Wendell that evening on the pretext of informing him about progress in the investigation of Valya's death and see where the conversation went.

At 8pm he dialled Wendell's number from a public phone box. After a short while he answered.

"Residence of Senior US Political Counsellor Wendell Randall III. Wendell Randall speaking."

"Good evening, Wendell, it is Will here, the British student. Sorry to disturb you, but I thought you might wish to be informed about progress in the investigation of Valya's murder."

There was silence on the line as Wendell internalised who was calling and why.

"Shhh, babe, I won't be a second," Will heard Wendell whisper to someone, presumably female, in his apartment, who was in the background.

"How'd you get my number?" snapped Wendell, clearly annoyed at being disturbed at a delicate moment.

"You gave me your business card once, don't you remember?" replied Will chirpily. "For Valya. Val. I forgot to pass it on. Sorry about that. Too late now since she is no longer with us. On it you wrote your private telephone number if you recall."

"Well, you should not be dialling my personal number, which is strictly confidential. And monitored. I am a top-ranking US diplomat here and I don't want you contacting me on this line. Is that clear?" said Wendell, annoyed that this British student had his private number and could call him at will.

"I do not want to take up any more of your precious time than necessary," replied Will sarcastically. "But since you had shown an interest in Valya, including accompanying her from the National Hotel just before she died, I thought you might want to hear more details about what happened to her."

Further silence on the line as Wendell again absorbed what Will had said.

"What you are talking about?" said Wendell. "Your facts are wrong."

"Oh, there must be a misunderstanding then as this is what I was informed by several members of staff at the National Hotel," responded Will, stretching the truth and deliberately trying to shake Wendell out of his comfort zone.

"Well, those Soviet blockheads made it up," said Wendell.

"Really? Never mind. There's one thing that I should mention, Wendell. An envelope with some information about the Soviet harvest has come into my possession. I have no use for it. But before I hand it over to my British compatriots here, I wanted to alert you, as I seem to recall that these matters might be of potential interest to you too."

Will had now dangled a juicy carrot right in front of Wendell's nose. How would he react?

A long silence passed, Wendell thinking fast about how he should respond.

"Hold back on that," said Wendell. "That, um… those data… those numbers… could be of interest to us. To me. More than they would be for the UK. Can we meet and discuss?"

"Certainly," said Will, smiling to himself that Wendell had nibbled the bait. "When and where?"

"Tomorrow at 7pm in the main bar of the Hotel Ukraina on Kutuzovsky Prospect. Near the Kutuzovsky diplomatic compound," replied Wendell.

"Fine. I will see you then," said Will.

"And bring the data with you," said Wendell, closing the conversation.

FIFTY

Hotel Ukraina

Will arrived well in advance of the planned 7pm rendezvous with Wendell to check the lie of the land. He took a tour round the ground floor of the building, one of the monolithic Stalinist high-rise 'wedding cake' structures, situated at a bend in the Moscow River. The hotel lacked the opulence of the Metropol or National Hotels and was frequented by less highbrow visitors and delegations to Moscow, mainly from Eastern Europe and Asia, who were consigned to hotels of lesser repute such as the Ukraina. Will positioned himself near the entrance to the lobby in a discreet place where he could see everyone coming in and leaving the hotel.

A few minutes late, Wendell arrived by his chauffeured car, which drove off immediately to park. Wendell walked briskly into the lobby and headed for the main bar. Well-groomed and business-like, he cut a figure of influence and authority. Will, by contrast, had put on a sports jacket but saw no need to dress up beyond that. He followed Wendell at a distance into the bar area. He decided he would make his move once Wendell began ordering so he could cadge a free drink off him. Wendell owed him one or two drinks anyway after Will had been cajoled into buying the second bottle of bubbly at the Metropol Hotel after the concert with Valya.

The barman approached Wendell and as he placed his order Will arrived.

"Beer and nuts," said Wendell to the barman.

"Hello, Wendell," said Will, sitting down beside him. "I'll have the same, thanks. Well, how are you, Wendell? How is your office? Busy?" Will had planned to engage in small talk for as long as necessary to ensure that Wendell made the first move.

Wendell brushed Will's mundane conversation filler aside and got down to business. "What can you tell me about the Val inquiry?" he asked immediately.

"Valya. OK. Well, yes, to be honest, it's proceeding very slowly, Wendell. The militsiya, who call me in every other day, say she was brutally strangled and her body dumped in the hills near by the Moscow River, which is where Tristan and I found her. They haven't established a motive, though they keep asking me if there was a handbag, papers or documents near her body. There weren't any such items," replied Will.

"I only met her once, when the four of us – me, Steph, you, Val – went to the Metropol Hotel, but she seemed a decent enough babe – shy though, like most Russians. She needed to loosen up and live a bit," said Wendell, lying.

"I agree with you, she was shy," said Will, letting Wendell make the running.

"Anyway, I'm sorry she passed. Too young. So, let's get down to business. Why don't you tell me about the information you have and then you can give it to me for safekeeping and future distribution? You did bring it with you, I assume," Wendell added, smiling condescendingly.

"Oh, yes, I thought you would raise that delicate issue," replied Will, smiling knowingly. "Well, to cut a long story short, Wendell, yes, a small dossier has indeed come into my possession. In it are the USSR's harvest forecasts for the main crops in 1975. In addition, there is a rather interesting document about the schedule of planned Soviet import of grains from the US, Canada and France in 1975/6, starting in a few weeks' time if my memory serves me well. Quite detailed, actually, with amounts of imports broken down by month." Will had decided to whet Wendell's appetite by describing the contents of the dossier in glowing terms.

"Finally, and to be frank, here I was astonished, there is a page of detailed forecasts of planned Soviet gold sales by the Ministry of Trade broken down by each month, through nominated banks in Zurich, to pay for the grain. Quite large sales, actually – more than a billion dollars of gold bullion is due to be sold over the next year if I recall correctly. That's a hell of a lot of lolly – wherever you come from – don't you agree, Wendell? Anyway, I thought the documents might interest the British Embassy here as they send regular economic reports back to London. Between you, me and the gatepost," said Will, winking, "I could imagine that a Western grain or gold trader looking for insider information about Soviet intentions might be interested in this stuff, as the documents could provide a basis for an effective trading strategy in these commodities over the next twelve months." Will had laid out the bait for Wendell to digest.

Will observed Wendell closely and he could see that he was salivating at the contents of the dossier and anxious to get his hands on it.

"These documents might be of interest to my authorities for sure," said Wendell, attempting to downplay his interest. "If you hand them over to me now, I will, naturally, make sure the Brits get a copy. We have a special relationship with HMG's ambassador here in Moscow. I do appreciate you contacting me on this issue, Will, and bringing the data to my attention. Much appreciated," said Wendell, confident that things were now on the right track and that he was about to get his own way. As always.

He took a gulp of beer. "Nut?" he asked Will, pushing the tray of cashews in Will's direction.

"Thanks," said Will. "Nothing like a good cashew nut with a beer. I prefer regular salted KP nuts, though." Continuing, Will said, "About the dossier, Wendell. Things are a touch less straightforward than you suggest. The information in this dossier has, I believe, directly or indirectly, led to the murder of two young people, both friends of mine. Its contents are politically and commercially explosive. That's why, to put it in a nutshell, I am not going to release this document to anyone until I know for sure how and why these two lives have been lost and who is responsible," asserted Will, strategically muscling himself into pole position in the negotiation and reducing Wendell to supplicant and demandeur.

"Two lives? Val – OK, one, yes. Sorry about that, as I've already said. And the second?" asked Wendell curiously.

"My friend Tristan, found drowned in the Moscow River a few days ago. In my estimation he was murdered by the same person or persons seeking the document we have been discussing."

"I don't believe it. Do you have evidence of this?" said Wendell, appearing genuinely shocked by this latest revelation.

"Not yet. Maybe you might have some useful information to tell me," replied Will.

"Me? Why the hell should I know? That Brit Tristan was an inveterate drunkard, a loudmouth, lecherous, womanising, arrogant bore, a real pain in the ass. But naturally," said Wendell, regaining his composure, "I wouldn't wish an early death on anyone."

Absent the drunkard bit, that seemed a pretty accurate description of Wendell himself, Will thought. *Takes one to know one.*

Will decided it was the moment to increase the pressure. "My hunch, Wendell, is that you are deeply involved in this affair. You have had contacts with some of the protagonists, or should I say, conspirators, involved in this grisly matter. And that is why, if we are to move things forward, together, in a smooth, harmonious, and consensual way, we are going to have to make a deal," said Will, seeking to take maximum advantage of the superior negotiating position that he now occupied.

"Deal? What kind of deal?" said Wendell, rattled.

"First, I want to know, in detail, all about your clandestine contacts with Valya, Kuznetsov and the other Russian in the group, starting with your meeting in the National Hotel. And…" said Will, seizing his advantage, "I am also curious to understand how all these activities tie in with your role as a senior US diplomat in Moscow."

Wendell, confronted with an imminent threat to his carefully crafted, upwardly mobile career which was at serious risk of unravelling at a stroke, was apoplectic. In a fury, he stormed out of the hotel bar, leaving Will to pick up the tab for the drinks.

Will had foreseen that Wendell might well fly off the handle once cornered. For once, though, Will didn't mind being saddled with the bar bill: he had achieved his purpose in rumbling Wendell, shaking him up and destabilising him.

Now he had to wait for the American's next move.

FIFTY-ONE

Serebryany Bor

Against his instincts, Will had to be patient. With Wendell out of town at a US diplomatic gathering in West Berlin, he decided to take up a longstanding invitation from Stephanie, Wendell's girlfriend, for a day out at Serebryany Bor, an attractive silver birch tree forest area with a lake, beaches and swimming area about fifteen kilometres north-west of Moscow. A popular spot with Russians throughout the seasons, in the autumn for mushroom-picking, in winter for cross-country skiing and in summer for picnics and bathing, it was also frequented by foreigners. Some embassies also had dachas there.

Will had kept up a friendly platonic relationship with Stephanie, despite her professed affection for Wendell. She had also kindly provided Will, from time to time, with some English delicacies he missed, such as McVitie's chocolate biscuits and Marmite, purchased from the diplomatic commissariat.

As they headed out of Moscow city centre in Stephanie's VW Beetle car, Will noted miltisiya blocpost towers situated along the main road at regular intervals. They recorded her diplomatic number plates and passed them on to the following one along the highway to anticipate the arrival of the vehicle. The car was travelling within the zone permitted by the Soviet authorities for Moscow-based foreigners, so no special permissions were needed. Nonetheless, strict surveillance of the movements of foreigners was still enforced by the Soviet authorities within this zone.

Leaving the Moscow suburbs, Will asked, "Is anyone following?"

"Not that I can see," replied Stephanie, glancing in her rear-view mirror, "though there is a car a long way behind us. It's maintaining a safe distance from us, though."

Will looked nervously over his shoulder. The car was half a mile away on the straight road and unidentifiable.

After about twenty minutes on the main road Stephanie turned sharp right into the fringes of the silver birch tree forest and drove on a few kilometres down a bumpy one-lane road covered by overhanging branches of trees and unkempt shrubs before parking on a dirt layby. They got out of the car: Stephanie searched in the boot for some plastic bags.

"A surprise," she said. "I made us a picnic. Let's take a walk through the forest towards the lake and find a quiet spot to talk and eat lunch."

"It was very kind of you to do that," said Will. They wandered along a path for twenty minutes and found a secluded spot close to the lake. Stephanie unpacked the picnic consisting of salads, cold meat and cheese, and a chilled bottle of Italian white wine.

"So, Steph, how is Wendell these days?" asked Will, curious to know if information about their volcanic confrontation in the Hotel Ukraina had been passed on to her.

"A bit tense, I would say, Will, the last time I saw him," she replied. "The problem is that he has such a pivotal role in the US Embassy that he is often overburdened with work. The ambassador is very demanding. Wendell has such finely attuned political and diplomatic skills that he is constantly in demand."

Will wondered if she really believed this hype about Wendell's professional attributes which had evidently come from Wendell himself. He decided to probe a bit. "I don't know the fellow like you do, of course, but I am a bit puzzled why he is working here in the USSR at all when his true vocation seems to be making money and trading in commodities. He seems more attached to private business than to US-USSR relations."

Stephanie slipped on her dark glasses to combat the glare from the water before replying, "Wendell says he will indeed return to the commercial world after his current assignment. It is true that at heart he is a trader. He has many business ties and contacts in Zurich and Chicago, where he worked before, and he doesn't want them to lapse. He doesn't like it here. He doesn't respect the Russians and he hasn't found the time or inclination to indulge in the more pleasurable aspects of life here in Russia," responded Stephanie.

"Yes, I saw evidence of that recently when he exploded at his driver for being five minutes late in picking him up after a diplomatic reception. It was a bit excessive," said Will.

"For sure his temper can get the better of him. He is extremely impatient. He's a perfectionist. Everything must be slick, quick, well-judged, organised and efficient. But he compensates his professional rigour with many attractive personal qualities," uttered Stephanie, seemingly missing his presence already. Will wondered to himself what those qualities could possibly be. It was, perhaps, a good moment to alert Stephanie that he was embroiled in a dark affair and that he may need her help in the future.

"Steph, I may need some help as I am unwittingly caught up in some nasty business beyond my comprehension. You are aware that Valya, the girl who was with me when we went to the Metropol Hotel, was murdered. A few days ago I was summoned to the embassy to meet with my friend Tristan's father, who was in Moscow to accompany his dead son back to London. I believe that he, too, was murdered," said Will.

"Murdered? Tristan? Come on now! We all know he died after falling into the Moscow River dead drunk. And, frankly, having suffered from his boorish behaviour on more than one occasion, I find that highly plausible," riposted Stephanie.

"Steph, I want to assure you he was definitely not drunk when I left him a few hours before he died. Not at all. He was killed, Steph: I am sure of it. And I want to prove it," replied Will.

"And how on earth are you going to do that?" Stephanie enquired.

"I'm working on it. But I may need some assistance at some point." Will took a swig of white wine from his glass. "I knew Tristan well, Steph. He was headstrong, argumentative and, when fired up, did not know when to back off in a confrontation. He drank, smoked to excess and was an inveterate womaniser. He had a wild, reckless streak in him, which he himself recognised but couldn't do anything about. To all intents and purposes, it was uncontrollable. But he also had a very sensitive side to him which outsiders rarely glimpsed. He was deeply moved by Valya's death and Russian funeral rites. My bet is that after we split up on the evening he died, he was accosted on his way home. He decided to take his attackers on and fight back, and paid for it with his life. His body was then dumped in the Moscow River. No proper investigation of his death has taken place, nor do I believe it ever will," said Will.

"This is just too far-fetched, Will. What evidence do you have?" said Stephanie.

"Not enough so far. But I want to smoke out the perpetrators and find out who is behind this whole grisly affair."

"You need to be careful," said Stephanie, adding, "This is dangerous stuff."

They finished lunch, stretched out and relaxed for an hour or so in the warm sun before setting off back towards the car. Will had put to the back of his mind the possibility that they may have been followed into the forest, but returning to the car, he proposed taking a different path from the one they had used when setting off for the lake. While still some distance from Stephanie's vehicle Will noticed a largish strong-looking man inspecting the car from the inside. The two front doors of the Beetle, the bonnet and the boot were open. Will ushered Stephanie behind a bush, put his hand across her face and beckoned towards the car. They crouched behind thick shrubbery in total silence as the man continued his examination of the vehicle, all the while giving the impression that this was not a random search but a well-honed professional operation. The examination went on for some minutes. Eventually the man emerged from the vehicle, locked it up using duplicate car keys and walked away towards a dark Volga parked under some trees in the distance. This car left after a short while.

Will had not got a clear look at the individual concerned but could see he was a well-built man in his forties, dark hair and upright with a military bearing. He looked very similar to the unnamed operative who had occupied a back seat at his last interrogation from Isakov. But Will couldn't be sure.

Will approached Stephanie's car very cautiously, fearing that it might have been tampered with in some way, a listening device inserted or, even worse, some sort of explosive device wired up. He was very nervous and cautious.

"We need to check it out, Steph. Give me the keys, please, and keep your distance," said Will.

He slowly opened the driver's door and cast a first glance at the interior of the vehicle. Nothing different was noticeable except a mild odour of cheap aftershave. Will then opened the rear of the car where the engine and battery were housed. No additional wiring was visible. He then carefully inspected the front boot which was empty except for the spare tyre and some muddy plimsols and a plastic bag from the *Beryozka* hard currency store. He looked under the vehicle by lying longwise on the ground and at the gravel and dirt on which it stood. Again, nothing untoward was discernible.

While everything looked OK superficially, Will couldn't vouch for possible listening devices. Embassy experts would have to check for these. Insofar as he could ascertain from a cursory once-over inspection, Will felt reasonably certain that the car was safe.

Will called Stephanie over and they examined the car again, this time together.

Satisfied, Stephanie got in the driver's seat while Will walked around the side to help her manoeuvre the car out of the layby.

Stephanie got her car keys out from her handbag but inadvertently dropped them onto the floor of the car. Her hands were shaking. Nervously recovering them and sliding them into the ignition block, she gingerly turned the key to the right to start the Beetle's 1300cc engine.

FIFTY-TWO

Farewell to Svetlana

A day before the trip to Serebryany Bor, while waiting for Wendell to act, Will had decided he needed to talk to Svetlana Antolevna one more time to try to obtain any additional information from her. He didn't have to wait long as she arrived unexpectedly the morning after his confrontation with Wendell, knocking at his door and entering discreetly.

Dressed sombrely in a black smock and belt, Svetlana gave the impression of someone hollowed out: she did not resemble the plucky and spirited lady he had met eight months before. And she was limping. Her bad knees were becoming an ever-increasing impediment to her movement.

She made tea for them.

"Svetlana Antolevna, I am pleased you are here. I wanted to see you before I leave for home in a few days' time. I sincerely regret I will not be able to be with you on the fortieth day of Valya's death," began Will.

"I thought you would be leaving soon, which is why I came round," said Svetlana. "Your stay here in USSR has been marked by tragic events. Always there is tragedy and death in Russia, and you have unfortunately witnessed this. As have so many others. It is etched in the soul of our country."

"The suffering to which you have been subjected pains me greatly, Svetlana Antolevna. I understand that the militsiya inquiry is making some progress," replied Will, deliberately exaggerating the positive aspect of the inquiry to elicit, hopefully, some more information from Svetlana.

"What progress?" she asked plaintively. "It won't bring Valya back. Kuznetsov treated my daughter badly. But I find it difficult to believe he killed her, though."

"I don't think they have concluded that he is responsible. The militsiya's investigation has been thorough. They need to ascertain the facts. Otherwise, the case wouldn't stand up before a trial judge," said Will, deliberately simplistically.

Svetlana looked at Will with an expression suggesting that the young man was very naïve. Her demeanour said it all: things just don't work like that here in the USSR.

"The only question, Vill, is *Kto vinovat?* – who is guilty? – not who perpetrated the crime," murmured Svetlana.

She poured some more tea for them both and passed the saucer with raspberry jam to Will to flavour the brew.

"Svetlana Antolevna, you have expressed doubts that Kuznetsov killed your daughter. Who then could have done it?" said Will, deliberately naïvely.

Svetlana shuffled uneasily on her seat and took a sip of tea before replying. "Kuznetsov was a rough individual, greedy and, at one time, regrettably, had affections for my daughter, although I don't think his interest was in any way reciprocated by Valya. Whenever I saw him, which was not often, he was always complaining about his salary, never being able to buy nice things, never having the money to be anything other than an average Soviet citizen. He was frustrated and felt he deserved more. I was glad when Valya rejected him and his schemes finally."

"So, if Kuznetsov was not Valya's killer then… who do you think it was?" asked Will abruptly.

"I do not know for certain if there were others involved. Gatherings used to take place occasionally in town – Kuznetsov, Valya… I turned a blind eye. Valya never told me much," replied Svetlana.

"So, Svetlana Antolevna, there were discussions to plan things, if I understand. You kept your distance from the scheme. Did you inform the militsiya of this? And the names of the people present?"

Svetlana's attention was elsewhere. Hey eyes were watering as she thought of her daughter. "*Konyeshno* – of course," she said. "They have the names."

"Then why have there not been arrests?" asked Will, deliberately assuming the role of the naïve foreigner who understands nothing.

"As I said before, this is Russia," said Svetlana. "It doesn't matter who is actually responsible but who is guilty. That is the end of the matter."

"So some people are above the law then. They are protected. Is this what you are saying?" asked Will with emphasis.

"*Nu-Da.* Well, yes… perhaps," replied Svetlana.

"Was one of these people, tall, dark-haired, slim, military bearing?" asked Will.

"Possibly," said Svetlana, shifting again in her seat, becoming progressively more uncomfortable and looking around to see if anyone was listening. She wasn't prepared to go further.

"One final thing: I still don't understand why Valya asked you to pass the envelope on to me? Why me?" said Will, anxious to clear up one aspect of the affair that really puzzled him.

"Valya liked you. She liked your shyness and your respect for her. She trusted you. You were different… she made a mistake… she was just trying to find a way to support her mother," at which point the tears began to flow down Svetlana's cheeks. "*Vot i vsyo*, here is everything – but now what?" continued Svetlana, barely able to continue. "Valya is no more. And me – adrift, alone, with few means to support myself… she did what she did for the right reasons, but how I wish it were not so. We would still then be together," Svetlana said softly, taking out a handkerchief to wipe the tears from her reddening eyes.

Will was unnerved by what Svetlana had said about Valya's feelings towards him. It was the first time he had ever been complimented in such a way and by someone who, culturally and socially, came from such a different background. Evidently, Valya had been very vulnerable and frightened. Will's lack of awareness of her plight was now painfully obvious to him and a personal embarrassment.

Will composed himself before saying to Svetlana a few last words. This simple lady had been a source of great warmth and friendship to him in Moscow. He was fond of her and distressed by her predicament. He knew he would likely never meet this lady again.

"Dear Svetlana Antolevna, I appreciate what you have just said. And I thank you for your kindness and friendship during my stay here in Russia. I will always remember you and Valya with great fondness and respect. I will have only good memories of you both. This has been a formative part of my life, and you and your daughter were at the centre of it," said Will, himself feeling rather emotional, his eyes watering. "Take good care of yourself."

"I will remember you too, Vill. Please write to me when you are back home safely in England," said Svetlana.

"For sure I will," said Will, taking Svetlana's hands and stooping to embrace and hug this simple, diminutive but courageous Russian woman who had led such a brutally hard life.

If he could have done something to help her at that precise moment, he would have not thought twice about it.

FIFTY-THREE

In the Silver Birch Tree Forest

In all her time in Moscow Stephanie had never had a problem starting her VW Beetle, even in the depths of a Moscow winter, but as she turned the ignition key this time nothing happened. The ignition motor did not spark into life or function in any way. It was as dead as the proverbial dodo.

"Shit, that's all we need," said Stephanie, turning the ignition key frantically and pumping the accelerator pedal for all it was worth.

"Let me have a try," said Will, who proceeded to follow the same drill as Stephanie had undertaken with the same negative result. The car would not start. Will, whose mechanical knowledge of cars was scant at best, opened the rear boot where the engine was housed to see if there was any obvious cause of why the ignition system of the car would not spring into life. Either the starter motor and/or the battery or both were kaput, or they had been tampered with or something else was the cause. He poked around the engine but saw no evidence of wires being cut or leads being displaced.

"There's only one thing for it, Steph, we'll have to jumpstart the car, pushing it as fast as we can and then trying to engage first gear once we've got up a head of steam. You will have to clamber in and engage first gear." They managed to turn the car round so it was facing the direction they were headed and straightened it up along the single-lane track.

"Right, Steph, you push from the driver's side, and I'll do it from the passenger side: you jump in once we've got going and hopefully it will start." They started pushing but the car veered off the path. After getting it back facing forward Will suggested that he push and direct from the driver's side and Stephanie push from the rear. This time they got going in a straight line and once speed had picked up Will jumped in and engaged first gear. The VW juddered and convulsed, a puff of smoke emitting from the exhaust pipe, but the ignition failed to engage.

"Let's have another go, Steph, it almost worked last time. This time there is a slight downward slope which should help us get some momentum." They pushed as hard as they could, and this time the car's speed was greater. Will clambered in again. More juddering but this time the engine bumbled haltingly into life. Will revved up the car to its maximum before easing down on the accelerator, the engine reverting to a normal idling speed as he put the gear stick in neutral.

"Hallelujah, *slava Bogu*, thanks be to God," cried Will as Stephanie caught up breathless and perspiring heavily in the humid heat. "That was a close-run thing. Let's get the hell out of here." He began to move over to allow Stephanie to replace him in the driver's seat, but she objected, saying she would prefer him to drive as she was shaken up.

"OK, but I have no documents, insurance or whatever, and I've never driven a Beetle before. But it can't be much different from my old English banger at home – my dilapidated old burgundy-coloured Ford Anglia. So here goes then."

Will gently engaged the clutch, fearful of stalling the vehicle, and the car inched forward. They had three kilometres or so to go to get to the main road from where things should get easier to manage. Will kept the car in second gear with high revs to avoid any risk of it stalling and coming to a halt. Things were fine for the first kilometre or so, but, upon turning a corner, they saw in front of them a Moscow Militsiya Volga car blocking the road at right angles to the asphalt road.

"Oh, shit, what is this?" exclaimed Will as he slowed the Beetle down. A militsiya officer emerged in front of the vehicle straddling the road and waved them to slow down.

"Steph, play the diplomat card to its maximum," underlined Will.

The Beetle slowed down, its engine ticking over, about twenty yards from where the officer was standing with a traffic truncheon in his hand.

Saluting, the officer asked for their IDs. Stephanie's diplomatic ID and Will's Soviet ID *udostovoreniye lichnosti* were handed over while they remained in the car. The officer took their documents and went to check them with his authorities by radio, not in any sort of hurry. Ten minutes went slowly by. Most likely the officers knew who they were even without their IDs since they had likely been trailing them since the morning.

After another five minutes sitting doing nothing, Will, getting increasingly irritated, decided to alight from the car and strolled towards the militsiya vehicle to see what was going on. Apart from the officer who had spoken with them and who was still in radio communication with his HQ, there were two others poring over their documentation.

Will decided to interrupt this pointless perusal of their ID papers. "Officer, who is in charge here? What is going on? Why are we waiting here?"

One of the officers replied, "This is a normal security patrol."

"In a silver birch tree forest? Two kilometres from the main road? Fifteen kilometres from Moscow? In that case why did you not apprehend a black car whose driver we saw pilfering our own vehicle thirty minutes ago?"

"There was no black car. We have been here for one hour. Yours is the first car we have stopped," the officer replied.

"Have you been following us?" suggested Will.

Another officer replied, "Why would we do that? Not at all. Purely routine security patrol work. You can take your IDs back now and return to Moscow."

Will snatched the IDs back and returned to the Beetle, whose engine had been ticking over for fifteen minutes.

"Pure official harassment," Will said to Stephanie, "designed to provide a security screen for the occupant of the black car to bugger off and send us a message that we are under surveillance." He depressed the clutch, engaged first gear, slowly pressed down on the accelerator pedal and continued their journey onto the main road and onwards to Moscow.

"I would get your car checked out by security guys, Steph, in case bugs – or other listening devices – have been placed in the vehicle," said Will as they neared Moscow. Once in the centre of the city Will pulled over to let Stephanie drive the rest of the way to her apartment in the diplomatic compound.

Before separating, Will broached the subject of Wendell again. "Steph, I would be grateful if everything that happened today and what we talked about remains between us. I would not want to worry or inconvenience Wendell when he returns from West Berlin, especially as he is so occupied with other things in his important diplomatic work," Will said, hoping Steph would play ball.

"Wendell is a possessive, jealous kind of a guy. He wouldn't appreciate that we spent the day together any more than I would tolerate him having a fling on the side. So I don't plan telling him much," replied Stephanie, much to Will's relief. "I will just say I went with some friends, including you, to the forest and had a picnic, and that on the way back we were stopped by the militsiya. OK?"

"Hmm, that sounds fine, Steph. I know how loyal he is to you," said Will, clearing his throat. *On reflection, perhaps it wouldn't be such a bad thing if Wendell knew that he had spent time with his girlfriend. It might increase his nervousness and prod him to accelerate his next move.*

FIFTY-FOUR

Deal?

Time was passing. The clock was ticking.

Will had not heard back from Wendell. Such was his distrust of him that, in the absence of any proof to the contrary, Will wondered if the American may have been implicated in, or at least aware of, the planned ransacking of his room to find the missing dossier. He decided to take a calculated risk to force the pace some days after Wendell's arrival back from West Berlin.

Will called Wendell's private number again from a public call box.

"US Senior Political Counsellor Wendell Randall III's residence. Wendell Randall speaking."

"Wendell, it's Will here. How was your trip to West Berlin? You have had plenty of time to reflect so I was expecting to have heard from you by now. And to be frank, I'm a bit disappointed that I haven't."

Silence on the line.

Will spoke again: "Wendell? Are you there?"

"Sure. I have nothing to say to you. Get off my private line, you asshole," answered Wendell aggressively.

"Oh, is that it then?" responded Will.

"You bet," replied Wendell.

"Well, if that's the case I will have to find alternative ways to get to the bottom of the murders of my two friends," answered Will.

"What alternative ways?"

"I'm not revealing my hand: options include developing contacts with European and US members of the Western press corps here. And, of course, pursuing contacts with the UK and US Embassy diplomats. Documents are ready for their perusal," said Will, upping the ante in this evolving game of chicken.

"Listen, you blackmailing scumbag," shouted Wendell into the telephone, "if you goddamn think I am going to fall for your bullshit—"

Will interrupted him before he could go any further: "You haven't grasped what is going on here, Wendell. I want to know what happened to my two friends. And you have a choice. You can either help me unravel the truth or deal with the consequences when I go public. Your career is on the line, cowboy, and my patience is running out. Should you change your mind and want to talk, I will be in the British Embassy Bar tomorrow at 8pm. It's the last-chance saloon," stated Will bluntly, leaving Wendell no doubt about the path on which he was set. He slammed the phone down.

Let him stew in his own juice for a while, thought Will.

It was a very risky strategy.

Tristan would have thoroughly approved of it.

FIFTY-FIVE

Showdown

Will positioned himself in a very prominent position at the British Embassy bar on Kutuzovsky Prospect the next evening just in case Wendell – should he decide to show up – had plans for any rough stuff or attempts at intimidation. He waited. He picked up a copy of *The Times* lying around on the bar counter and read about the hot weather impacting England. *Not the only place in Europe affected by the heat*, Will thought to himself.

Thirty minutes later Wendell arrived with two beefy, uniformed crew-cut companions in tow, presumably US Embassy Marine guards, who proceeded to position themselves at the other end of the bar within clear sight of Will. This was an effort to intimidate and warn him.

"Shall we step outside, where we can speak in confidence?" asked Wendell.

"No, we will not," replied Will. "I'm fine here. It's quiet."

"OK then," said Wendell. "What is your proposal?"

"My proposal? I rather thought you were going to make me a proposal," asked Will.

"Look, I want this matter brought to finality. I regret the

233

passing of two young people. How can we close it out? I'm ready to cut a deal if the information is good. And the price is ballpark ok," replied Wendell.

"That's all well and good," stated Will. "But first you must stop lying to me and tell me what happened when you met Valya and her companions at the Hotel National and why Valya left that meeting with you."

"Oh, that was nothing. Just a friendly talk with Val and Kuznetsov. I just offered Val a ride. We were going in the same direction," said Wendell.

"A ride in a US Embassy car with diplomatic number plates? An American Government taxi service in Moscow? An ordinary Soviet citizen would never agree to this unaccompanied," replied Will.

"Well, in the event, she didn't take up my offer of a ride," said Wendell.

"What happened next?"

"She had to go back to work," replied Wendell.

"Was this when you expected to receive the document you had commissioned from your Soviet pal Kuznetsov?" blurted out Will.

"What document?" said Wendell with a straight face.

"The document I told you about, the one now in my possession containing information on harvest forecasts, planned imports and gold sales. The one that you, Wendell, had agreed to purchase. Things went awry because Valya changed her mind for whatever reason and didn't produce it after all. How many dollars, by the way, did you plan to pay the conspirators?"

"Is there no end to your fantasies, Billy boy. Are you hallucinating? Are you high on drugs? Grass? Coke? Man, what bullshit. The US Government doesn't pay for commercial information like this," said Wendell, attempting to bat away Will's allegations and recuperate the high ground.

"True, perhaps the US government would not pay," retorted Will, "but market traders will pay. And you, as a former professional market trader, are linked to grain and gold markets, as you never cease in telling us. Maybe you were buying this information on your own personal account to be passed on to your associates with a view to them making large trading profits based on exclusive insider information and knowledge of Soviet grain imports and gold sales. The problem – your problem – is that the whole racket that you had planned with Kuznetsov and his partner backfired when Valya pulled out of the deal."

Wendell dismissed this theory as an outright fabrication. He was getting nervous and edgy, though. And Will wasn't going to let him off the hook.

"So how do I get the document you keep referring to, whatever it is worth? How much do you want for it?" asked Wendell. "Let's make a deal."

"Who killed Valya and Tristan? Once I know that maybe I can enter into negotiations." Will was playing hardball.

"Are you crazy? Do you think I am implicated in this shit? I had nothing to do with any Soviet violence," pleaded Wendell.

"Maybe not, but your insider trading scheme was indirectly the cause of their deaths, Wendell. Your greed and your dishonesty. So don't give me a load of sanctimonious bollocks about being an outsider to what has happened: you're in it up to your neck, buddy. So, let's start with the names of those whom you met at the National Hotel," underlined Will.

"If you think I am going to get picked off by you, Billy boy, slice by slice, like from an Italian salami, while getting nothin' in return, you can forget it, sonny. You think I'm some kinda stupid Texan cowhand?" said Wendell. "Name your price."

"Very well. I want names. Plus $10,000 cash. Clear?" said Will.

Wendell was flabbergasted. "Outrageous and totally unacceptable. Blackmailer. Take a hike," said Wendell, getting up and preparing to move towards his crew-cut escorts drinking Coke at the other side of the bar. At that moment British diplomats arrived.

"Oh, hello, Wendell. How are you?" asked Charles Fortescue

from the embassy, wearing his ubiquitous tweed coat, as he approached the bar. "Can I get you a drink?"

Wendell, distracted and ill at ease, declined Fortescue's offer.

"Oh, sorry, old chap," Fortescue continued, addressing himself to Will. "How dastardly rude and remiss of me. Can I get you something?"

"Thank you, Charles. A pale ale would be nice."

"Pale ale and a G&T then," Fortescue said to the barman. "So what's new in your world, chaps?" asked Fortescue.

"Oh, nothing very much," said Will. "I'm just completing my research on Soviet agriculture and the Soviet grain harvest before I leave Moscow in a few days' time."

"How about you, Wendell?" asked Fortescue politely.

"Politics. Helsinki. No agriculture – not my beef and—" said Wendell.

"Really, Wendell? You are really far too modest," interrupted Will, twisting the knife in. "You seem to know an awful lot about the subject, if I may say."

Fortescue, sensing that there was more than a bit of needle between the two 'W's, judiciously withdrew from the stilted conversation to seek more cordial company with colleagues at the other end of the room.

"You aggravating asshole, Billy boy," sneered Wendell in a blind fury.

"Did I say something wrong, Wendy—" said Will, feeling sure that this diminutive form of Wendell would drive him ballistic. He was right on that point.

"Don't fucking call me Wendy. I'm Wendell. Geddit?"

"And I'm Will, not Billy boy. Get it? Now let's get serious: there's only one question: are you going to play ball or not, Wendell? Or do I give the whole dossier to Fortescue and the press? Your call. And that call has got to be made right now," said Will, ramming home his advantage.

"I'll cut a fair business deal. But first I want the document in my hands for perusal and verification," said Wendell.

"No. First, I want names. Then I will exchange the document – but only for $10,000 in cash. On my terms," Will spat out.

Wendell, disorientated, sweating and worried that the severely compromising knowledge that Will held could seriously damage him professionally, made a last attempt to negotiate a better deal. "What is your proposal? I need an exchange process, a path to a fair business deal and a fair price," he said.

"We will meet tomorrow afternoon at 3pm at the Sadunovsky Banya, the famous Moscow bathhouse, where we will undertake the trade. It is a public and busy place, and no-one will notice us. You will come alone. At the *banya* you will inform me of the names of the Soviet consortium you have been dealing with. Otherwise, the deal is off and I go straight to the Brits and the press. Yes, or no?" said Will.

"The price is way too high. Five, max. Final offer, Billy," replied Wendell.

Will decided not to push his luck too far. "I'll take five thousand but all in used hundred-dollar notes. Otherwise no deal," retorted Will.

"It's a deal. I'll be there tomorrow," sighed Wendell.

Will could sense the gnashing of Wendell's teeth. The ultimate dealmaker had been cornered by a nobody and it infuriated him.

Wendell stomped off, realising he had no choice but to comply with Will's arrangements otherwise he was at risk of being exposed and disgraced.

Will had him right where he wanted him.

FIFTY-SIX

Wendell Reflects

Wendell was used to things running smoothly, in accordance with his planning and at the pace that he – and he alone – decided. He had to be in sole charge, the centre of attention, the one around whom everything gravitated. To find himself, therefore, in the hands of that irritating, haughty and condescending English pup, Will, infuriated him. How had he so mismanaged things that his future career was to all intents and purposes hanging by a thread and subjected to the whims of this unyielding, scheming Brit?

Wendell had reflected on trying some strong-arm tactics to get hold of the secret dossier from Will, but that have would involved bringing in the embassy's Marine security staff and having explain to them and to his ambassador how he had become aware of the dossier, how it had been generated and who was supplying it. Eyebrows would have been raised in the embassy at his apparent willingness to fund an illicit deal with some rogue Soviet Ministry of Agriculture officials, one of whom was now dead. Yes, the dossier could be of interest to the US Government, the more so as it laid out planned Soviet grain purchases from the US, but its most important potential use was commercial. He would be under suspicion for procuring commercially sensitive information for exploitation by his family's firm and for using the US Embassy as cover for a private commercial scheme at a highly sensitive time in US relations with the USSR. That would not look good and would damage his political and business career prospects.

The alternative, of course, was to junk the whole project and walk away from it. Will would then be left holding the 'baby' with no obvious outlet for it except, possibly, the Brits and the press. This aspect really worried him: Will could spill the beans, leak the document and damage him at any time. As to journalists – well, they were always poking around looking for a story and his name could easily be dragged into the dirt.

In the light of these considerations, and uneasy though he was about going through with the deal, Wendell decided that the least risky – although still risky – course was to buy the dossier off Will and get it to his uncle. Assuming no hitches, he could expect to profit handsomely from it: his uncle was a generous man. Millions of dollars beckoned if things went according to plan, a prospect that made him purr with satisfaction. It would propel him into the big league of market traders, open doors politically for him in the Republican party – he harboured a long-term goal to become a US senator – and offered much more besides. He had always wanted to buy a home in the Bahamas, rubbing shoulders with the global glitterati there and swimming in the turquoise blue waters.

The Russian triumvirate he had been dealing with were, all things considered, now completely out of the picture. They had failed to deliver anything except a dead young woman. It was a pity about Val for sure. The other student, de Fallières, appeared to be just collateral damage in the affair. Wendell wasn't interested in the slightest how he had been topped. The guy had been an irritating, drunken pain up the ass.

Wendell recognised that Will was all het up about what happened to these two young people. This was complicating the deal, but they were not his problem. His conscience was clear: he had simply entered, in good faith, into a straightforward business transaction with some clandestine Soviet contacts anxious to make some quick bucks. It had gone awry, but now, happily, it was back on track. Wendell had thought about scaling back what he was ready to spend to get possession of the dossier – $5,000 was not a snip, after all – but, in the end, he decided against prolonged negotiations as he didn't want to provoke more trouble with Will who, regrettably, still held the whip hand.

As he reflected further Wendell determined that he would never let himself get caught between a rock and a hard place again and be exposed, as he had been in this matter, to the whims of one scheming individual. Control was key. No more loss of control in future business transactions. He had learned his lesson. Henceforth, Wendell pledged to himself, his deals would only be fully 'legit'. No more shadowy stuff under the table. Too risky.

FIFTY-SEVEN

At the Banya

The Sadunovsky Banya, the most famous one in Moscow with its marble Baroque columns, Roman pools and Turkish baths, was, at the best of times, a wonderful venue for enjoying a traditional Russian bath with friends, to eat, drink, steam, sweat, cleanse, wash and be merry. However, these were not the reasons why Will had chosen this unusual location to seal the deal with Wendell. On the contrary, he wanted to take Wendell out of his comfort zone, unaccompanied by US Marines or any other back-up supporters and place him slap bang in the middle of a highly frequented, public and alien Russian environment. This would make any planned skulduggery on his part more difficult to undertake and enable Will to control matters.

Will had been to the Sadunovsky Banya several times. It was an enjoyable, fun experience once the body had acclimatised to the hot room and the plunge pools to cool off in. But, on this occasion, it was business first.

Will arrived well in advance of Wendell to suss out the lie of the land and plan his moves in the main changing-room area. From the attendant he rented towels and a large cotton loincloth and chose two lockers as far apart as possible, one close to the entrance, which he would use, and the other by a bench at the other side of the changing room. He then selected and paid for another two lockers close by the entrance to the changing room in the same row as his own one.

On a very hot day in Moscow, he had deliberately come to the *banya* very lightly clad – just a T-shirt, loose-fitting linen trousers, underpants and moccasin shoes without socks. He placed his wallet in the pocket of his trousers. This, crucially, held his July monthly bus ticket which he would need to take the 87 bus home. He had also brought his battered briefcase with him.

Will put his T-shirt in the locker nearest the entrance and wrapped the cotton cloth around his waist. He then put the grey-coloured Ministry of Agriculture file in the distant locker and jammed it between shelves at ground level, so it would not be immediately visible once the door was opened. He placed a bench in front of the locker so he could recognise where it was.

There was still a good hour to go before Wendell was due to arrive in the *banya*. Will reserved a table close to the entry of the changing room and ordered hot tea, beer, biscuits and honey to be delivered in an hour's time. These typical refreshments ordered by *banya* clientele were normally consumed after a session in the hot room and a plunge in the cooling pool. Indeed, at the adjoining table a group of corpulent middle-aged Russians were drinking heavily and eating similar snacks. They had just ordered more bottles of vodka and cognac as supplements. Much ribaldry and laughter came from this group, who were becoming progressively more inebriated.

Will decided to have a quick session in the hot room to loosen up before his rendezvous with Wendell and headed off there, having stripped naked except for his cotton wrap. Reaching the top level of the hot room Will was requested by a smallish man to beat his back and legs with a *venig* – thin birch sticks and leaves bound together – to increase the temperature on his skin and impregnate it with an agreeable forest scent. This he duly did. After sweating heavily for five minutes Will left and plunged into a cold pool to cool off. He recovered his now-damp wrap and headed back to the table he had reserved. After cooling down he went to his locker and put on his underpants, his loose-fitting summer linen trousers rolled up to his knees and his moccasins, leaving just his T-shirt and briefcase in the locker. He rented another dry cotton wrap, which he wound round his waist.

The refreshments arrived. Wendell was due in five minutes.

This time Wendell arrived on time. He was wearing a very smart, immaculately pressed lightweight black business suit, belted trousers and red braces, white shirt and patterned silk tie, tie pin, and shiny brogue shoes.

"Why are we meeting here in this stinking Soviet sweat hole?" Wendell said, looking around the changing room, in an accusatory and abrasive tone.

"It's neutral territory. I thought it would be more secure for both of us. Have you not been here before?" asked Will. "It's a good place to meet privately, have a hot bath, cleanse oneself and talk. And give yourself a good beating with a *venig*. A relaxing Russian environment. I suggest you strip down like me. We can do business now or later after a session in the hot room. As you prefer. I arranged a couple of lockers in the adjacent row for you if you want to change. Here are the keys. Please put the money in one locker. I have put the secret dossier in a separate locker too."

"Oh, why the hell not? It's unbearably hot and steamy in here," said Wendell, and headed off to change. This took quite a while, as he meticulously folded his suit, shirt and other clothing items to ensure no creasing. Eventually he returned barefoot with the cotton wrap around his waist.

"Tea?" asked Will. "Honey goes well with it. Biscuit? Beer?"

Wendell, somewhat disarmed, took some tea and sat back. Meanwhile the group of Russians at the adjoining table were in an even more drunken if not paralytic state, telling jokes, making toasts, and laughing so much that two of them, heads resting on the table, could barely move or speak.

"A typical Russian *banya* crowd," said Will, sipping tea and smiling. "I already had a short session in the hot room and plunged into the cooling tank before you arrived," said Will, shaking his wet hair to make the point. "How about a session in the hot room to get our juices going before consummating our deal?"

"I wanna get down to business immediately," replied Wendell impatiently. "I don't have that long. Unlike you, I'm working."

"Very well," said Will, smiling courteously, anxious to build mutual confidence and avoid an immediate confrontation, "but you really shouldn't miss out on having a hot bath: it's a great experience. You feel great after it. So, Wendell," continued Will, "let's begin our discussion. As I said to you before, I want names. I want to know who killed my two friends."

Wendell hesitated. He sat forward. "OK, I'll come clean with you, Billy. Yeah, I made contact with that Ministry of Agriculture guy, Kuznetsov, when he came to the reception at Spaso House. We firmed up a deal later. The idea was to get some confidential data on the Soviet harvest, grain orders from the US and Soviet gold sales, which my uncle needed for his grain brokerage. Val was nominated as the conduit and courier. She had the job of stitching all the data together in one dossier. I don't know how she had gotten it all."

"So what happened next?" asked Will firmly.

"After sealing the deal at the National, Val went on her own by metro to her ministry to pick up the dossier. I was to meet her near there: that's where the exchange was to take place. But it all got screwed up. She was cute, a tad shy, and I had plans for the two of us…" Wendell continued, oblivious to Will's own affections for Valya.

Will could barely restrain himself from taking a full-blooded swing at Wendell there and then. After exhaling several times to calm himself and regain control of his emotions, Will managed to regain his composure.

"Then, for some reason, and out of the blue, the stupid bitch changed her mind. She never showed up at the rendezvous. Kuznetsov later pleaded with her, but the stubborn gal would not relent. Val was turning her nose up at some quick and easy greenbacks. The dossier was primed and ready to trade, but she wouldn't release it."

"If she knew where the dossier was, why kill her?" asked Will.

"Believe me, I was goddamn shocked when I heard she had been murdered. The only answer I got later from Kuznetsov was that his business partner, a KGB-type operator, fearing betrayal and exposure, took matters into his own hands," said Wendell.

"Betrayal? Are you serious? Who was Kuznetsov's business partner? Who killed her?" insisted Will.

"I do not know who Kuznetsov's business partner is. And I don't want to know. I suspect he was a past or present security guy, a hired hand, Military, KGB or something like that," replied Wendell.

"You met him at the National Hotel. What was the hatchet man's name?" asked Will.

"I don't know for sure. Someone once said Leibovitch or Milevich, something like that," replied Wendell unconvincingly.

"And his Christian name? Patronymic?" said Will.

"One time, I think I heard the name Yeremevich. Another time, I caught something like Pavel or Dava. I don't speak Russian. That's all I could pick up," responded Wendell.

"And Tristan. Did this guy do him in as well? How and why was he killed?" said Will, eyeballing Wendell and trying to ascertain in his mind if this duplicitous Yank was telling the truth.

"No idea," said Wendell. "Not my issue. Not involved. Period."

"Two young people have lost their lives, Wendell. Valya's mother is devastated. Her life, her hopes and dreams for her daughter, lie in ruins. And all because you wanted to get your grubby hands on some insider information on Soviet harvest forecasts so you and your sleazy Chicago associates could make a ton of money trading in grain and gold. It's deplorable," said Will.

Wendell, indifferent to the damage he had caused, continued, "Of course I regret the loss of life. But what about the money-grabbers on the Soviet side looking to line their pockets by stealing state secrets and make a quick killing at my expense? Did you ever think about them? Can't you see it was just a normal business transaction that had gotten into difficulties…" Wendell continued in this vein, seeing himself as victim rather than perpetrator of a criminal conspiracy and seeking to avoid any responsibility for his role in what had transpired.

"If that is 'normal' business, Wendell, I hate to think what an abnormal business transaction is," Will blurted out.

Wendell didn't give a damn about Valya or Tristan, thought Will. He had shown no remorse for his appalling behaviour and actions. A pumped-up narcissist, he had just one objective – to extricate himself from an unholy mess of his own making without any collateral damage to his own career and reputation.

"One final thing, Wendell. Why did Kuznetsov – and you – go on denying that the harvest outlook was poor when you knew full well that the opposite was true?" said Will.

"Kuznetsov insisted on confidentiality. Harvest forecasts are a state secret. No leakages. He feared exposure. The Soviets didn't want bad news seeping out on the eve of the Helsinki Conference on pan-European security next week – that would be hugely embarrassing for them. So stick to the Party line," Wendell offered as the explanation.

For once, Will thought, *he might be telling a grain of truth.*

"OK, Wendell. I've heard enough. Now, let's talk cash," said Will, turning to the business side of the equation. "I want to see and count the money. All $5,000 of it."

FIFTY-EIGHT

The Exchange

Wendell, relieved that Will had finally backed off from pursuing further information about his Soviet business partners and about the two murders, was not going to be a soft touch as far as the rest of the deal was concerned. Fed up with being outmanoeuvred and placed on the back foot, he decided that now was the time to 'play offense'.

"Not so fast," said Wendell, reasserting himself with the aim of disrupting Will's control of the encounter. "It takes to two to tango. We need a process of exchange here. A procedure. I wanna see and verify the contents of the dossier first."

"And I want to be sure that you have brought $5,000, in cash, as agreed, in used hundred-dollar notes. Where is it?" replied Will forcefully.

"It's here, right with me, Billy boy, in my second locker. But first, hand over the dossier," insisted Wendell.

"Look," said Will, foreseeing that Wendell would play hardball on the logistics of the exchange, "why don't we, separately but simultaneously, confirm what we each committed to deliver? Then we can be mutually satisfied that there is no jiggery-pokery at play."

"You mean no double-dealing?"

"The same thing," replied Will. He continued, "Just a word of explanation. When I came to the *banya* earlier the place was absolutely packed and there were no free lockers. So, I had to wait for one to become available. Happily, it's a bit quieter now. I took the first one that came free and I put the dossier in it. So it's in a locker over there," said Will, pointing vaguely towards its location. "Number 115. Here's the key. You can check the contents of the dossier there. Give me the key to the locker where the money is and I will count the dollar bills and certify that the amount is correct. We can then meet back here at our table in a jiffy to cement the deal and celebrate by drinking some tea. Or beer. And maybe have a steam bath together. Does that sound OK?" said Will, smiling. It was all very polite and respectful.

Wendell, manifestly wanting to get the whole excruciating affair terminated as soon as possible, agreed without thinking to this convoluted way of proceeding.

"May I have the key to the 'dollar' locker, please?" said Will. "What locker number is it?"

"Number 9," said Wendell, handing it over to Will. Concurrently Will handed over key 115 to Wendell.

Wendell, with key in hand, stood up, bare-chested and clad in a cotton wrap, and began heading towards the locker at the other side of the changing room.

FIFTY-NINE

Wendell in the Steam

Reaching the far side of the changing room, Wendell searched for locker 115. Once he located it, it took him a few seconds to shove the bench in front of it aside and insert the key into the tall, thin, rectangular locker. He opened the rusty lock and looked inside. At first he couldn't see anything but then he noticed a grey dossier in the right-hand corner at ground level, wedged awkwardly between two shelves. He took it out, sat down on the bench and opened it. Inside, to his astonishment, were just five blank sheets of white paper. With nothing on them at all except for a handwritten Russian phrase 'с лехым паром' on the first page, a phrase which meant nothing to him.

For a moment Wendell thought there must be some mistake. He had been expecting a document with numbers and words in Russian outlining the Soviet Union's grain forecasts and import strategy as well as statistics on planned gold movements. Something was seriously amiss. Bewildered, he turned rapidly and headed back quickly towards the lockers where he and Will had planned their exchange. What the hell was going on? He looked left and right and the other side of the lockers. There was no sign of Will.

Wendell ran immediately to the entrance of the changing room and looked around. Still no glimpse of Will. *Where did that*

English shit go? To the men's room, perhaps? Wendell rushed to the *Muzhchiny.* No sign of him there either. He retreated back to the reception desk in a blind panic.

One of the drunken Russians who had been on the adjacent table was propped up on the counter talking loudly with the changing room attendant.

"*Gdye* – where – *chelovek* – man?" asked Wendell urgently.

The Russians looked at him without understanding a word of what he was saying, ignored him and continued their conversation.

Wendell pointed to the page with the Russian expression on it and showed it to the Russians.

"What does it mean, what mean? *Znacheniye?*" Wendell asked.

The Russians looked at the words and laughed out loud, pronouncing the phrase several times and putting their thumbs up. They attempted to show him what it meant by pretending to wash and rub themselves and expressing satisfaction.

"Aaaargh, *otlichno, otlichno*… wonderful!" said the Russians.

Baffled, Wendell returned to the lockers. It was slowly beginning to dawn on him what had happened. He opened locker number 9, which still had the key in the lock. It was empty. The envelope with the $5,000 had gone. There was no sign of Will except for his discarded cotton wrap on the floor.

Wendell stood there stupefied.

The bastard had run for it.

He was minus $5,000 and plus five useless sheets of blank white paper with just one Russian phase on one of them.

He had no idea where Will was.

He had been taken for a ride.

Duped.

Conned.

Big time.

Standing there with a cotton wrap tied round his body, he was furious with himself for having been so goddamn stupid.

SIXTY

Exit from the Banya

As soon as Wendell began heading purposefully towards the far side of the changing room Will immediately turned and put the key in locker number 9, which was in the same row as his own.

Twenty-four seconds max, Will reminded himself, the time he calculated it would take Wendell to return to the starting point.

He saw straightaway a buff envelope on the upper shelf of the locker, its edges sealed with Sellotape. He ripped a small tear in the middle of the envelope. Inside he saw what appeared to be a wad of green dollar notes. He had no time to count the money but was as satisfied as he could be at first glance that the dollars were there.

Holding tightly on to the money, he turned to his own nearby locker, number 15. He had left the key in the lock to gain time. He threw his cotton wrap to the ground, grabbed his T-shirt and his briefcase, and ran for the exit ten metres away, shoving the buff envelope into his briefcase as he went. Briefly glancing over his shoulder, he saw that Wendell was still grappling to open the lock of number 115, having lost precious seconds pushing aside the strategically positioned obstructive bench.

Will descended the ornate *banya* staircase rapidly to make

251

the fastest exit possible but then found himself confronted with an unexpected hurdle in the form of a cleaning lady methodically washing the stairs with a large soapy bucket and blocking his descent.

"*Odyevaityis pravilno molodoi chelovek* – dress yourself properly, young man!" she said sternly as Will pushed past her and her large aluminium pail, which he inadvertently knocked over, resulting in a minor torrent of dirty foamy water cascading down the stairs towards the *banya's kassa*.

"*Izvenitye* – sorry," said Will, exasperated, continuing his descent.

"*Khuligan, khuligan!*" screamed the cleaning lady in a screeching voice as Will continued down the stairs at maximum speed, taking as much care as he could to avoid slipping on the soapy stairs.

At the bottom Will stopped and pulled on his T-shirt and rolled down the legs of his trousers, losing precious seconds. Will rushed past the *kassa* and into the sunny street outside. He darted in and out between pedestrians and, without drawing excessive attention to himself, headed towards his next destination, two kilometres away, which he planned to reach on foot. Arriving at the corner of a major road junction he quickly looked back. There was no indication that he was being followed. In any event, he surmised, it would take Wendell some moments to realise that he had bolted and even longer to dress himself in his fancy business clothes, which would be an impediment to his rapid departure from the *banya*.

For the time being Will was in the clear.

And, most important of all, he had the money.

SIXTY-ONE

Afternoon at the Militsiya

Will kept walking quickly and was soon sweating profusely in the late afternoon sun. Heat and sun reflected blindingly off the sticky Moscow tarmac and pavements. He arrived at his destination, Central Moscow Militsiya Headquarters, his T-shirt thoroughly wet through. A familiar building which did not hold good memories for him.

Entering the building, he addressed himself to the officer on duty. This one, minus tie and cap on a hot day, was absorbed in a book of crossword or number puzzles. He barely noticed Will's arrival.

"You've come to the wrong building, citizen. This is the Central Militsiya Headquarters," he said without looking up.

"I've come to the right building, Officer, and I have an appointment with Chief Inspector Isakov," replied Will, lying about a meeting which had not been arranged.

"He's not here," said the officer.

"Well, go and find him then," said Will. "Tell him Gospodin Lawrence wants to talk to him."

"He's on another case. Come back another time," said the officer disinterestedly.

"Tell him I have new information about the murder of Valentina Michaelevna Dontsova," said Will, desperately trying to get the officer's attention.

"What information?" asked the officer, still looking at his crossword and showing little interest in what Will was saying.

"Confidential information for Chief Inspector Isakov, not for any Tom, Dick or Harry, Militsiya Officer," said Will without thinking.

"Gkharry? Ick?" the officer replied, confused.

Yes, thought Will to himself, *there are some English expressions that are not easily translatable into Russian and vice versa.*

"Never mind. Just get Isakov. Tell him it's urgent," said Will bluntly.

The officer, still unconvinced, called an internal number and mumbled something into the phone about the Dontsova murder. And resumed his crossword puzzles.

Will waited. And waited.

Half an hour later one of Isakov's sidekicks emerged from the bowels of the building and asked what Will wanted. Will explained again. He disappeared but not before indicating that Isakov was in the building but was busy. "*On zanyat.*"

Will waited another thirty minutes, by which time he had cooled down. His T-shirt had dried but was freshly scented with his pungent body odour.

Finally, he was escorted upstairs to the same interrogation room he had been in before.

Will waited.

Fifteen minutes later Isakov finally appeared.

He looked Will straight up and down but said nothing. He sat down with an assistant officer to Will's right and indicated that Will should sit as well.

"I did not expect to see you again, Gospodin Lawrence," said Isakov in a voice, by his standards, not too gruff or aggressive. "The last time I warned you not to interfere or obstruct our investigation or the consequences could be severe. So, I hope you have not come here to do that – for your sake. Have you bought the document with you?"

"No, Chief Inspector, I have not. I do not have any such document. I just thought I would drop in before leaving the USSR in two days' time to inform you who killed Valentina Michaelevna Dontsova and Tristan de Fallières and why. I presumed you might possibly be interested in that," said Will cheekily.

Isakov, who looked pale, tired and drawn, was not an idiot and certainly did not want to be made a fool of by Will, especially in front of his young assistant. Any suggestion that he and his colleagues in the militsiya were incompetent, while this impertinent English student had solved the Valentina Michaelevna murder, would not be tolerated.

"If you have more information on the Dontsova case reveal it now. The de Fallières dossier is closed," said Isakov.

"Very well, Chief Inspector. Here is what happened. For what it is worth," replied Will, who proceeded to lay out the basic deal – cash for information about harvest forecasts, grain imports and gold sales – without mentioning names. Valya was silenced when she had second thoughts about supplying the secret information, thus exposing the Soviet conspirators to arrest. Tristan followed the same fate because he confronted and stood up to Valya's attackers, who were searching in desperation for the missing dossier, their route to a dollar bonanza.

"Names. I want names," said Isakov.

"Kuznetsov, Alexei Vladimorovitch from the Ministry of Agriculture was one of the conspirators but not the killer. The latter, I believe, is from the security services – a name and patronymic something like Dava or Pavel Yeremevich. Surname something like Milevich. More details, I don't know. But there can't be too many people around in the USSR's security services, past or present, with those names. Perhaps you could check him out. It shouldn't be too difficult as I believe the individual concerned sat at the back during one of my recent interrogations in this building," said Will.

"What security services?" questioned Isakov.

"KGB most likely… this guy came from one of their branches," said Will confidently.

"This is pure speculation devoid of substance. We don't have state security agents running round killing people in our country or anywhere else for that matter. This is not America. Where is the stolen secret document?" Isakov asked.

"I have absolutely no idea. It appears to have totally disappeared. I never saw it, in any case," said Will, lying with a straight face.

"And the cash? How much was to be paid? And by whom?"

"$5–10,000. By a consortium of US grain brokers. I don't know who the instigator was," said Will, thinking that Wendell should be grateful to him for covering up for his misdemeanours.

"Was the American Embassy involved?" asked Isakov pointedly.

"This was a rogue private sector operation," replied Will.

"Where is the money?"

Will, feeling his briefcase nestling against his right leg with the envelope containing what he presumed to be $5,000, was tempted to say, "Right here, Chief Inspector," but refrained from doing so.

"I don't believe the money was ever paid to the conspirators by the US grain consortium," said Will. "I mean, would you, Chief Inspector, pay thousands of dollars for stolen documents that you never received? The transaction was aborted because of Valentina Michaelevna Dontsova's refusal to go through with it. That is what I believe," replied Will confidently.

"We will judge that. You have not provided me with any useful facts or considerations that could be helpful in solving the murder investigation. It's all hearsay and speculation. We will continue our investigation into this crime. You may leave now," said Isakov, closing his dossier with a snap. He shook Will's hand and left the room.

Will made his way out of the Militsiya building. He sensed that Isakov knew everything about the conspiracy and that what he had told him had just confirmed his suspicions. He hadn't probed the US connection – maybe because it was too delicate a matter at a sensitive time in US-USSR relations. Neither did he show any interest in Will's information on the identity of the killer. Was this guy untouchable? He recalled what Svetlana had said – the important thing was *Kto vinovat?* – who is guilty? – not who actually committed the crime.

There was little more that Will could do to bring the perpetrators of the two murders to justice. It was out of his realm. He needed to leave the USSR. He had an exit visa from his academy, so in principle, he could depart anytime.

Will gathered himself in the lobby of Militsiya HQ. The officer on duty at the reception was still fiddling around with his crosswords and, as before, paid him not the slightest attention.

It was after 7pm and he needed to make his way home.

He walked to the Lenin Library, recovered the secret dossier he had left there for safekeeping and put it in his briefcase.

He then walked towards the bus stop by the Bolshoi theatre and jumped on a battered blue and white-coloured 87 bus in which was seated a sprinkling of waiting passengers, fanning themselves with whatever was at hand to cool down after a swelteringly hot day.

Will sat down on a bus seat, equally exhausted. He clutched his briefcase tightly on his knees, knowing that it contained everything that the conspirators and the militsiya were after.

Six stops before his normal stop on Listvennichnaya Alleia Will got off and changed buses.

Resuming his journey after a fifty-minute detour, Will alighted at his residence. It was the last time he would take the trusty 87 bus to Listvennichnaya Alleia.

SIXTY-TWO

Isakov's Challenge

After Will's departure from the Central Militsiya Headquarters Isakov returned to his office with the latest files on the Valentina Dontsova case under his arm. He plonked them down on his heavy, dark wooden desk with a thump. He was deeply unhappy and very concerned. A man under severe pressure. He reviewed the situation he found himself in.

The English student Lawrence had told him nothing new in his unexpected reappearance at Central Militsiya HQ that he didn't know already about the Dontsova case – or about the other student, de Fallières, for that matter.

The whole affair stank.

His instructions from his superiors had been clear from the start.

One, the deaths – the murders – were to be kept quiet. A scandal had to be avoided at all costs. The fates of the two deceased people were an irrelevance in the grander scheme of things and, as far as the Soviet state was concerned, both individuals were expendable. People, Isakov was reminded, were at the service of the Soviet state, not the other way round. State interests came first.

Two, more importantly, the matter had to be kept out of the clutch of the international community and especially the voracious Western press. The leadership of the Party was focused on the diplomatic triumph it would proclaim at the signature of the Helsinki Final Act at the Conference on Security and Cooperation in Europe in a few days' time, confirming the post-war division of the continent. They did not want adverse publicity about another economic failure in the USSR resulting from a poor grain harvest, accusations of Soviet plundering of US grain stocks, nor any tittle-tattle about Western cash for Soviet economic secrets, let alone trivia about the murders of two irrelevant young people, one of them a British citizen, to deflect interest from their diplomatic triumph.

Three, Isakov's instructions were clear: get on top of the affair, manage the investigation, conclude it and, most important of all, bury it from any external scrutiny.

These orders were contrary to nearly everything that Isakov had stood for and carried out in his thirty-year professional militsiya career. He was committed to the USSR, to socialism and to the enforcement of Soviet justice. His core professional and personal values derived from his belief in the rightness of the work of the CPSU to construct, on behalf of the people, a communist society. But in this case, Soviet interests, defined on high by top Party officials and imposed on him, trumped his principles and values. He was deeply uncomfortable. He felt compromised and used, a pawn in a much bigger game. He reminded himself that he had become a police officer to apply Soviet law, not to subvert it by burying criminal cases.

Fulfilling his instructions had been straightforward as far as the secondary case regarding the student de Fallières was concerned. The student was, by reputation, a wild type and it was easy to conclude he had fallen drunkenly into the Moscow River and accidentally drowned. The deep crack in his skull caused by the violent blow of a heavy object was a slightly awkward element but explainable by a possible collision with something adjacent to, or in, the Moscow River. Of course, Isakov knew perfectly well that this was not what had happened. Kuznetsov's partner in this 'cash for information' racket, Pavel, an old classmate of his from Leningrad in the 1960s, had in all likelihood taken matters into his own hands, probably employing some of his roughneck KGB comrades to beat up the student and demand where the secret dossier was being kept. De Fallières probably resisted and was hit on the head with a metal pipe or by some other heavy object. Whether these ham-fisted bunglers meant to kill the student is unclear, but that is what they had succeeded in doing. There were some signs of a struggle close to the path from the beer bar back to Moscow University, not far where de Fallières had met Lawrence, and indications of two or three people carrying a heavy load – perhaps his body – down to the river to be dumped.

As a militsiya chief inspector of long experience he would have expected the immediate relatives and the British Embassy to kick up a fuss and insist on a thorough investigation. To his great surprise, however, they did not. In fact, they seemed just as complicit in wanting the affair to be quietly parked and kept out of the spotlight. The Soviet Foreign Ministry had swiftly taken the matter in hand, and before long, what happened to de Fallières was a closed chapter. No further questions asked. Matter concluded, dossier archived, end of story.

The case of the young Soviet comrade Dontsova was more problematic. She was a Soviet citizen with no past criminal record. Manifestly she had a falling out with her co-conspirators Kuznetsov and Milevich. Why she had decided not to go through with the carefully planned transaction was unclear. But she had followed the correct course and was entitled to feel she would be protected. The opposite had occurred.

Milevich's enforced presence at one of his interviews with Lawrence had infuriated Isakov, but once again, orders had come from on high to accommodate him and let him witness the interrogation. If the idea was to intimidate Lawrence it hadn't worked any more than his clumsy 'casing' of the British diplomat's car in Serebryany Bor and his search for the missing documents in Lawrence's room. Militsiya officers had been called upon to intervene by blocking the road and providing cover for the inept Pavel Yeromovitch as he made his getaway.

Most threatening of all to Isakov, the secret ministry file containing toxic information about planned Soviet grain purchases and gold sales remained unaccounted for, with the potential to cause severe embarrassment if it fell into the wrong hands. It was this that senior Party authorities and his bosses were most nervous about. They did not give a measly kopeck about the murders. However, failure to locate documents with the potential to impugn and ridicule the economic performance of the USSR at a time of heightened international focus and proclamations about the superiority of the socialist system, would lead to retribution being exacted from those considered *vinovat*, or guilty, for not fulfilling the Party's orders. Blame, demotion, a cut in his pension and even worse could await Isakov. He was the main target of the wrath of the USSR's higher authorities and their anger was ratcheting up a notch every day.

Isakov rested his head in his hands and then leant back in his chair, exhausted by the strain of events that were now out of his control. His thirty years of honourable public service in the Moscow Militsiya, doing his job in a professional and, most would argue, skilled way, steering clear of trouble, personnel disputes and avoiding conflicts with other Soviet agencies and the KGB, could go up in smoke. A dishonourable discharge from Militsiya HQ for incompetence would sting him after all his efforts and successes over the years in solving civil cases including murder, rape, embezzlement, child molestation, protection rackets, drug-dealing, criminal gang warfare and more besides. He had done his job professionally and had kept out of political matters. But now he was in big trouble.

Isakov had to find the dossier assembled by Valentina Dontsova at all costs and get it out of harm's way. If the Americans got hold of it all hell would break loose. He had been warned by his authorities that senior party leaders would not tolerate the USSR being ridiculed publicly at a major international conference; he could imagine the headlines… 'Triumphant Communists unable to feed their own people again', the Americans would crow, and, worse, the USSR would be accused of preparing to loot Western grain markets again. The country's entire trading strategy to make up for any harvest shortfall would be exposed to renewed international scrutiny. Prices of grain would rise on world markets and the USSR would have to ship more gold to pay capitalist traders, forcing world grain prices up and gold prices down to the detriment of Soviet economic reserves and the Soviet people's well-being.

His neck was on the line.

Nothing about this whole matter was in any way fair. As far as the higher Party echelons were concerned Isakov's career was about as irrelevant as the two young people whose lives had been tragically ended by freelancing agents of the state.

Isakov's gloomy and bitter reflections were interrupted by a knock at his door.

"*Shto* – what?" snapped Isakov.

In walked his assistant Yuri Leonidovitch Ternak, a mousy-haired, obsequious junior officer, just two years into his militsiya career, always anxious to please, who had been present at the Lawrence meeting that had concluded a few minutes ago.

"The witness Lawrence has now left the building, Comrade Chief Inspector. Shall I write up the minutes of the meeting for insertion into the Dontsova file?" asked Ternak, pleased with himself for taking the initiative to offer to assist the chief inspector who, Ternak had noticed, appeared to be very tense and nervous these days.

Isakov reflected. "No," he replied, "I will do it myself, as I want to add some commentary and analysis."

In fact, Isakov had no intention of reporting on the meeting at all as it would be imprudent, if not dangerous, to include any reference to Lawrence's allegations of possible KGB or security service involvement in the case.

As Ternak turned to leave his office Isakov asked him suddenly, "Yuri Leonidovitch, why did you choose to join the militsiya?", catching him off guard.

"Comrade Chief Inspector," Ternak replied, choosing his words with care, "I believe in our country, I believe in socialist legality and I believe that our citizens should live in a society where the rule of law applies in furtherance of the aims of building a truly communist society. It is the militsiya's job to protect Soviet citizens and I am proud to be an officer."

"Good. That is all. Dismissed," said Isakov.

Ternak saluted and scurried promptly out of the chief inspector's office.

It all comes down to ends and means, Isakov thought to himself. In the USSR 'ends' come first. Projecting the ambitious targets, the shining image of the state and its heroic leaders will always be determinative and take precedence. The labour of ordinary Soviet citizens and officials is just the 'means' to achieve the 'ends' set down by the Communist Party, those 'ends' supposedly chosen on behalf of the people but, in reality, reflecting the preferences and priorities of the Soviet political elite – the *nomenklatura*.

In this case, obedient Soviet officialdom had been swept aside and marginalised for loftier goals. *How can this be right?* Isakov argued to himself. *If simple justice is discarded will this not lead to the unravelling of all the principles and values I have spent my life working for? Can a state operate in this way for the good of its people?*

Isakov's head was throbbing. He was confused and anxious. He couldn't answer his own questions; he couldn't think straight anymore.

SIXTY-THREE

Break Up

Kuznetsov and Pavel met the same day at an outdoor café near the centre of Moscow. Both were in a highly stressed state of mind.

Their cast-iron scheme to enrich themselves had spectacularly backfired. The document on the USSR's harvest projections had gone missing and, consequently, they had nothing at all to trade with the American, who, to all intents and purposes, had abandoned them because they had failed to deliver on their side of the bargain.

Pavel reviewed the situation. "We tried to force a confession from the student de Fallières about where the document was by intercepting him near Moscow University, after his drink in a bar with Lawrence. We naturally assumed that de Fallières would be drunk, but we found out, surprisingly, that he was sober. Unwisely, he resisted all our reasonable demands for information." Pavel sighed, shrugging his shoulders, suggesting that what happened next was inevitable but not his responsibility.

"We then proceeded to rough him up a bit – nothing too violent, at least initially – but the fool resisted and just wouldn't consent to our demand for information about where the dossier was located. No amount of verbal persuasion elicited any positive results."

"So what happened next?" asked Kuznetsov in trepidation about what was now going to be revealed.

Pavel, looking nervously around him to make sure that no-one was listening, continued, "Foolishly the student then tried to make a run for it. That's when things got, well, a bit violent. To quieten him down a few blows to the head were administered by Slava, a loyal comrade, but, as so often when this operative is involved in any incident requiring force, the violence was overdone and the student fell unconscious. He couldn't be revived. We decided to dispose of his body in the Moscow River. The three of us carried him down there, pretending we were helping a drunken comrade get home. The student was all skin and bones, so it wasn't a troublesome operation moving him. We had to obscure the bloodstains to his head when a curious passer-by dawdled around in our presence before moving on after our assurance that we were just supporting a paralytically drunk young Moscovite. Dumping de Fallières' body in the river was not the outcome we had planned. More importantly, it hasn't helped us to locate the missing dossier."

"Two deaths and we've still got no idea where it is?" asked Kuznetsov incredulously.

"Every effort has been made to locate it," retorted Pavel. "Earlier I instructed another two reliable comrades, for $50 cash each, to undertake a comprehensive search of the student Lawrence's room in his academy. The security authorities there were told to get lost for a few hours. Our search was not helped by an irritating busybody, Lyudmila Alexandrovna, a resident in Lawrence's corridor. She had to be ordered to keep quiet for her own good while the operation – a Level 4 search – was carried out. This involved ripping up floorboards, dismantling window frames and slashing matrasses. Maddeningly nothing came to light. No sign of the dossier."

Kuznetsov's concerns were mounting as Pavel recounted what he had been up to.

"That's not all," Pavel added, endeavouring to convince Kuznetsov that he had left no stone unturned. "I myself tracked Lawrence and some female British diplomat on their excursion by car to Serebyanny Bor. I personally searched the car from top to bottom but, infuriatingly, once again, nothing could be found there either. So, where could the dossier be?"

"Lawrence must know," said Kuznetsov. "Otherwise, it's gone missing."

"Yes," said Pavel. "My conclusion too. We've searched everywhere. We'll have to pick him up and pressure him. It's our last chance."

This prompted an immediate reaction from Kuznetsov. "I don't think we should do that. This affair has spiralled wildly out of control. Two young lives have been lost already. I don't want to proceed any further. Let's drop the whole matter now and admit we failed, before we get into even deeper water."

Pavel, conscious of Kuznetsov's diminishing appetite for measures to bring the deal to a conclusion, exploded in a series of vicious, foul-mouthed insults. "You duplicitous scumbag, Alexei. I thought you were my brother-in-arms. My blood comrade. Instead, what do I see before me? A traitor to the cause, a spineless turncoat. I've invested all my hard-earned savings – $1,100 – in this deal and I'm not giving up now. Neither are you – or there will be severe consequences to pay," responded Pavel, red-faced as he spat out the words menacingly.

Alarmed at what he was hearing, Kuznetsov looked at Pavel, who was incandescent with rage. Was this hothead before him the same childhood friend and comrade that he had known for nearly forty years? What had turned him into the abusive, violent thug that he now was?

"I'll decide what I do, not you, Pavel Yeremevich," retorted Kuznetsov contemptuously in reply. "Your violent methods have led nowhere. The only concrete results are two pointless murders. I regret ever mentioning this business opportunity to you. So much for your professionally honed methods of persuasion. Looks more like rank incompetence and gratuitous KGB violence to me. So, I'm getting out. Out. I want no more of this fool's escapade. If you want to pursue the missing file, you're on your own." And with that Kuznetsov threw down a three-rouble note on the table of the café where they were meeting and walked away in disgust.

That gesture of contempt was the last straw for Pavel. He had been betrayed by his long-time friend Alexei and squandered $1,100 of his own money for no financial return.

Smouldering with indignation at being double-crossed but clear-sighted enough to identify a way forward, Pavel determined to exact retribution in two ways. The first casualty would be Kuznetsov himself.

He walked to the nearest telephone box and dialled the number of the Moscow militsiya. A receptionist answered.

"Who is calling?" asked the receptionist testily.

"KGB, Seventh Directorate, Milevich, Pavel Yeremevich," replied Pavel. "Get Chief Inspector Isakov immediately."

The call was transferred. After a while Isakov picked up.

"Milevich, Pavel Yeremevich here. KGB. This is official. Take note. Alexei Vladimirovich Kuznetsov, Director in the Ministry of Agriculture, has just confessed to the murders of Valentina Michaelevna Dontsova and the British student de Fallières. Kuznetsov also organised the theft of state secrets relating to Soviet harvest projections, imports of grain and planned state gold sales with a view to selling them for $10,000 to a Western speculator. My office was charged with undertaking surveillance on this case, and I was the assigned officer. You are hereby instructed to arrest Kuznetsov forthwith and indict him with these offences within twenty-four hours. You are also charged to recover the missing state documents and return them to the Central Committee of the USSR. Is that clear?"

"*Ladno* – clear," replied Isakov wearily. "*Ponyatno* – understood."

Isakov put the phone down. *Total lawlessness*, he thought to himself. *Will this flagrant criminality and violence, perpetrated by those purporting to act in the name of the state, ever end?* Isakov asked himself. *The business transaction was illegal for sure. But Kto vinovat? Who is really guilty?*

Isakov felt the rug had been pulled from under his feet. Events were spiralling even further out of his control.

Job done, Pavel now focused on implementing the second track of his recovery strategy. He was going after the Englishman, Lawrence. No holds barred.

SIXTY-FOUR

Flight Preparations

Arriving at his home bus stop, after his short detour, Will decided to drop in to see Zina and Natalia, who had met him on his arrival in Moscow, to say goodbye.

As he walked along dusty Listvennichnaya Alleia by the rows of larch trees in the rapidly fading light, clutching his briefcase, he was alert enough to notice, out of the shadows behind him, a black Volga car, like the one he and Stephanie had observed in Serebryany Bor a few days before. Glancing backwards again, he saw that the vehicle, with two people in the front seats, was creeping slowly along behind him. Although he readied himself to take evasive action in a hurry should that be necessary – *Am I just imagining things?* he wondered – he was nonetheless taken completely by surprise when the car suddenly accelerated at great speed, rose up onto the pavement and attempted to hit him square on from behind. Alerted by the high revs of the Volga's straining engine, Will had just enough time to avoid being struck by the vehicle by diving headlong off the pedestrian path into some thorny bushes, his briefcase flying into scrub nearby. He felt the roar of the engine and the scattered dust from the path as the car narrowly missed him and sped up Listvennichnaya Alleia at high speed.

In shock at avoiding what was clearly intended to be a fatal assault, Will, shaken up, scratched and bruised, with dust all over his T-shirt, linen trousers and face, recovered his briefcase and staggered to the nearest building to clear his head. A few passing onlookers on the other side of the street asked if he was alright but they did not hang about. They put the incident they had witnessed down to dangerous driving, not to any attempt to kill or maim him.

Will had a different view.

He abandoned the idea of seeing Zina and Natalia and instead headed back to his room by a less direct path, away from Listvennichnaya Alleia.

It was clear to him that Kuznetsov and his accomplices – *Is Wendell implicated too?* he wondered – were in a rage at being thwarted in their quest for a significant sum of hard currency and were intent on exacting revenge. As darkness enveloped the surroundings he retreated to his room and packed a small carry case of essential items and a few notebooks. The rest of his stuff, including virtually all his clothes, would have to be abandoned as he was going to have to leave in a hurry.

His main concern now was the presence of the same unmarked black Volga car which had parked and was now visible from the kitchen in the front of his *obshezhitye* looking out towards Listvennichnaya Alleia. Its two occupants remained there keeping a watch on the building. He was fearful that at any moment they would move for him. His fate rested on what happened in the next hours. He needed to get out.

Who could help him?

He called Natalia. No reply. An hour later she appeared at the door of the *obshezhitye* to bid him farewell.

"Dear Will," she said, smiling, "you did not come round to see us this afternoon as you promised! I wanted nonetheless to wish you *do svidaniya!* – goodbye!"

"Natalia, I am so sorry. I was delayed. But I am very happy to see you and thanks for coming round to say goodbye. I appreciate all you have done to make my stay a pleasant one here. Please come in," said Will, looking over Natalia's shoulder at the hovering black Volga. "Natalia, since my room was broken into, I have been in a state of some nervousness. I have been followed – I don't know why – but come to the kitchen and look behind the curtains and you will see a black car that has been there for over an hour with its occupants watching the building," added Will.

He steered Natalia towards the kitchen window, and she discreetly took a look. They went then to Will's room.

"Natalia, I need you to help me again."

Will recounted the background to the murders of Valya and Tristan, the search for the secret document that underlay the ransacking of his room, the attempt on his life. Natalia sat there open-mouthed, unable to believe that these things could happen in her country, in her town and on Listvennichnaya Alleia.

"Natalia, this is the truth. I need to get to a safe place. I cannot simply walk out of the door here as I will be seen and apprehended by the men in that car. I need to escape through the courtyard at the back of the building. There is no back door, so I have to exit by the front door and turn immediately left to walk by the side of the building and get to the courtyard beyond. There is no other way," said Will nervously.

By now it was well after eleven at night.

At that moment Natalia, an amateur actress in her teens, had formed an idea in her mind on how to create a diversion. She began to rehearse.

"Get me what alcohol you have," she said, and she proceeded to drink the lot.

271

SIXTY-FIVE

Flight

The next day at 10am Ambassador Mansfield walked briskly into a meeting room on the ground floor of the British Embassy.

"So, Lawrence, we meet again. I understand you have again been in a spot of bother…" began Ambassador Mansfield in the suave, measured and calm tones redolent of the experienced senior British diplomat he was. "…not foreseen in your studentship with the British Council, was it? So, what are our Soviet friends up to?" he asked.

"Ambassador, it has not been my intention to disturb you or your colleagues during my stay in the USSR," began Will.

He outlined the discovery of Valya's body with Tristan, his interrogation by the Moscow police authorities, his realisation when he visited Valya's mother that she had been removing sensitive documents on forecasts of the grain harvest, Tristan's unaccounted-for death and the wider conspiracy involving US cash for information. The US political counsellor was implicated together with two Russian officials.

He continued, "Quite unwittingly, I found myself sucked into something beyond my control and comprehension. My life has been threatened: just yesterday early evening I was nearly killed by a black Volga car accelerating at speed behind me over the pavement just yards from my residential bloc."

The ambassador listened attentively before responding in clipped tones. "US cash for grain trade secrets? A maverick cowboy diplomat in the US Embassy? Death of a British student to boot? Difficult to fathom. I'll have a word with our American cousins. Names, details needed. Sounds as if you have bitten off far more than you can chew, Lawrence. Very disappointed you didn't keep us far better informed. I will put it down to inexperience and immaturity. All this has been taking place while preparations for the big political signing ceremony at Helsinki are underway. Unacceptable. The Soviets won't want any negative media coverage denigrating the USSR at this triumphal moment of post-war Soviet diplomacy solidifying the post-war division of Europe. And they certainly wouldn't want an unwelcome spat with the Americans to muddy the waters even further. Nor would HMG, for that matter," said the ambassador in a revelatory aside. "We'll have to get you out of Moscow and back to London ASAP."

An aide was instructed to speak to BEA Airlines and get Will on the next plane to London. The ambassador continued in clipped tones, "Special request from the ambassador. Tell them it's an emergency – code 34ADL. Passenger's father dying, needs to return home immediately. Book an embassy car to Sheremetyevo Airport, two-man security detail. Stephanie will also accompany."

Will spent most of the day at the British Embassy feeling like a duck out of water. He went over in his mind his escape from Listvennichnaya Alleia and how he had taken a number of buses before arriving at Belorussky station, where he spent the night pretending he was waiting for an early morning train. He figured that he would be safest in a large public concourse before making his way to the British Embassy in the morning. He found a quiet corner in a waiting room, but that didn't prevent all sorts of drunks and misfits bothering him, some of them seeking money to buy vodka. Will tried to remain as inconspicuous as possible by constantly shifting from place to place while keeping an eye open for any potential assailants. The night passed very slowly. It was not until 8am that he made his move towards the embassy.

He departed for the airport at 4.30pm. The embassy car in which he travelled was followed all the way to the airport by a black Volga car which had been hovering around the gates of the embassy compound since that morning. Stephanie and the officers had been instructed to see Will physically onto the plane via the VIP check-in and to board it with him, leaving the aircraft only moments before the outer door shut.

As they walked towards the departure gate Will noticed, much to his relief, a yellow *Pochta* post box. This was his last opportunity to post something before boarding the aircraft. He took out from his briefcase a thickish buff envelope, containing five sheets of densely typewritten paper in Russian, on which he had affixed the last of his Soviet stamps. The *desinataire* of the envelope was Chief Inspector Isakov at the Central Moscow Police Headquarters. Will deposited the envelope in the postbox.

Moments later he arrived at the departure gate and boarded the aircraft. As the last BEA ground staff left the aircraft prior to its departure Will embraced Stephanie and thanked her for her help and friendship.

"And say goodbye to Wendell for me," said Will.

Recalling what he had written in Russian on the first page of the otherwise blank five sheets of paper he had left in locker 115 in the Sadunovsky Banya the previous day, Will added, "The Russians have a nice expression, '*s liokhim parom*' – '*have a good steam bath*'. Do pass this thought on to Wendell, Steph. I'm sure he will understand and appreciate it."

"I'll pass it on when I see him this evening," said Stephanie, somewhat perplexed. "He leaves for Washington tomorrow for a 'mid-posting' performance review at the State Department. He's expecting a big promotion. I shall miss him terribly. He should be back in a week, though. We'll celebrate his advancement in style," replied Stephanie.

Hmmm, I wonder, thought Will to himself, as he turned and settled into his aisle seat for the journey to London. *I wouldn't count on it, Steph. More likely your Wendell is going to find himself in very hot water. The steam will be coming out of the ears of his superiors.*

SIXTY-SIX

Waiting on Listvennichnaya Alleia

The first part of Pavel's operational plan to strike the second Englishman, Will Lawrence, from behind to punish him for his interference in the 'Cash for Harvest Information' affair and to open the way for further searches of his room had misfired. Lawrence had escaped, though not without being shaken up. While Pavel and his comrade Slava maintained their surveillance of Lawrence's residential block, some stupid drunken postgraduate girl celebrating the end of her academy studies had flopped onto the bonnet of their black Volga and been sick all over it, causing a stinking mess. He and Slava had to prop the silly bitch up against the car and clean up the puke, which reeked of alcohol. There was nothing much worse than being splattered with someone else's vile, alcoholic-soaked vomit. Fortunately, Pavel and Slava had an oily rag in the boot of the car, which they used to get rid of the mess before chucking it in the undergrowth. It was disgusting but all over in five minutes or so.

The girl began to moan about a painful stomach. *Her own stupid fault*, thought Pavel. In the old days in the army, he would have been tempted to take advantage of her and send her packing. However, he was now a more circumspect and mature agent;

furthermore, he wouldn't have wanted to give that bonehead Slava any excuse to snitch on him. That would worsen even further his dwindling career prospects in the KGB.

"Just go home, *devushka*, and sober up," said Pavel impatiently.

"Aaargh, I don't feel well," replied Natalia, placing herself strategically in front of the two KGB officers and blocking their arc of vision to the front of Will's residence. She then collapsed in a heap by their feet, obliging the two men to pick her up and stand her up leaning against the car.

"I think I'm going to be sick again," said Natalia, emitting an exaggerated retch which didn't produce much from the remaining contents of her stomach except a bit of spit. *Surely*, she said to herself, *Will would have had enough time to make his getaway by now.* She collapsed again. *That should do it*, she thought.

Thanking the men and endeavouring to continue to distract them, she wobbled theatrically round the vehicle seeking to find her non-existent handbag.

"My bag, my bag, where is my bag?" asked Natalia.

Pavel and Slava looked around the car but, not surprisingly, couldn't find one.

"There is no bag, *devushka*. Now, scram, will you? Piss off, you stupid, drunken bitch," said Slava, resorting to his habitual roughneck vocabulary. With this, Natalia, unsteady on her feet, wandered off. She had done her job to perfection.

To avoid a commotion in the middle of the night Pavel and Slava decided to make their final move for Will around dawn while keeping his building under surveillance in the meantime.

At around 5.30am at first light they barged into the residence, woke up all the occupants of the *obshezhitye* and demanded the location of the student's room. Their intent was to settle matters once and for all with Lawrence and force him to hand over the secret dossier which he must have in his possession.

"End of the corridor on the right," said the ubiquitous Lyudmila, who had opened the front door of the residence and was sleepily curious to know what consequences awaited Will Lawrence from this early morning call.

Pavel and Slava banged on the door, shouting for Will to open it, waited five seconds and then tried to force their way in. The lock was jammed with a small barrel device designed to prevent unauthorised access.

"Shit. No chance of picking this lock," said Slava. "We'll have to break the door down."

The two strong men launched themselves at the door several times, causing an even greater racket throughout the residence. The door hinges began to creak before four of the five holding the door in place gave way to the combined assault by the two hefty men. They stumbled into Will's room to find it unoccupied.

"Where the fuck is the bastard?" blurted out Pavel.

No-one had slept there that night. Papers, files and household utensils were spread around. Two large suitcases were on top of the cupboard. Slava pulled them down and searched them. They were empty. The cupboard was half full with winter clothes and shoes. Nothing of any interest here either.

Pavel looked disconsolately at the scene in front of him.

Reality had caught up with him.

The student Will Lawrence had flown.

Pavel wasn't going to get his hands on the dossier.

His savings had been wiped out for nothing in return.

His gamble to increase them fourfold had failed.

He had betrayed his closest friend who now faced twenty years in penal servitude for crimes for which he was only partially responsible.

He was too numb to take it all in. He slumped against the wall.

"Let's fuck off out of here," said Pavel. "That English bastard screwed us, no doubt about it. So much for doing business with capitalists. Anything here worth taking with us?"

Slava, never one to skip an opportunity to get his hands on a quality Western product, spotted some items in Will's cupboard. His eyes fell on a tin of Gillette shaving foam.

"What's this then?" Slava asked.

"Some kind of perfume spray or mousse?" replied Pavel.

"Mousse? What for? *Konfeti* – confectionary?" replied Slava.

"Why don't you taste it?" suggested Pavel.

Slava pressed the top of the can and the shaving mousse poured out.

"Take your finger off the top, you idiot!" shouted Pavel.

"It tastes lemony," said Slava. "I don't like lemons. Ever since I was young. Hate them."

"Sod it, I'll take it then," said Pavel, figuring that he had spent $1,100 for one can of mousse.

They walked down the corridor towards the entrance of the *obshezhitye*, leaving the door of Will's room hanging on one rusty hinge and the room in a ramshackle state.

Lyudmila, ever aware of what was going on in the corridor of the residence, popped her head out of her door. "*Vsyo v poryadke gospada* – everything in order, gentlemen?" she asked in her busybody, inquisitive way.

"*Absolyutno. Vsyo v poryadke,*" replied Pavel, brushing past and ignoring her as he moved purposefully towards the front door and out into the sultry morning air in a foul mood.

SIXTY-SEVEN

Special Relationship

On the day of Will's departure from Moscow, British Ambassador Mansfield had been invited for early evening drinks by his US counterpart, Ambassador Thomas Powell. Their get-togethers were part of a regular dialogue in Moscow between representatives of old allies constituting the 'special relationship'. It was the turn of the American Ambassador to host. The two settled themselves comfortably in the blue and gold wallpapered library of his splendid residence, Spaso House.

Thomas Powell, US Ambassador since June 1973, a GOP Republican through and through, was a political appointee who had been rewarded with one of the State Department's plum ambassador posts because of his substantial financial support to the Nixon campaigns in 1968 and 1972. Powell's donations to the GOP amounted to nearly $100,000, making him one of the party's largest donors, the money coming from his successful Wall Street brokerage. Wealth and privilege oozed out of every pore of him. He was 'well in' with the current political powers in Washington and had his eye on a cabinet position – Interior Affairs or the CIA – should President Ford decide to reshuffle his pack before the next

US general election in November 1976. He had certainly let it be known to the White House that he had earned his spurs after two difficult and not hugely enjoyable years in Moscow and that he was ready to move on to a higher calling.

The ambassadors exchanged views about the political situation in the USSR and talked about which senior Soviet apparatchiks they had met recently and what they had gleaned from them about the condition of the Soviet Union. They also touched on what impact the CSCE conference – about to begin in Helsinki – would have on European security and on US and British interests.

"Another G&T, perhaps, Archie?" asked Tom.

"Delighted as always!" the British Ambassador responded as the white-jacketed waiter removed his long glass for replenishment, adding a generous portion of gin and flavouring it, as before, with a squeezed wedge of lime and a plentiful dollop of crushed ice cubes. *These American chaps may be a bit rough at the edges*, Mansfield thought to himself, *but, my goodness, they do at least know how to make a decent drink.*

After taking a gulp Mansfield said cautiously, "Tom, absolutely don't want to scuttle our friendly chat – always delighted to see you, of course – but am obliged to raise with you something a smidgeon on the delicate side…"

"Sure thing, go right ahead. I'm all ears," said Powell, not expecting anything of any great significance from Mansfield, whose unctuous, suave and superior manner cleverly camouflaged his reluctance to provide any useful nuggets of information to the US.

"Here we go then, Tom… Look, old boy, it has come to my notice that one of your embassy chaps has been engaged in a bit of financial skulduggery with the Soviets over the last few weeks… I thought I ought to put you in the picture because, as I am sure you will agree, notwithstanding the exceptionally bad judgement of the individual concerned, this affair has the potential to cause us – and you in particular – a spot of bother and some political embarrassment…" said Mansfield.

"Keep going, Archie," interjected Powell, his curiosity aroused.

Mansfield outlined in detail the attempt by one of Powell's US Embassy staff to buy sensitive data from three rogue Soviet Ministerial employees to pass on to his family's firm for personal gain. He drew the US Ambassador's attention to the fact that two young people had lost their lives because of this nefarious scheme, one of them, deplorably, a British citizen.

"Two deaths? For some statistics on grain and gold? You can't be serious, Archie? I'm totally shocked," replied Powell. "Who is this rogue US Embassy staffer?"

Mansfield took a small notebook from his pocket – he was terrible at remembering names, Russian or Western – adjusted his half-moon glasses and said, "I believe he goes by the name of Mr Wendell. Randall Wendell III or some variant thereof. Not a name one would encounter in Blighty, I would venture."

There was a silence while the US Ambassador absorbed what he had just been told. After a short pause for reflection, he responded, "You must mean Wendell Randall III, Archie." Powell spoke slowly. "Surely not, buddy. He is one of my smartest political counsellors. A savvy operator. Works closely with me in my private office. Energetic. Intelligent, a top staffer. Political appointee, family is from Chicago – big supporters of the GOP. Big career in front of him. I personally selected him for Moscow. Can't believe what you just told me. Sure you got the right guy?"

"Absolutely," replied Mansfield. "Look, Tom, far be it for me to tell you what to do about black sheep on your ranch but duty obliges me to say that HMG wouldn't want a scandal brewing up over this matter. Not now of all times, on the cusp of Helsinki. The fact that one of our students unwittingly got ensnared in the affair and lost his life makes it highly sensitive for us, especially given his family background. We've managed to put a dampener on our side of the pond, but I'd be grateful if Foggy Bottom could also ensure that things are taken in hand, if you take my meaning. With your 'hire and fire' culture I'm sure things can be arranged in DC without too much fuss."

"Mr Randall will be leaving for Washington for a personnel review tomorrow. I'll pass a word to my colleagues in State," said Tom, still reeling from the revelation that one of his top aides – whose appointment, moreover, he had promoted himself – had behaved with such reckless irresponsibility. There was a risk that the affair could even rebound on Tom's own political career prospects if he didn't take the matter quickly in hand and ensure that Randall's employment contract was terminated forthwith.

"Don't worry, Archie. I'll process the Randall issue. Goddam idiot," responded Tom.

"By the way, Tom, there were two Russians involved in this affair, one a hapless mid-ranking Ministry of Agriculture official of no interest to us, the other a rather nasty KGB-type hatchet man. Perhaps your chaps could make sure he doesn't surface anywhere he shouldn't… if you take my meaning," added Mansfield.

"Sure thing," replied Powell.

"A grubby affair hopefully put to bed then," said Mansfield, smiling condescendingly. He had alerted his US counterpart to a troublesome matter in time for corrective measures to be taken; Tom now owed him a favour. He would cash that chip in later. Taking another sip of his delicious G&T, Mansfield added, "More generally, Tom, this affair illustrates the appalling deterioration of standards in public life in the Western world. Everywhere, that is: and I don't exclude the UK. Diplomats exploiting the shelter of an official position in a top embassy to engage in some greedy personal profiteering with the Soviets is bad enough. Next up we'll be dealing with ministers breaking the law by steering state resources and contracts into the arms of their political supporters and getting rewarded with backhanders and gongs. Need to nip such scurrilous, corrupt and contemptuous behaviour in the bud now before it spreads like cancer," added Mansfield.

"After Watergate I couldn't agree with you more," said Tom by way of a response, still reeling from Mansfield's revelations.

"Now, Tom, on a happier note, you and Sherie just must join us for dinner at our dacha in Serebryany Bor. Maggie gave me the strictest instructions that I was not to leave Spaso House without your agreement for a BBQ next Saturday, for which she promised to make your favourite pecan pie *à l'anglaise*. Don't let me leave Spaso without a yes."

"It would be a pleasure, Archie. What we just discussed will be behind us by then," said Tom, raising himself from his chair and escorting Mansfield through the splendid reception rooms of Spaso House to his waiting black Rolls-Royce.

SIXTY-EIGHT

Birmingham, 31 July 1975

Will's parents met him at London Heathrow Airport and drove him to their home in Birmingham, arriving around 8pm. He went straight to bed after a light supper, exhausted, not saying much about his experience of living in the USSR.

That weekend the family – Will, his parents and his younger sister Lizzie – gathered around the oval-shaped mahogany table in the dining room for a traditional Sunday roast beef lunch. Will's mother had been busy all morning, without any help, preparing the meat and vegetables (carrots, turnips, fresh peas), Yorkshire pudding, roast potatoes and gravy, and for dessert, getting the ingredients together for her legendary 'Queen of Puddings', consisting of meringue over a lemon-flavoured sponge base with jam, served with lashings of double cream. The family Aga cooker, requiring constant replenishment of coking coal, had been working overtime that morning.

Will arose late and skipped breakfast. His father had bought a couple of bottles of claret and Muscadet for lunch from the local off-licence to celebrate Will's return.

"Well, it's good to have you home son, safe and sound and back in the family fold," said his father, raising his glass. "Cheers." They raised and clinked their glasses of Muscadet before tucking into the smoked-salmon starter.

"So, what was it like there?" he asked.

"That is a long story, Dad," replied Will.

His mother's assiduously prepared food was delicious; Will was pleased to tuck into his first British roast meal for a long time with relish, lubricated by a glass of warm claret, while continuing to tell a few stories about life in the USSR.

"Did you meet any nice Russian girls?" asked his sister Lizzie cheekily.

"Plenty. But no romances, you will be disappointed to hear. Just platonic friendships," replied Will.

Will continued talking to his family like this, limiting himself in what he said, sticking to facts and experiences but avoiding any mention of Valya, Tristan, Chief Inspector Isakov, Wendell, Kuznetsov, Pavel et al. He didn't want to alarm his parents; they would have been horrified at his escapades.

Looking around his parents' comfortable, homely, middle-class family dining room with a grandfather clock ticking monotonously by a Victorian mahogany sideboard, the corner tables with displayed Chinese antiques, the thick red-patterned carpet, green curtains and faux chandelier, Will was disconcerted by a feeling that everything familiar to him actually felt different compared to nine months ago. While the rest of his family had continued living their lives broadly in the same way as before, he had changed. He was no longer the same person he was before. Home felt different: a friendly place to visit and meet his family but no longer his safe harbour and refuge. He had awakened and moved on.

He doubted his parents would grasp that he was no longer emotionally dependent on them, at least not immediately. It would take time.

Will already found the atmosphere at home rather stifling and determined that he would have to leave quickly and head to London in search of full-time work.

As formative as his experience had been in Russia, this chapter of his life was now closing. There was a bigger world out there. And he wanted to discover it.

SIXTY-NINE

Debrief, London, 7 August 1975

A few days later, Will arrived at British Council Headquarters in Spring Gardens near Trafalgar Square for a debrief on his studentship in the USSR.

Three people were present in the meeting room to which he was escorted; Colonel Roger Torrington retired, Director of External Programmes, Mrs Pamela Nugent, Director of USSR and East Europe programmes; and Miss Anne Brown, a young, attractive, brunette notetaker with a nice smile.

The colonel welcomed Will back and said that the Council were pleased to see he had returned in one piece. Mrs Nugent had been debriefed by the Foreign Office on the circumstances of his rapid exit from the USSR, but they would like to hear Will's version of events.

Will began formally, "I have benefited professionally and personally from the experience of spending nine months in the USSR, so I thank you for this opportunity. I was well received in my academy and by people whom I visited outside Moscow. The research was worthwhile, though I had to leave some materials behind.

"I had not set out, of course, to get embroiled in controversy, and I well remember Mr Longmore's instruction to us at Liverpool

Street Station on the day of our departure in November last year to stay out of trouble. It was my misfortune to discover the body of a young woman in the hills by the Moscow River whom I had been expecting to meet a few hours earlier. What happened thereafter was unforeseeable and, at times, terrifying, culminating in the death of my friend Tristan de Fallières in very mysterious circumstances."

Will then proceeded to outline the sequence of events that had dominated his last weeks in Moscow.

"Yes, tragic indeed about de Fallières," said Colonel Torrington. "Wild sort, I understand from the Foreign Office, temperamentally unsuited to living in the USSR. We do try to weed out bad eggs in our selection procedures, but we don't always succeed unfortunately. Lessons to be learnt for us here in the BC, Mrs Nugent. Need to tighten up our recruitment procedures. Make sure we get the right calibre of chap."

Pamela Nugent shifted uneasily in her seat, evidently disapproving of Torrington washing the Council's dirty linen in front of Will. Her expression left no doubt that Torrington, a typical ex-British army buffer, should have kept his counsel.

Colonel Torrington's disparagement of Tristan stung Will. To all intents and purposes there had been a cover-up regarding the circumstances of his death.

Continuing, the Colonel asked what could Will have done better? Director Nugent asked if, in the event that his research notes are lost, would he be able to complete his thesis?

To the second question he answered affirmatively but it may take more time.

"Could I have acted better – yes, in some respects. However, I was unaware, until too late, of the entangled US and Soviet dimensions of the affair. I have learnt about law and justice. It is my hope that the relationship between state and people will change one day in Russia. Who knows, one day communism may end. Dare one hope that it will not be replaced by anything remotely comparable?" Will hypothesised.

A spell of silence ensued.

"With regard to Tristan," said Will, choosing his words carefully, "I have a much more positive appreciation of him. He was a good and loyal friend to me. Yes, he was a risk-taker and his behaviour was, on occasions, reckless, but he was an intelligent and sensitive person who understood Russia, Russians and the USSR very well. That specialist knowledge is now forever lost to our country. His death was a total shock to me and has not been fully explained. I should add that I am seeing his father for lunch later today."

Colonel Torrington broke another awkward silence by saying, "Well, I am pleased to hear that. Peter de Fallières is a good friend of mine so please pass on my best regards to him."

Another silence before Torrington continued, "Well, I think we're done for today, Lawrence. We wish you success in completing your thesis. And we look forward to receiving, in the next week or so, a full report of your studentship. About two thousand words should be pukka. Double spacing if you would. It should be one of the most interesting contributions we will have received from a BC student returning from the USSR."

Will shook hands with the Colonel Torrington and Mrs Nugent and departed the building escorted by Miss Brown.

SEVENTY

Reform Club, Pall Mall

Will headed to the nearby Reform Club in Pall Mall for lunch with Tristan's father, who was waiting for him in the lobby.

Peter was more brightly dressed than when Will had last seen him in Moscow. This time he was wearing a beige-coloured, sharply pressed summer suit, pink shirt, Old Westminster pink and blue-striped bow tie, and immaculately polished dark mahogany brogues. A matching blue and pink silk handkerchief had been fluffed up and thrust into his top pocket.

"Delighted to see you again, Will," said Peter. "Let's go and have a pre-lunch cocktail in the lounge. What would you like?"

"Oh, thank you, Mr de Fallières, yes, well, maybe a glass of dry white wine? And, before I forget, greetings to you from Colonel Torrington whom I just met at the British Council's offices," responded Will.

Turning to José, the Portuguese waiter hovering nearby, Peter intimated that it was the 'normal' for him, i.e. dry martini on the rocks with tonic water and a twist of lemon peel plus a glass of house vin blanc for Will.

"As we were, Torrington, yes..." said Peter, reflecting. "Between you and me he's a bit of an old windbag, but he does buy the odd print from me from time to time. In the cheaper range. Do call me Peter, by the way."

The drinks arrived quickly and were served by José with a small bowl of mixed cashew and salted peanuts.

"Cheers," said Peter, and they clinked glasses. "And here's to Tristan. Welcome back to London, Will. I trust you survived your last weeks in the great Soviet Paradise unscathed... I heard they were action-packed," continued Peter.

"Oh yes, thank you, Peter," said Will, not intending to reveal what had happened to him in those last weeks but puzzled that Peter appeared to have acquired some prior knowledge about his more recent experiences. "I got most of what I wanted to do accomplished in time. May I ask if all the arrangements with Tristan worked out?"

"Yes, absolutely," Peter replied quite cheerily. "We got him home in one piece alright at the back end of that dreadfully sad and traumatic week in Moscow. The ambassador was most helpful in a frightful situation. All in all, I was well looked after by the embassy there."

"And where, if I may kindly ask, has Tristan been laid to rest? I would very much like to visit his grave. He was my closest companion in Russia. I was very fond of him," said Will.

"Actually, we cremated him after a small family service at a local church near where I live in Hampshire. Tristan hadn't drawn up a will. Why would one at his age? And he always hated graveyards. We have scattered his ashes around his family home. We also laid some ashes in a beautiful glade in the Lake District – Glenderaterra Beck – by the River Greta near Latrigg and Skiddaw, through which streams of water flow down from the surrounding hills and make their way towards Keswick. An idyllic, calm and peaceful spot in the Lakes which Tristan loved," replied Peter.

"So, that means there is no permanent grave or memorial to him yet?" asked Will.

"No, not for the time being. In time we will erect a plaque or something, somewhere, to remember him. It's all a bit raw right now, frankly. His mother, who lives in Geneva, wants to do something for him there too," Peter said matter-of-factly without showing the slightest emotion.

Will was taken aback by the way in which Tristan's father had disposed of Tristan's remains and had given so little thought to commemorating him. Did he just want his only son to be expunged from his life and memory? Did he have no feeling for his son at all?

Unlike Valya, thought Will, *whose spirit had been so carefully nurtured under Russian Orthodox traditions prior to her final commemoration after forty days, Tristan had no permanent resting place.* Will broke the silence, saying, "I experienced the commemoration of death in Russia in accordance with Orthodox traditions. It is highly ritualised compared to our practices in the UK but very moving," said Will reflectively. "But whatever the exact funeral arrangements, the loss of any young person in their twenties is a great human tragedy. It can only mean an unfulfilled life, a loss of potential, unrealised expectations and dreams. Tristan had so much in front of him. He would have gone places. He was courageous; he was not afraid to speak his mind and face the consequences. He understood Russia and respected its people," continued Will, reflecting on the positive qualities of his friend. "He taught me to be more confident and assertive and stand up for what I believe in. I only have good memories of him. He was a wild spirit but a loyal friend to me."

Peter de Fallières listened to Will carefully but, instead of welcoming these reflections, appeared to be ill at ease talking about his son's memory.

"He was certainly a go-getter sort of chap. A daredevil. Bright, energetic, but, as you say, a terrible risk-taker. A restless spirit. A 'must have now' not a 'will wait till later' type. Never happy. He didn't really fit into our world of traditions, order, discipline, rules and conventions," said Peter distractedly.

Will concluded that Peter had constructed an image of his son that suited his own purposes. Where was any warmth of feeling towards him? As far as Peter was concerned, Tristan had veered wildly off course. He had little understanding of his son or of his fate. He had pretty much disowned his own flesh and blood.

"Shall we go for lunch?" Peter said, draining the remnants of his martini cocktail in one gulp. "José," he said, beckoning to the waiter who was standing nearby, napkin draped over his left forearm, waiting to escort them to their table. "We will proceed *à table* now. Oh, and by the way, José, my dear man – and this is not the first time I have said this to you – do make sure in the future that my cocktail is a fifty-fifty mix and not drowned with fizzy tonic water. Today's martini on the rocks – if I can call it that – lacked zip and punch. And no lemon pips in the drink, please – nothing worse than a mouthful of fiddly pips at lunchtime. Or at any time, for that matter. One never knows where to put them, does one?" said Peter, breaking out into a condescending smile to make the point.

"Very well, sir," replied José obsequiously, disappointed at having been reprimanded by de Fallières, a longstanding but tight-fisted club member, whose regrettable admonition would inevitably impact the size of his gratuity.

At lunch, in the formal dining room, they opted for the daily set menu of avocado cocktail with shrimps, sole meunière, boiled potatoes and peas, and a slice of Bakewell tart with custard for dessert, washed down with a dry, zesty Chardonnay from Burgundy – 1972 vintage. At lunch Peter asked Will about his future plans while Will asked Peter about his work as an antique dealer in nineteenth– and twentieth-century European art.

"Sometimes we get a decent Russian canvas or two in our business – an average quality Levitan, a Repin, Serov or a Goncharova – but there's not much demand for these works in today's international art market. Too obscure. And Russian. French impressionism – that is what the market can't get enough of: Matisse, Pissarro, Monet, etc. I must go and see the Russian holdings of these great French masters in the Hermitage in Leningrad one day. Tristan and I had actually planned to do this at the end of his trip. He liked art," said Peter.

"The collection is stupendous," said Will. "Nothing though beats Rembrandt's masterpiece *The Return of the Prodigal Son*. The great Dutch artist manages to convey with great tenderness a father's forgiveness of his errant son. It is deeply moving. Is there any other artist who has succeeded in capturing this fundamental human value – 'forgiveness' – so sensitively and with such poignant beauty?" asked Will pointedly.

Peter did not comment.

Having quickly disposed of their avocado and shrimp starter, they proceeded to tuck into their entrée. As they did so Peter leaned slightly forward and quietly said, "You had an awful time in Russia, Will. I do regret you had to put up with so much. I heard from… well… sources, that you handled yourself admirably… most important of all, you emerged unscathed. A touch of *sangfroid*, as the French would say…"

Peter paused to take a sip of wine before continuing, "This Burgundy is quite smooth on the palette, by the way, I do hope you are enjoying it… as I was saying, qualities such as cool headedness and good judgement under pressure are ones that… some close associates of mine attach importance to…"

"You mean bidding under pressure for high value works of art?" asked Will, interrupting.

"No, no, my dear fellow… good Lord, no… no, I am talking about discreet, intelligence types who assure our nation's security… chaps who work with the Foreign Office and MOD… that sort of area," replied Peter, chasing a pea round the rim of his plate with his fork. Having eventually speared it, he added, "They might be interested to talk to you."

Will, under scrutiny from the other side of the table, took a few moments to digest what Peter was hinting at. It was a subtle testing of the waters from which both sides could still retreat without any engagement on either side.

"And if I was interested...?" asked Will.

"Leave it to me, old boy. I can make the necessary contacts," replied Peter, his blue eyes focusing intently on Will.

Will did not react and wanted to mull over in his mind whether to pursue this potential opening. At one level he did not warm at all to Tristan's cold-hearted father and did not want to get involved in any undertaking with him. On the other hand, he needed to explore options for the future.

The conversation moved on to other subjects.

After a shared cafetière of coffee and cream – they declined José's proposal to take a brandy or cognac – their luncheon began to draw to a close.

Peter leant over the table again and touched Will on the arm, for the first time showing some signs of human warmth. "Well, Will, it was a pleasure to meet you again, on home turf. Tristan would have certainly approved of us getting together here at my London club. Do keep in touch. And, of course, I will inform you, once we decide as a family, where, when and how we will commemorate Tristan," said Peter.

While perusing the bill discreetly placed by José on a small plate by his right elbow, Peter murmured, without looking at Will, "I take it from our little side discussion during the main course that your response is a no. Quite understand. No hard feelings whatsoever from my side."

"Thank you for the luncheon, Peter. Please do tell me about the commemoration plans for Tristan and the place you decide upon. I would like to visit it and honour my friend. I think about him a lot," replied Will. "As regards our side discussion," he added, choosing his words with great care, "I would not want you to take my initial reaction today as a no."

"Understood. I'll be in touch then. Well, goodbye for now," said Peter, smiling and shaking Will's hand.

Will sat at the table quietly reflecting. He lifted the crisply starched-white table napkin lying on his lap and shook a few breadcrumbs off it. He meticulously and neatly folded it into a rectangle, before positioning it parallel to his unused cutlery and untouched glass of water on the dining-room table.

Emerging into the bright Central London afternoon, Will put on a pair of sunglasses and headed across the Mall to St James's Park where workers, returning to their offices, were mingling with tourists relaxing and enjoying the splendours of the park and Buckingham Palace. He found a blue-striped deckchair and moved it into the shade by a large oak tree, having paid an attendant five pence to rent it for an hour. He adjusted the chair's back to its lowest rung, put this head back and stretched his legs out to relax and take in everything that had occurred that day.

His thoughts turned immediately to Tristan and Valya.

Will silently mourned the loss of his two 'Russian' soulmates who had fleetingly touched and left a mark on his life.

They were gone now. But memories of them would remain with him forever.

He thought of Tristan, his outrageous behaviour in the sprats restaurant, his life lived on the edge but also of his honesty and sense of bravado.

Will then took from his wallet the small black and white passport-sized photograph of Valya given to him by her mother, Svetlana Antolevna, now curling at the edges. What might have developed with this mysterious and troubled Russian woman, prone to frequent changes of mind, whom he had only just begun to get to know?

Valya was adamant at their last meeting by the Kremlin that she would never sell state secrets. Yet she had allowed herself to get embroiled in the 'cash for information' conspiracy. But then, mysteriously, she renounced her participation in the deal and reverted back to her position of principle. Why?

He would never know.

SEVENTY-ONE

Valya's Decision

After parting from Wendell outside the National Hotel, Valya walked to the nearby Okhotny Ryad metro station to get the train to her office in the Ministry of Agriculture and carry out the arrangements that had been agreed with the American and her Russian co-conspirators. Her office was only three metro stops away so, in all probability, she would arrive there well before the American.

At the bottom of the steps leading to the metro she stumbled upon a veteran of the Great Patriotic War propped up against one of the walls by the station entrance. His left leg was amputated at the knee and the rounded end of his stump was visible through the torn trouser leg. His two soiled walking sticks were lying at obtuse angles on the floor beside him. *Soviet militsiya patrolling Moscow's streets and Moscow metro service staff would not tolerate this display of pitiful deprivation if they saw it,* thought Valya, as it was completely contrary to the image of the USSR the authorities wanted to project in central Moscow; the man would be given short shrift and told to move on, irrespective of his disabilities.

"*Ya Veteran, veteran velikoy otechestvennoy voini...* – I am a veteran of the Great Patriotic War....!" the man cried out, extending his cupped right hand, turning to look at Valya forlornly. Valya noticed that a Soviet war medal – *Za otvagu*, for courage and bravery – was attached flimsily to his filthy shirt by a badly torn grey ribbon with a blue border. It was hanging on by the slimmest of threads. As she bent down to give the man five kopecks Valya saw the blank expression in the veteran's eyes: he was not just missing a limb but also blind.

The plight of this veteran, struggling to support himself against all the odds at the bottom of the Soviet heap, jolted Valya. The poor man had to all intents and purposes been abandoned, despite having fought for his country.

Comparing the desperate state of this destitute man with her mother's own predicament tipped Valya into reassessing the risks inherent in the cash for secret information deal. This had been nagging at her for some time. She was the one in the most vulnerable position and, if she was caught, she would be facing twenty years in jail. Her mother would then be in dire trouble, unable to support herself; she could even end up like the veteran on the streets in front of her. It would finish them both and everything they had lived for.

Valya had only got embroiled in this shady scheme to help her mother. She had no interest in making money for herself. If Svetlana Antolevna did not get a medical operation on both of her badly swollen arthritic knees soon, she would be unable to walk and would have to abandon her work which, though it was poorly paid, was important in getting her out and about, keeping her socially active and maintaining her self-esteem.

In a severe quandary, Valya wondered if there were safer, more legal – or less illegal – ways to earn some hard currency in Moscow. Maybe she could get another job at the weekends. A school friend of hers made a living out of buying and selling Imperial Tsarist silver items, such as *korobochki* or snuff boxes and medals, to tourists. Valya could help her do this. Alternatively, she could take up trading – a *fartsovshchitsa* – in Western goods such as jeans, LP records of famous pop stars, cosmetics, tights and other female clothing, or even become a currency trader – a *valutchitsa*. A lot of people in the USSR moonlighted in these shadowy areas. The downside was that it would take time to accumulate an adequate dollar reserve to help her mother by engaging in any of these black-market activities. But wouldn't it be safer, a less risky strategy than one based on a one-time big dollar payoff that required her to act disloyally and betray the Soviet state?

But what would be the consequences of changing course at this late stage? Valya was up to her neck in the conspiracy together with two Soviet officials, one most likely a KGB thug. These co-conspirators would not take kindly to her suddenly changing her mind on grounds of conscience.

Is there any way out of this predicament? she asked herself.

The train rumbled on and arrived at Krasnaya Vorota, the nearest metro station to her ministry situated on Orlikov Pereulok. Standing by the automatic doors, which had opened moments before, she hesitated to alight from the train onto the platform. She then heard the warning signal: "*Ostorozhno, dveri zakrivaitsya, sledoyoushaya stantsiya...*" announcing the imminent closing of the metro car doors before the train headed for the next station up the line.

Standing transfixed on the threshold between the station platform and the metro car, with just seconds to make up her mind, Valya decided on the spur of that moment to abandon her role in the conspiracy. She would not undertake what she had committed herself to do. She stood motionless and did not leave the train.

The thick rubber seals on the metro car doors slammed shut with a familiar loud thump. The train accelerated away towards Komsomolskaya, the next stop on the Sokolnicheskaya orange line.

Valya had an immediate sense of relief. But what she should do with the dossier? It was locked in a safe in her office. To leave it there would be perilous. She would have to remove it as soon as possible. She couldn't do it that day as the American would be hanging around the ministry. She resolved to recover it first thing the next morning and take it home. She would put it in the little alcove behind the Orthodox icon in her mother's bedroom. No-one would dream of looking for it there. And if anything happened to her, well… she would tell her mother what to do with it in such circumstances. Maybe give it to Will?

Valya would explain her decision to withdraw from the business deal in a calm and measured way to her co-conspirators. She would make it clear that they could do whatever they wanted: but she was not going to risk her life – nor that of her mother – by undermining the principles and values of the Soviet state.

Logically, the matter would then be dropped, she would be left alone and she could get on with her normal life as before.

Such was her reasoning.

SEVENTY-TWO

St Nicholas Church Cemetery, Moscow, 7 August 1975

Svetlana Antolevna, her sister Masha and other relatives and friends gathered at the grave of Valentina Michaelevna Dontsova, 'Valya', at a cemetery on the outskirts of Moscow on the same day that Will was in London. It was forty days after her death. The morning was hot and humid with a light scattering of clouds in a hazy sky. At the back of the modest black marble tombstone placed horizontally over Valya's grave stood a vertical Russian Orthodox cross. In the middle of the tombstone was a small, smiling picture of Valya, the same one as in Will's wallet. Beneath the picture was recorded Valya's date of birth, 25 January 1951, and her untimely death on 28 June 1975 at the age of just twenty-four.

Svetlana Antolevna quietly greeted the fifteen of so people who had assembled at the graveside, the women clutching flowers, which they proceeded to place gently and neatly in bunches around the gravestone and the cross. There were some quiet murmurings, much crossing of bodies in accordance with Russian Orthodox tradition, and plenty of emotional support for Svetlana Antolevna, who was bearing up stoically. She had linked arms with Masha, who had arrived from Krasnodar that morning for the ceremony.

Svetlana did not weep: the time for cascades of tears had passed. In her pocket she clutched her small silver and enamel Czarist-era icon depicting the Holy Mother and Infant. Valya had given it to her ten years ago.

She stood by the grave quietly.

"Valya will always be with you," whispered Masha to Svetlana in a barely audible voice.

Inured to grief, Masha's words, heartfelt and sincere though they were, did not register with Svetlana.

She did not care any more about who had killed her daughter or whether they would be apprehended by the authorities: she doubted it.

She didn't care about the Soviet state, the authorities, the militsiya or any other local official, nor about what they said or did.

And she didn't believe in miracles. Not for one moment did she imagine that some guardian angel was going to miraculously save her from her fate, the outlook for which was dire.

Svetlana's only concern was that the soul of her beloved daughter, Valya, would leave this earth in peace and tranquillity, to find its rightful place in the afterlife, and that she herself would retain, until she herself passed away, everlasting and happy memories of the years they had spent together.

That was all that mattered – her love for her daughter.

Svetlana reached for her bag and slowly took out the white towel that had lain untouched on the windowsill of her apartment for forty days since Valya's death.

A single teardrop formed in Svetlana's right eye and slid slowly down her cheek leaving a slight transparent, glistening trace on her face powder as it descended towards the corner of her mouth. She made no attempt to interrupt its unsteady passage.

The moment had arrived.

Svetlana unfolded the white towel with great care until it opened fully into its rectangular shape.

She then shook it vigorously for some seconds. The grey dust on the ground surrounding the grave scattered in all directions.

Silence followed.

Valya's soul was released.

She had left her mother.

Forever.

SEVENTY-THREE

Zhizn Prodolzhayetsya – Life Continues

The forty-day mourning period to mark Valya's passing had come quietly and reverentially to a close.

The best period in Svetlana's life, her time with her daughter, had ended.

How short it had been, Svetlana thought, as she walked slowly and in pain towards the exit of St Nicholas Church Cemetery, arm in arm with her sister Masha.

Her close friends and fellow mourners followed respectfully behind them in silence.

Svetlana Antolevna crossed herself several times as she approached the outer iron gates of the cemetery, the threshold between the past and the present, clutching Valya's icon in her right hand.

On the busy street outside, cars and laden vehicles rumbled noisily by in both directions.

Standing on the pavement outside the cemetery while waiting for everyone to assemble, a mundane thought suddenly popped into Svetlana Antolevna's head.

Some days ago someone had rung her doorbell and left an unaddressed, thickish buff envelope with a small tear in it on her doormat. Probably something official from the commune relating to Valya's death.

Still in mourning, Svetlana didn't have the heart to deal with tiresome paperwork wrapping up Citizen Valentina Michaelevna Dontsova's personal affairs. So she put the envelope aside on her bedroom dressing table to be looked at later.

With a deep sigh, Svetlana resolved to open it when she returned home.

"Life must go on," she whispered to herself.

Life must go on.

For writing and publishing news, or
recommendations of new titles to read,
sign up to the Book Guild newsletter: